Accidental Doctor Daddy

A Silver Fox Ex-Boyfriend's Dad Romance

Unintentionally Yours

Mia Mara

My ex hated my curves.
But his silver fox dad? He loved every inch of
them. All. Night. Long.

I went on vacation to forget my toxic breakup.
And ended up in the bed of a ridiculously hot older man.
Dominant. Sinful. And insanely good with those experienced, surgeon's hands.

It was one wild, nameless night...
Then sunrise hit... and so did the shocking truth:
I'd just slept with my ex's father.

Yeah... so I ran.

Fast forward to me, pregnant with twins, standing in his ER, mid-contraction.

"Ella?" he says, eyes wide.

Oh, *Doctor*. If you think you're shocked now,
wait until you see your babies.

Chapter 1

Ella

I wonder how many cocktails it takes to mend a broken heart.

Seabirds squawked overhead as the tropical sun dipped below the horizon, its last rays painting the sky in a breathtaking palette of oranges and pinks.

I sat alone at the beachside bar with my toes in the sand, cradling a Halekulani—a complex cocktail of bourbon, pineapple juice, and a hint of lemon that promised forget-fulness in its sweet, potent embrace.

Forgetting was all I really wanted.

This vacation was my boss-prescribed remedy for my wounded heart. Would it work? I had no idea. But I liked the drinks and the sights and sounds of The Blue Pearl Resort and Spa. This was my chance to find some kind of peace away from the hustle and bustle of New York City.

As I sipped the cocktail, the soothing rhythms of a steel drum band blended with the gentle crash of the waves, a soundtrack designed to wash away sorrow. When was the last time I merely sipped a cocktail?

The question brought back memories of too many nights in kitchens, barking orders at staff, only to be met with a begrudging, "Yes, Chef!" Too many nights on the line doing vodka shots between services...kitchen life isn't for everyone, but I wouldn't have it any other way. Being assistant head chef meant I had almost as much authority as the actual head chef, and that irritated some people.

Mostly men.

Forget men, Ella. That's why you're here.

If only I could forget men.

After my last break-up, I would gladly never look at another man, if given the choice. But seeing the shirtless guys playing the steel drums, I knew I was screwed. I still couldn't help but count their cobblestone abs and wonder what it'd be like to run my tongue along the grooves between each muscle.

Worse was the guy next to me.

My hormones had clocked him the moment he sat down.

Tan, tall, silver-haired, with the darkest eyes I've ever seen. He wore an open white Guayabera shirt over a white tank top and khaki shorts. Muscular, but not overly so. And, unfortunately for me, he was also incredibly handsome. Strong jaw, prominent nose, and lips that I could suck on for a day.

He was also older than me by a good fifteen years, so there was no way he'd be into me.

No wedding ring, not that those can't come right off. But there was no wedding ring tan line, either.

When he ordered a gin and tonic, I had expected a

British accent, but nope. New York. And he spoke with authority, immediately making me want to take his orders.

Lust is an ungainly beast.

To my further dismay, the beach was alive with people, each lost in their own world of laughter and flirting. I had no privacy to sulk in, no quiet contemplation. I was among others, yet I felt disconnected, as though I was an observer of joy rather than a participant.

It was not unlike how I felt in New York. Surrounded by people and utterly alone.

The sun sunk beneath the waves as torches were lit along the beach and the palm-thatched bar. *That can't be safe—the palms will catch fire! What are they thinking...I doubt there are any fire codes here.*

A group of performers spread out through the crowd, each in a palm frond-printed top—shirts for the men, bikini tops for the women—and grass skirts. They moved with an almost supernatural grace, their bodies twisting and turning to the rhythm of the music.

Then—whoosh—a flame shot upward from the middle of the group.

I startled, my elbow knocking my glass clean over.

The cocktail splashed in a vibrant sunset streak across the bar...and straight onto the lap of the ridiculously hot older guy I'd been pretending not to notice all night.

His deep laugh rumbled through the humid air. "And here I thought I was already too warm."

The orange liquid soaked into his crisp white shirt, blooming like a target I'd just painted on him.

My cheeks flared hotter than the flame thrower. "Shit! I am so, so sorry. Let me—"

3

He cut me off with a slow smile, his eyes dragging over me like silk. "No harm done." He glanced at the spreading stain, then back at me. "Let's call it... a creative icebreaker." He extended a hand. "I'm Dominic. Or Dom, if you prefer. Most people who douse me in booze earn the privilege."

I laughed, already reaching across the bar for club soda and salt like I'd done this a hundred times before. "Take off your shirt, and I might be able to save it," I said, flashing him a playful grin. "I'm Ella, by the way."

His slow smile turned wicked. "Nice to meet you, Ella."

He peeled off his outer layer, handing it to me like we weren't surrounded by tiki torches and half a resort's worth of tourists.

My mouth went dry.

I was wrong. There were far more muscles under that shirt than I had initially thought.

Oh those biceps.

I focused on blotting the bourbon and pineapple out of the fabric, but my pulse didn't get the memo. "Almost as good as new," I said, clearing my throat. "Though I'd let the hotel dry-clean it if I were you."

He held it up, inspecting the shirt in the flickering fire-light before flashing me another grin. "You've got a knack for managing chaos."

I shrugged, trying to sound breezy, though my heart was still doing backflips. "Occupational hazard."

"Lemme guess," he drawled. "Disaster response team?"

"Close." I shot him a wink. "Chef."

"That explains it." He looked me up and down, and I felt it on my skin as if he was touching me all over. "The fire dancers made you jump?"

4

"I didn't know they were fire dancers—thought they were regular ones. When you see an unexpected fire in a kitchen, that's never a good day."

"Understood." He flagged the bartender down. "Another for the lady on my tab."

The bartender got straight to work.

"I don't know about that," I said, trying to...well, I don't know what I was trying to do. I felt bad for spilling my drink on him, and I didn't want him to think he had to do anything for me. "Maybe I've had enough. I'm already spilling drinks—"

"That was hardly your fault."

"You're being generous. Thank you, but—"

"Here we are," the bartender set the next one on the bar for me.

Dom raised his glass to mine, voice rich as velvet. "To happy accidents."

I echoed him softly, clinking my glass to his. The bourbon burned pleasantly as it slid down, but it was nothing compared to the heat simmering in my cheeks. "Thanks again for the drink."

His eyes glittered. "Why does that sound like you're giving me the brush-off?"

I smirked, drawn to his candor. "I figured you were just being polite, and I didn't want to distract you from your night."

He leaned in, voice dropping. "Ella, I'd gladly let you distract me from anything."

My throat went dry, and his words curled around me, making me feel something I hadn't felt in ages. Desired. For the first time in months. I met his gaze, steadier than I expected. "Is that right?"

He nodded once. "Isn't that why anyone comes to a place like this? A diversion from the everyday?"

"I certainly did." I murmured, finishing my drink far too quickly, chasing the warmth pooling between my thighs.

He sipped his, watching me like I was already dessert. "Tell me, Ella. Will you let me be your distraction tonight?"

My breath caught. The air between us stretched taut like a pulled thread ready to snap.

My ex never looked at me like that. Not once in the last year, anyway. He stopped touching me and I'd become invisible to him. A body he barely looked at.

A body that was too soft, too full, too much.

Yet here was this man—this sinfully handsome stranger —gazing at me like I was the most captivating thing on the island. Like he wanted me. And God help me, I wanted to be wanted. Even if it was just for one night. Even if I'd wake up tomorrow alone.

Maybe Carrie, my boss, was right. Maybe I did need to run away. Maybe what I really needed was this—someone to make me forget what it feels like to be unwanted.

"Yes." It slipped out, breathless and sure.

His large hand brushed my knee, warm and certain, before sliding beneath the hem of my tropical dress. I tensed instinctively. *Here it comes,* I thought. The part where his hand would hesitate, where he'd realize just how soft my thighs were compared to whatever fantasy he'd built in his head.

But... he didn't flinch. His touch roamed higher, slow and deliberate, like he was savoring every inch. Like my curves weren't a flaw but an invitation.

Heat bloomed under my skin as his fingers found their mark, and my breath hitched. A thrill of disbelief mingled with the arousal curling deep inside me. He wasn't put off. He was *devouring* me with his touch, his gaze, his every move.

He leaned close, not for a kiss, but to whisper in my ear. His stubble grazed against my cheek. "Come with me to my room, and I'll distract you. All. Night. Long."

I nodded, pulse thrumming wildly. He withdrew his hand, rose from the barstool, and offered me his hand like he'd just invited me into something far more dangerous than a hotel suite. His grip was steady, warm, commanding.

Silence wrapped around us as we walked through the resort's glowing corridors, a blur of carved wood, hibiscus flowers, and tiki torches that felt worlds away from the chaos inside my head.

I didn't need to escape the island. I needed to escape *me*. And God, I hoped Dom could help me forget everything—even if it was only for tonight.

Inside his presidential suite, everything was soft lighting and expensive, masculine touches—dark woods, cool stone floors, and an endless balcony overlooking the ocean. But none of it mattered. Not when Dom's eyes locked on mine like I was the most luxurious thing in the room.

The door clicked shut with a nudge of his foot, and in the next second, his hand curled around the back of my neck, pulling me into a kiss that melted every ounce of hesitation.

Electric. Heady. Hungry.

The kind of kiss that made me forget my name and remember every inch of my skin.

His hand slid down my back, gripping my ass in a possessive squeeze that left me breathless. I stiffened, a flicker of insecurity cutting through the heat. *He's going to notice...* But if he did, it didn't show. No hesitation, no retreat. Just him claiming me like he couldn't get enough.

When he tugged my head back, his fingers threading into my hair, I whimpered softly, tilting toward him, dizzy under the weight of his touch.

He finally eased back, and I found myself clinging to his shirt, biting his lower lip like I needed to mark him.

His grin was sin incarnate. "You're a feisty one, aren't you?"

"You'll see," I whispered, surprising myself.

Clothes came next, a frantic blur of fingers and fabric. I was too caught up in him to stop, but that nagging voice in my head was still there, whispering, *What if he notices? What if he changes his mind when he sees you naked?*

But Dom didn't falter.

When I stood bare before him, vulnerable and exposed, he stepped back like he needed a second just to take it all in. The air shifted. The heat in his gaze deepened into something almost feral.

His slow, reverent stare dragged over my curves like he was savoring every soft inch of me. His wolfish smile stole the breath from my lungs.

"My apologies, Ella."

My heart stuttered. For a heartbeat, panic gripped me. Regret? Pity? "Apologies?" I rasped.

His voice dropped to a dark, delicious growl. "I'm going to ruin this beautiful body tonight." His tongue slid across his lower lip as his eyes darkened. "And I'm afraid you won't be walking straight tomorrow... so I thought I should apologize ahead of time."

Dom peeled off the rest of his clothes, and I swear my breath caught somewhere in my chest.

He was... *magnificent.* All hard planes and honed muscle, carved like he spent his free time bending steel with his bare hands. His chest was broad and dusted with dark hair streaked with specks of gray—subtle but impossible to miss. A reminder that he was older, more experienced, and somehow twice as devastating because of it. His abs were tight, his body powerful and disciplined, like he knew exactly how to use every inch of it.

My gaze dropped, and heat pulsed through me.

Jesus.

His cock stood thick and heavy between his thighs, impossibly big, and straining like he'd been aching for this as long as I had. Veined, flushed, and undeniably intimidating —but every instinct in me screamed *yes.*

And his hands... God, those hands. Big, strong, masculine. The kind that could easily pin me down and make me feel small, yet steady enough to trace every inch of me like I was something precious.

I couldn't help but wonder—*what does a man with hands like that do for a living?* And more pressingly, *what is he about to do to me with them?*

The thought alone sent a rush of heat straight to where I needed him most.

He launched at me—all muscle, heat, and rough hands —gripping, touching, biting, until he backed me onto the bed. I landed on my ass and elbows, breathless. Looking up at him from beneath, everything about him made my pulse stutter. That body. That cock. The dark, hungry gleam in his eyes that promised I wasn't leaving this bed the same woman who walked in.

He caged me in with his arms, his powerful frame towering above mine as my legs dangled helplessly over the edge of the bed. He didn't settle on top of me right away, and at first, confusion fluttered beneath my ribcage. Then it clicked—he was holding back. Careful, measured. Like he didn't want to crush me, like I was delicate.

But I wasn't delicate. I was burning up inside.

That won't do.

I needed him just as wild as I felt.

Dom dipped lower, hovering just over my lips. His breath fanned against me, his voice dark velvet. "Last chance to say no."

My heart thundered. I wanted him to take everything. "I never back down."

A slow, knowing grin. "Neither do I."

The first kiss wasn't sweet. It was claiming. His mouth on my chin, down my throat, tracing my collarbone like he was memorizing me with his tongue. One strong hand slid from my shoulder to my breast, and instead of groping, his touch ghosted across my skin like silk. Barely there, yet more intoxicating than anything bold.

I squirmed beneath him, arching into every whisper of touch, desperate for more friction. He chuckled against my belly. "You're a needy thing, aren't you?"

"Yes," I whimpered, hating how empty I felt without his full weight on me.

"Good." His approval slid into me like another caress.

When he finally spread me wide open, his hands—those

strong, capable hands—molded to my hips and thighs with reverence. "So soft," he murmured, almost to himself, like he'd found his favorite thing and couldn't believe his luck.

A sharp gasp escaped me as his fingers teased the outer edge of me, coaxing out every shiver until my entire body clenched and released under his care. Then, without warning, his mouth was on me—licking, tasting, *owning*. His tongue and fingers worked in sync, and when he hooked a thick finger inside and stroked just the right spot, I forgot how to breathe.

The orgasm came hard and fast, wiping away every scrap of self-doubt until I was boneless beneath him.

Dom didn't stop. He growled against me, low and sinful, like he *needed* this as much as I did, dragging me right into another orgasm that shattered me even harder. When he bit the inside of my thigh, marking me, a strangled cry broke from my throat.

His gaze locked on mine, wild and ravenous.

Dom slid up my body and dragged me up the bed with him, his cock—thick and burning hot—pinning me down as I wrapped my legs around his waist. His lips were glossy with my release, and when he kissed me, I tasted myself on his tongue.

He pressed his forehead to mine, voice rough and sure. "You're mine now—your mouth, your body, every filthy little sound."

I smiled, breathless. "Prove it."

His answering bite to my bottom lip made me whimper, and then he was inside me with a single, savage thrust that had me crying out into his mouth.

He swallowed every sound as he built a rhythm, fucking

me deep and steady, each stroke carving pleasure into me like a brand.

I'd never been taken like this—consumed whole.

I'd forgotten what it was to surrender, or maybe I'd never been given the chance.

Dom *gave* it to me.

He took control, hooking my thigh and spreading me wider, his cock slamming deeper, dragging me up into another climax that burst like lightning across my skin.

"Look at me," he demanded, voice thick with dominance. "Give it to me."

And I did. I shattered beneath him, eyes locked on his as he milked every last aftershock from my trembling body.

But he wasn't done.

Dom flipped me onto his lap, facing him. His hands— huge and commanding—gripped my ass, lifting and driving me down onto his cock with brutal efficiency. His hips snapped up, filling me impossibly deep, forcing me to clutch at his shoulders like I might fall apart.

I never would. Not with those hands holding me steady.

He wouldn't let me.

My cries turned raw as he bounced me harder, faster, until another orgasm coiled tight inside me and detonated with violent force.

I barely had time to recover before he spun me around, seating me reverse on him, legs spread wide, fully exposed. The angle was too much, the pressure perfect.

"I can't—" I gasped, shaking my head.

"You can," Dom growled behind me. "You *will*."

His hand worked between my thighs, relentless, coaxing pleasure out of me whether I was ready or not.

My orgasm slammed into me like a tidal wave, ripping another scream from my throat.

Dom shifted us again, pulling me to my knees as he pounded me from behind, rough and precise, until my muscles trembled with exhaustion.

Finally, Dom pulled out with a low growl, only to grab me and flip me onto my back like I weighed nothing at all. His strength made my pulse race as I hit the mattress, dazed and breathless, limbs loose with pleasure.

But he didn't move right away.

He knelt between my spread thighs, looming above me with that dark, possessive glint in his eyes, his chest heaving, his cock standing thick and flushed. The weight of his stare pinned me down harder than his hands ever could.

"Look at you," he rasped, voice deep with hunger. "Completely wrecked... and still so fucking beautiful."

Heat roared beneath my skin. I tried to catch my breath, but all I could do was lay there—open, exposed, dripping, and utterly undone. I could feel the tremors still racking my thighs, the wet heat pooling between them, and still, Dom took his time, dragging his gaze over every inch of me like he was memorizing the aftermath of what he'd just done.

He leaned forward, slow and predatory, and pressed his hands to either side of my head, boxing me in. His body radiated heat and power, and I realized just how much control he still held over me. And how much I craved it.

"Ella," he murmured, his voice like gravel over silk. "I'm not done with you."

I whimpered beneath him, fully aware of how exposed I was, how thoroughly taken—and still aching for more.

Then, instead of entering me, he reached down,

grabbed his cock, and dragged the thick head along my swollen clit.

I gasped, my hips jerking involuntarily, but he pressed me down with one strong hand on my stomach. "No," he ordered gently, but firmly. "You stay right there and take it."

His cock slid along me again, slow and teasing, smearing my wetness across his length as he toyed with me, keeping me right on the brink. Over and over, he circled and rubbed against me until my muscles tensed and tears threatened behind my eyes.

I was shaking, desperate, hovering on that knife's edge between pleasure and madness.

"Dom, please..." I barely recognized my own voice.

He leaned down, his forehead brushing mine, eyes locked on mine. His lips brushed the corner of my mouth. "Watch me."

I forced my eyes open, heart pounding as he guided himself lower and—inch by inch—pushed inside.

The stretch was maddening. The slow, deliberate drag of every ridge and vein as he filled me again felt like he was claiming me all over, but this time with intention.

"Good girl," he whispered against my lips. "Feel how deep I am?"

I moaned, nodding as my body clenched tight around him.

His thrusts deepened, growing rougher, faster, but never losing control. His cock dragged over that sensitive spot inside me with punishing precision, each movement wringing more sounds from my lips.

The pressure was too much, the fullness too deep—and I shattered. The orgasm ripped through me like a shock-wave, stealing the air from my lungs as my vision went white-hot. My whole body convulsed beneath him, wrung out and shaking, my muscles locking as if I could break apart under the sheer force of it. It wasn't just release—it was *obliteration*. The kind that left me ruined and gasping beneath him.

Dom's eyes locked onto mine, dark and feral. His grip on my wrists tightened as his pace turned relentless, driving into me like he couldn't get deep enough. His jaw clenched, sweat beading along his temples, and that familiar, animalistic growl rumbled low in his chest.

I could feel the tension coiling inside him, sharp and electric, his whole body straining as he fought to hold back.

"Dom..." I breathed, helpless beneath him, completely pinned and undone.

His gaze flickered down to where our bodies joined, watching himself disappear inside me over and over. "Fuck, Ella," he gritted out through clenched teeth. "You're so tight. So perfect."

He drove harder, faster, until I felt the sudden swell of him inside me—the undeniable telltale sign that he was about to lose it. His rhythm faltered for a split second, then sharpened, desperate and hungry.

"Mine," he growled, voice hoarse and raw. "This body is fucking *mine*."

With one final, brutal thrust, Dom buried himself to the hilt, hips grinding against me as his entire body tensed. His breath ripped from his lungs in a guttural groan, deep and savage.

I felt the heat of him flood inside me as he pulsed, coming hard, filling me as he shuddered through his release.

His forehead dropped to mine, his weight settling just enough to make me feel fully, deliciously caged beneath him.

His breath was ragged against my lips, but he didn't move—not right away. Instead, he stayed buried inside me, still holding my wrists, as if he needed the anchor of my body to ride out the storm of his orgasm.

And when he finally opened his eyes, that dark, wild gaze softened just enough to steal what was left of my breath.

Chapter 2

Dom

The fine white sheets were a tangled mess around us, a testament to what had unfolded moments ago. Lying beside Ella, I still felt the echo of her touch against my skin, that lingering warmth fueling an insatiable desire.

This woman was dangerous. Addictive.

Her head rested on my chest, and her chocolate brown hair spilled in waves over my arm. Deep rhythmic breaths fell over my scant chest hair like she was close to falling asleep. But I wanted those hazel green eyes open again. They'd been so wary and wide when she spilled her drink on me like she thought she was in trouble.

I could have taken pity on the girl, but I wasn't ready for sleep. My mind raced, already plotting the next step in this unexpected game we found ourselves playing. I wanted her in every way possible.

Normally, I dated within my social set. It would be unseemly for me to be with a woman like Ella. But women my age weren't usually this carefree with themselves. They had more obligations and things to consider than a girl in her twenties. Back home—

But I'm not home. I don't have to worry here. No one knows me on the island.

Maybe that was the magic of vacation sex. Nothing to consider, no responsibilities. Just fun. Ella The Chef was the perfect vacation hookup.

And I wanted more.

Waves crashed outside, the sound filtering through the open balcony door. I should have smelled the ocean. Instead, I smelled her all around me. Vanilla and sugar and something undeniably female. I wanted her here, in this moment with me, indefinitely. Her presence was intoxicating.

"Ella," I began, my voice low as I traced my fingers along her arm to outline the small whisk tattoo there. Her skin was like silk. I wanted to know her. Not only her body, but the woman she was. "Tell me something about you that no one else knows."

She chuckled at my request and yawned. "I hate underwear."

I barked a laugh. "Something tells me I'm not the only person who knows that."

She shifted slightly, propping herself up on one elbow to look at me. The moonlight cast her face in a soft glow, highlighting the curiosity in her eyes. "Something no one knows? That's a big ask from a stranger."

"I don't see the point in making small talk. Life's too short for that."

Her lips curled into a thoughtful smile. "That's true." She laid back down on my shoulder. "When I was a girl, I used to write poetry. Silly stuff, really. About dreams or boys I liked, the kind of things you think will never really happen."

I smiled, tightening my hold on her. "Why wouldn't the boys happen?"

"I was a late bloomer. Didn't have my first boyfriend until I turned twenty."

"So, this was two, three years ago?"

She laughed. "Ten."

"You're thirty?"

She nodded, then took a bite of my pec.

I swatted her ass for that infraction, and she giggled and released me. "What was that bite for, young lady?"

"You're not supposed to ask a woman's age, and thus, you had to be punished."

"Oh, I'll show you punishment, if you like."

Her breath hitched at that. "Maybe later."

I liked that she had an adventurous streak in her, even if only for the night. It was my nature to push for more—to know more, feel more, own more. With Ella, every piece of information felt like a piece of her soul she was handing over, and I was eager to collect as much as she was willing to give.

"Promise me I'll get to punish you again."

"What we did didn't feel much like a punishment to me."

"Promise me."

She laughed, a sound that was part music, part magic. "Maybe," she teased, leaning in to kiss me softly. "If you're lucky."

The kiss deepened, and I rolled over, pinning her gently

beneath me. My body was ready again, my desire for her reignited by the mere sound of her voice, the taste of her lips. "I don't rely on luck," I whispered against her mouth. "I make my own."

"That's why I have a four-leaf clover tattoo on my ankle. I had to make my own luck a long time ago."

"Sounds like there's a story there."

She smiled, and it was enough to take my breath away. "Yeah. But I already gave you one of my secrets. Tell me one of yours. Something no one knows."

"That's not how this game goes—"

"It is when you play with me," she said sharply. "Unless you don't want to play with me again—"

"Fine, fine, a secret for a secret. Brat."

She grinned. "You bring the brat out in me."

Lucky me. "My secret, if it can be called that, is that I miss simpler days."

"How is that a secret?"

"Because anyone who knows me would think I have the perfect life. The truth is, I miss the old days when I was starting my company."

"I assume that means you're a big success now?"

I chuckled. "If you've ever had surgery for a heart murmur on the East Coast, there's a significant chance the hospital used some of my company's equipment."

Those hazel green eyes go wide for a flash. "Oh, wow. Impressive."

Shrugging off her compliment felt wrong but accurate. "Thank you, but I miss the days from the start of things. Twenty years ago, when things were sketchy, and we didn't know if we were going to hit the way we wanted to...it was me and two partners working with manufacturers and others to move our products to market ourselves instead of selling to one of the big corporations. Those are the days I miss."

"That sounds terrifying. Why would you miss it?"

There were some secrets that I couldn't tell her, so I kept things as clean as possible. No sense in dragging her into my sorrows. "Back then, the company was small and nimble. The three of us against the world. I was finishing my degree in Chicago when I met my partners, and that's where we started the company. Life is simpler there than in New York. I assume that's where you're from, too—"

"Born and raised."

"Same. I love New York, but Chicago has a Midwest charm. People there are friendlier and warmer. Things move at a slower pace. I miss that."

"What's so different about things now?"

"Now, Morbinski Incorporated is a behemoth by comparison. Over two hundred employees, a board to answer to, all the trappings of corporate life. My partners sold me their stake in the company, so I own all of it, and there are days it is more than I want to handle. So—"

"Simpler sounds better."

I nodded once. "I'm here to escape...that and my son. He has refused to go to rehab again, and we had a shouting match about it. Again. What about you? What brought you here?"

She sighed and laid back, taking her delicious warmth with her. So I laid on my side to be closer to her. She licked her bottom lip, a hesitation. "I don't want to bring you down. Don't—"

"Whatever you're holding back, there is nothing you could tell me that would diminish the high of having you in my bed."

"You sound very sure of that."

"I am."

She bit her lip once more before blurting, "Bad breakup."

"What happened? If it's bad enough that you needed a passport to escape your breakup, you likely need to talk about it."

Her smile died. "I guess that's true. We dated for two years, give or take. Things were mostly good. Kind of. Anyway, I thought we were really gonna be something, you know?"

"What went wrong?"

"Recently, God, I guess it's been almost a month now— he told me he couldn't see himself settling for someone like me."

"Settling?" I didn't have the time to blink before the anger set in. "What precisely did he mean by that?"

Her voice cracked, and she gave a tight, embarrassed laugh. "That I'm... not exactly his type anymore." She shrugged, but it didn't hide the hurt flashing in her eyes. "Too soft. Too much of me, I guess."

All sense of satisfaction evaporated upon hearing those words. "That son of a bitch—"

"He has a lot of problems," she said as some sort of explanation.

"He's about to have another."

She laughed. "Stop. It's not the first time some guy has said something rude to me about my body, and it won't be the last, I'm sure of it. He's a big pill head and drinks too much, one of those artists who take the Hemmingway approach to life, you know what I mean?"

"All too well."

"He mixes too much of one with the other, and sometimes, it makes him mean. He says...rude things. I'm not trying to excuse what he said—only trying to explain it."

"You don't need to do either for my benefit, Ella. No context excuses what he said to you."

She shrugged. "Anyway, my boss told me I needed to come here and get my head straight. She and her husband come here to get out of the city, so she recommended this place." She rolled onto her hip to face me. "I'm glad she did."

"Enjoying your stay?"

"Tonight in particular."

I traced along her collarbone and down her sternum, losing my fingertips in her cleavage. "Tonight has been especially good."

Her breath hitched in her chest. "Agreed."

I loved seeing the effect I had on her. Every inch of her had been so responsive, and knowing she'd likely been neglected by her bastard ex-boyfriend, I made a silent vow to make up for his mistakes. "I owe you another punishment."

Her smile turned playful. "But I thought I had been so good."

"The punishment isn't because you were bad. It's because I've been good."

Her pupils blew as her breaths increased. "You have been."

"Stay here." I exited the bed and fetched a pair of robes from the closet. "Put this on."

"What kind of punishment requires a robe?"

"Put it on and find out," I said as I put mine on.

She huffed and took the robe. "All right, but this better be good. Someone promised to distract me all night long."

"Yes, well, you were five minutes away from falling asleep not long ago, so I'm not sure you could keep up with me."

Her indignant laugh made me smile. "Oh, bullshit! You've got ten years on me—"

"Eighteen, actually."

That stopped her for a moment before she tied the robe. "You're forty-eight?"

"Is that a problem?"

"Not even a little. I was just surprised. Now, what is the robe for, Dom?"

I took her hand and led her to the balcony. When she saw it, her appreciative gasp was all I needed to hear. She leaned on the decorative railing for a better view of the ocean. It was why I had picked the suite—I liked a good view.

"It's beautiful out here."

A private beach was flanked by jungle on two sides, but the sandy beach stretched before us. The water was black and glittered beneath the stars and a half moon. There was little light pollution from this end of the resort, so the natural surroundings shone all the brighter for it.

But then the sound of drums pulsed out from the corner of the building. I had timed this just right. I pressed myself against her ample backside and held the railing on either side of her. "We're just in time."

"The resort's nightly parade?"

"Indeed."

She giggled. "Didn't think that'd be your scene."

"It's not." I slipped one hand from the railing to place it inside her robe.

She startled and stiffened for a beat before relaxing against me. "Oh."

The adults-only nature of the resort made me worry less about pushing the boundaries of propriety. Guests and employees walked around the building every night at eleven. Musicians and dancers carried torches or instruments, while the guests usually carried their third or fourth cocktails as they laughed and danced. Not a large parade, but usually several dozen people long. Enough for a hint of risk.

I'd always enjoyed public play, so I hoped she wouldn't object. My fingers splayed over her belly, the tips barely grazing her softness down below. "Anyone could look up here and see that my hand vanished into your robe. So, you better be quiet, young lady." My hand dipped lower, my thumb on her clit as she mewled behind closed lips. "Wouldn't want to get caught, would we?"

"No," she whispered.

I experimented with my touch until I found the motion that made her go tight against me. "What a pity you don't want them to see this. A pussy this pretty should have an audience."

"Oh God."

"Have you ever played in public, Ella? Have you let people see you come?"

"No."

I hooked a finger into her, and she shuddered and arched ever so slightly to take me deeper. I nudged her hair out of my way and exposed her bare neck to bite her there. Not hard—just enough to satisfy my need to own each part of her body. She whimpered and opened her neck to me, making it easier to sink my teeth into her.

She was mine only for the night, and I intended to take everything I wanted.

"Dom, please."

"Please, what? Tell me what you want."

"I need to come. Please."

Even if Ella wasn't the most addictive woman I'd met in a long time, hearing her beg for orgasm was enough to hook me. I opened the front of my robe and lifted the back of hers. "Lean forward and watch the parade, Ella."

"What are you—"

I entered her from behind, earning a surprised yelp from her sweet lips. Fuck, she was so damn wet and tight. I moved as if dancing to the parade music, and she gripped the railing. "Dance with me."

"Oh my fuck—"

The sound of a trumpet cut her off. The parade leader liked to come through and wave at all the people on the balconies as he played his trumpet. Sometimes, he had a pair of women with him to toss beads to the balcony spectators.

I was delighted to see them again tonight. I grunted. "Smile and wave, Ella. Give them a show."

"Can't—gonna come!"

I pounded into her to the rhythm of the parade, just another dancing spectator lost to the music. When she clenched on me, she nearly yanked me over the line. But I held back. I had other plans.

The bead tossers threw some necklaces our way as the parade wound around the other side of the building. When the last of them vanished from view, I pulled out and tucked myself away. Ella leaned back on me for balance.

"What...the fuck?"

"Don't like a little danger in your fucking?"

Slowly, she turned around to face me. Her face was flushed, sweaty. If I didn't know better, I'd think she had a fever. "I don't...never...wow."

I took her hand in mine again, this time leading her back to the bed. "Lay down for me."

"Don't have much choice. My legs are still shaking."

I unwrapped the robe from around her and kissed a trail from her exquisite, full tits to her thick thighs. "You are a vision. Never let anyone tell you otherwise." And then, I feasted on every inch of her.

Once was never enough. With a woman like Ella, it could never be enough.

As our physical connection ebbed, I held her close, feeling a proprietary satisfaction in the heat of her body against mine. "Stay with me tonight," I murmured into her hair. The thought of her leaving, this room growing cold by her absence, was unacceptable.

Ella looked up at me, her eyes searching mine in the dim light. After a moment, she nodded, her smile soft. "I can't think of anywhere else I'd rather be."

As sleep finally claimed us, I was content in the knowledge that she was here, safe in my arms, and for now, mine.

Chapter 3

Ella

The first light of dawn made the sky lavender through the white sheers of Dom's suite. I lay awake, the sheets wrapped around me like the thoughts spinning through my mind. I'd woken up early, unable to rest once the thought struck me.

Dom's company's name was familiar, and I couldn't think of why.

The steady rise and fall of his chest beside me was a rhythmic contrast to the erratic beat of my heart. Last night, I felt a connection that transcended the casual nature of our encounter. But it was hard to believe it was anything more than amazing sex.

My body said something else. My head, however, was unconvinced. *Morbinski. His last name? But he said he had business partners...*

I couldn't take it anymore. I had to know.

Carefully, I slid from under his arm, feeling the cool air replace the warmth of his body. The only sounds were the distant murmur of the ocean and Dom's soft breathing, even as I tiptoed to my purse to grab my phone. Every step reminded me of our fun last night. I was, in fact, not walking straight to my phone. Once it was out, I googled the company's name on the hotel's slow Wi-Fi.

When it popped up, nothing significant showed itself on the landing page. I clicked the "About Us" button and scrolled through the board members to get to the founders. Robin Skiggs—a woman from Chicago, blah, blah, blah. Greg Binson—a man from Seattle, don't care about the details.

And then...

Dom's picture.

Oh.

Fuck.

The air sucked out of the room. My pulse hammered in my ears as I read the name beneath the photo like it couldn't possibly be real.

Dominic Mortoli.

The surname hit me like a punch to the ribs.

No. No, no, no.

My stomach knotted so violently I thought I might throw up. Every muscle in my body went slack, and I nearly fumbled my phone to the floor. Only the sharp jolt of panic —don't make a sound, don't you dare—kept my fingers clamped around it.

He was still asleep. Peaceful. Oblivious.

I stared at the glowing screen as bile rose in my throat.

Dominic Mortoli.

My ex's father.

I just fucked my ex's father.

Sweat pricked at the back of my neck as my mind

scrambled, unraveling into chaos. There would be questions. God, so many questions.

Why are you leaving?

Where are you going?

And how the hell do I explain this?

I sucked in a shaky breath, whispered, "Fuck."

Dom snorted as he reached for my side of the bed.

I moved my pillow close enough that he reached it and seemed satisfied. One tiny crisis averted.

Now, to make my escape.

As I dressed, a thousand questions flew through my head like the good sense I should have been born with. But they all boiled down to one.

Why did fate pair me with this family not once, but twice?

It was cruel. Fate had never been particularly kind to me, but this? This was bad, even by my standards. It's like the universe was trying to tell me something by repeating itself, and I'm still unable to hear it. Rationally, I believed in coincidence, but this was too much.

I slipped my sandals on, cautiously picked up my purse while I hoped not to make too much noise, and tiptoed toward the door. But my sandal slapped the bottom of my foot, and I froze.

Dom didn't even stir.

I stepped out of my sandals, opting for bare feet on the dark hardwood instead. The latch on the door didn't click until I closed it behind me. And then, I ran for my room on the first floor. I ignored the knowing smiles from the nosy staff as I made my way through the halls. I wanted to shout, "Yes, I had sex with a stranger last night! Are you happy?"

But shouting might have alerted enough people to wake Dom.

I could not be here when he woke up. I had to leave right now.

Once I got to my room, I remembered I didn't have much to pack. I changed back into the clothes I flew down in. Thankfully, summer in New York was almost just as hot as the weather in the islands, so when I went to the front desk in my shorts and tee, no one gave me a second glance.

"Yes, hi, I know I am booked for another three nights, but I have a family emergency back in New York, and I have to get home as soon as possible. How do we make that happen?"

"I am sorry to hear that and happy to help..."

Thankfully, the concierge made all the arrangements for me, and before I knew it, I was on a plane back to the States. I didn't like lying to get what I needed done, but technically, it wasn't a lie.

I had a family emergency. I'd fucked my way through two men in the same family.

Thankfully, Leo had no brothers, or Fate might have had even more fun at my expense. My head tipped back against the cushy first-class seat. How could Leo be so different from his father? For the past month, I'd told myself he must have gotten that shitty attitude from his dad. Wasn't that how these things worked? Guys hated women in front of their sons, so their sons mimicked that. Or so I had thought.

Dom clearly had no problem with my body. In fact, he seemed very, very into me. It was a pity he had spawned the biggest jerk I ever dated.

Leo had always said that his father was a neglectful asshole surgeon. Did Dom lie about his job? I wasn't sure. Leo being Leo, maybe he was too drugged up to explain what he meant. Surgeon had to be close enough to medical device inventor for him to confuse the two, or maybe Dom had been a surgeon before he invented—

You know what? It doesn't matter.

I had spent far too much time trying to dissect Leo's family from a distance, and I decided enough was enough. The Mortolis would get no more energy from me.

Except Leo had told me Dom worked at a hospital near the restaurant I worked at. That was why he never visited me at work—he didn't want to chance running into his dad.

Ugh. None of this lined up. As much as I didn't want to give them my time and attention, I hated it when I had more questions than answers. And Leo's characterization of Dom did not align with anything I had learned about him last night. He wasn't inattentive or cold. He was focused and hot.

So damn hot.

Stop that.

The whole thing left me confused. The intimacy we had shared was unlike anything I had experienced. As I replayed our conversations, his words echoed in my mind, revealing a man who could have been more than a hookup. He was someone I connected with.

Truth be told, we had more of a connection in a single night than I had with Leo for two years.

His son. He's his son. Get your head out of your ass.

It wasn't only about me at this point. Leo had a shitty relationship with his father. If he learned about last night...I shouldn't care what he'd do with the information, but I did. As much as he had hurt me, I still didn't want him to be hurt by this. More than that, I didn't want to be a wedge between Dom and Leo. Their relationship was hanging by a thread, and I heard the pain in Dom's voice when he spoke of Leo.

I couldn't be what drove them further apart.

Leaving without a word might have been cowardly at the time, but looking back on it now, it was the only choice.

For me and for them.

But that was cold comfort on the airplane. The intimacy we had shared was something I'd never forget. The kind of thing poets write about. And maybe I would one day. But maintaining a distance was a safeguard for my vulnerable heart.

The poet in me wondered a ponderous question. Was I protecting my heart, or was I running from the very thing I had longed for my whole life?

The truth was, it didn't matter either way. I had left Dom's room to save myself from admitting I'd nailed my ex's father and to maintain control over my life. If I had stayed, if I had told him the truth, what horrors would that have wrought?

I couldn't date Dom, no matter how much of a connection we had. Aside from being who he was, he had eighteen years on me. He started voting the year I was born. How could we possibly have had a relationship that was more than a punchline?

Logically, I knew some people had good relationships with big age gaps. But that didn't stop others from judging them over it. Hell, I'd judged people for that kind of thing before.

There was no possible way for us to work out. So, really, what was I worried about?

Never seeing Dom again.

Oh, shut up.

My inner voices only ever argued like this when I truly wanted something. I knew what that meant, and I knew that it didn't matter. Dominic Mortoli was off-limits, thanks to his son who had wasted two years of my life.

No. I had wasted that time with him. I could have left him at any time, but I had stayed. Since the breakup, I'd replayed a lot of moments between us, good and bad. The more I examined us, the more I realized how much we were together out of convenience.

With his artist's schedule of waking up whenever he wanted to wake up and having the freedom and money to do whatever whenever, I didn't have to worry about him not being available when I felt like seeing him. My schedule was the crazy one. I was the one with ambition and dedication to my job, and I couldn't work from home like he could, so my place was a convenient spot for him to escape his work whenever.

I cared for Leo. But it was never love. Neither of us had ever even tried to say the L-word to each other.

The first Christmas, I had asked about meeting his family. He told me he wasn't seeing them for the holiday, so I didn't need to worry about it. Then, last Christmas, he said they weren't inviting friends for the holiday.

Friends. Like that was all I was to him.

Dom showed more care for me in a single night than

Leo ever had. As much as I hated the circumstances, I was glad I'd met him and taken a chance. No morning's reality could wash away the memories of the night I'd had.

The realization that I might never see him again struck with an acute sharpness. Beneath the surface, a stubborn ember of hope glowed warm—the hope that perhaps this wasn't the end, that perhaps fate had more in store for us than a steamy night followed by a cruel morning.

No. I knew better than that. I was Fate's punching bag. Nothing more.

I made myself comfortable and asked for a flute of champagne as a balm for my bruised heart. The island had worked its magic. I'd gone from wounded to merely bruised, thanks to a fleeting connection and phenomenal sex.

Maybe that was all I could ask for out of life. Some people don't even get that. I should be grateful I met Dom at all.

But the thought of never seeing him again left me cold.

Chapter 4

Dom

Waking in a cold bed without Ella was unacceptable, but I didn't have a say in the matter. Somehow, I'd wrapped my arm around her pillow, and I suspected that was her doing. It was like last night was a fantasy come to life, only for morning's harsh light to illuminate the truth of the matter.

She was my fantasy. I wasn't hers.

I shook my head at myself while staring over the beach from the balcony. The connection between us was too strong for her to have pretended, and I knew for certain she hadn't faked her orgasms, so why did she leave me without a word?

I didn't understand.

And without her phone number, I never would.

At least she had left her scent behind on the sheets. Vanilla, sugar, and her. I'd never smell cookies or cake the same way again.

Perhaps this was all she wanted from me—a night of passion after a bad breakup. Something to soothe the hurt I heard in her voice when she spoke of her ex-boyfriend, the bastard. I hoped I gave her what she needed. She had certainly done that for me.

I should have been glad for the experience, and I was, but I had wanted more.

Truly, no matter how much waking up alone stung, it wasn't personal. We hadn't gotten to know each other well enough for this to be personal. She got what she wanted, and so did I. To an extent.

Until this morning. I had hoped for another round or two this morning. But I supposed it was not meant to be. We had spent my last night here together, which would have to be enough.

It had been a long time since I'd slept next to someone. The comfort found in the arms of another person was unique to that person, but still a comfort all the same. It didn't matter that we had been strangers, and to a degree, we still were. Spooning Ella had soothed something raw inside of me. Maybe it shouldn't have, but it did.

Packing my suitcase was a mechanical process, my movements automatic as the vibrant memories of the night replayed in my mind. Her laughter, the way she quaked under me. Laying in bed and talking about life or talking about nothing at all. The silent seconds of merely touching, before we started up again. Every moment with Ella had been special.

The tropical paradise that had seemed so inviting now felt empty, a sandy stage for a play that had ended too soon. The palm trees swayed outside my window, their silhouettes a stark contrast against the midmorning sky. This picturesque scene now felt like mockery.

I was both glad for my night with Ella and also glad to be leaving. I wouldn't feel grounded again until I was home.

But in New York, the city slammed into me like a steel door—horns blaring, crowds pressing in, the chaos too loud and too fast. Same old streets. Same old skyline. But everything felt…off. My high-rise apartment, once a badge of success, now felt like a glass box. A gilded cage.

I set my bags down and stared at the skyline. Concrete. Steel. Miles of cold indifference.

Nothing grounded me here—not when I could still feel Ella's warmth pressed into my skin.

I shouldn't have thought of my hometown that way, but it was hard not to. Perhaps not a cage, but a maze, and somewhere in the labyrinth was a woman who vexed me. The poet chef who gave into every one of my base instincts. Not merely gave into them, but enjoyed them as much as I did.

I would never meet another woman like her. It wasn't possible. Last night was a once-in-a-lifetime thing. Better to have that memory than to have nothing at all. Wasn't it?

I slept fitfully and woke up with my arm over the second pillow, a hollow imitation of the day before. I shoved that pillow off and got out of bed. There were lives to save. Another day, another night, another shift in the ED.

As a surgeon in the emergency department, I was used to changing gears quickly, but today, the weight of my thoughts made each decision heavier, each case more taxing. There should have been a transition day for returning from vacation, one in which you had half a caseload instead of the full monty, and people didn't try to force you to make conversation.

My lunch break was my only solace. I clocked out, hit

the cafeteria for a sad salad with grilled chicken breast, and ducked back outside. The hospital was one of the best in the city, and one of the best features was a small area with picnic tables and a tiny koi pond. The koi were happy to accept fish feed and anything else the staff tossed them. Their needs were simple and quiet. No confusing mixed signals with the fish.

As soon as they saw me, they swam to the edge of the pond, mouths gaping for food. I tossed them a few lettuce leaves and sat at the table nearest the pond. It was too hot out for most people to be out there, so I had the mini park to myself. A rare moment for this hospital.

When lunch was over, though, it was back to the grind. Inside was a blur of activity, as always. The sharp beeps of monitors and the sterile smell of antiseptic were suddenly more pronounced. My colleagues greeted me with nods and smiles.

All but Seth Bowan.

That asshole's customary head nod-slash-grimace combination was little more than the polite version of, "Fuck you."

But I was used to that from him.

Every interaction felt like a hollow echo of my usual routine. I navigated through a day packed with back-to-back surgeries and patient consultations, my professional mask firmly in place while, in my mind, I wandered the city in search of the enigmatic poet chef.

Where would I find such a creature again? I'd never know. It was a mystery I'd never solve.

New York City was unlike how the TV shows and films made it seem. People didn't incidentally run into each other all the time. You might see the same people in a diner every day, or see the same people in your neighborhood, but in a city of nearly nine million people, you were highly unlikely to run into your holiday hookup.

And if I ran into her, what would I say? Long time no see? Why'd you leave without so much as a word to me? Would you like to get a cup of coffee sometime? When can I fuck you again? The possibilities were endless, and none of it mattered because I'd never get to ask my questions. Whatever was between us was only for that night.

After a long day, the fatigue of mental and physical demands weighed heavily on me. I wasn't ready to be back at work and needed a release, a moment to disconnect. From myself as much as from the hospital.

I found my way to a familiar upscale bar, the kind where the clink of glasses punctuated sophisticated conversations. Stockbrokers and lawyers usually crammed the spot, but tonight, it was only half full for some reason.

Maybe today was a holiday and the world forgot to tell me. It was like that in the ED until holiday injuries started to pour in. I checked my phone to see if I'd missed another holiday. No—but it was one of the days the stock market was closed, so I assumed everyone else in here was a lawyer.

The bar was dimly lit, with plush leather seats and dark wood paneling, exuding an air of exclusivity. Ordering a Halekulani—the drink that Ella had introduced my shirt to —felt like a salute to her memory.

As I sipped the sweet, complex cocktail, I could almost taste the salty air of the tropics. I shouldn't have ordered it. The drink only made me miss her more. But sometimes, a little pain made a memory bittersweet instead of just bitter.

41

A heavy perfume wafted over me, and a feminine voice said, "I couldn't help but notice you seem all alone. Care to change that?"

I glanced to my left to find a classically beautiful woman standing there. She was tall with sleek gold-toned brunette hair and a graceful manner that matched the bar's upscale vibe. Her dress was elegant, a simple black number that hinted at curves without revealing much. Thin. Painfully so. In this city, she was as likely to be a model as an accountant.

She was all sharp angles and gloss.

Not like Ella.

Ella was warmth. Ella was weight and softness, laughter and poetry.

This woman was a glossy magazine spread. Ella was art.

I took in the polished exterior and the expectant tilt of her head. Something about her reminded me of the women I used to pursue—confident, near my age, perfectly put together. But tonight, her presence was an unwelcome interruption to my thoughts. I preferred my melancholy over her company.

"Thank you, but I'm not interested," I said firmly, my tone leaving no room for further discussion. She wasn't Ella. She didn't have Ella's wild laugh or the soft curves I couldn't stop imagining beneath my hands. This woman was sleek and polished. Ella had been messy and alive —*real*. No one else stood a chance tonight.

She lingered for a beat before returning to her table. Maybe to give me a chance to change my mind, or perhaps she wasn't accustomed to being turned down. If she was a lawyer, I could see her making an argument. Whatever the case, I was glad when she left.

Turning back to my drink, I let the rush of the bar fade into background noise. I had gone to the tropics to escape the pressure cooker of my job, where I was constantly competing for a promotion that seemed increasingly unworthy of the sacrifices required. Or maybe I was merely in a foul mood after a long day back at the grind, post-vacation.

That kind of thing never did anyone any good.

More pressing, though, was the strained relationship with my son, who was reeling from his own troubles. I had snapped at him out of stress and frustration right before my trip, worsening the rift between us. Leonardo needed rehab. I'd often considered employing one of those pseudo-legal groups to kidnap him and force him into rehab, but they didn't have good long-term success rates, and that was what he needed. My son had addiction problems, and he needed a life-long solution.

The irony wasn't lost on me. I had gone seeking solitude and contemplation, only to return with a distracting new addiction of my very own. Ella had taken hold of my thoughts, filling every quiet moment with a longing bordering on madness. It would have been different had she not been a New Yorker, that I was sure of.

But she was here in my city. Finding her again felt like searching for a needle in a haystack, and the concept was too close to stalking for my liking.

As the night wore on and the bar began to empty, I realized that my return to home was a façade. The city felt more alien than ever, each step homeward a reminder of what—

and who—I had left behind. Though, I supposed I had been the one left behind. Not her.

I'd make my peace with it eventually. But not today.

The streets were busy with the late-night crowd, the air hot and humid, the skyscrapers towering overhead like...I wasn't sure. But given her penchant for poetry, I was sure Ella would have devised a good analogy.

She wasn't just a fling. She had branded herself beneath my skin, an echo in my mind that wouldn't fade. How I was going to reconcile that with my daily life? I had responsibilities that awaited me. I couldn't remain hung up on a woman who left without a word. It was a puzzle I couldn't yet solve.

But as I walked the neon-lit streets of New York, her image haunted me—a beacon that kept the shadows at bay and fueled my determination to find her once more.

Chapter 5

Ella

Suivante was my home, the restaurant that had lifted me from sous chef to assistant head chef. The clatter of the restaurant kitchen was the soundtrack of my life, and it energized me from the time I walked into the restaurant until I walked out. Until now.

This morning, everything felt off. I couldn't explain it.

The lunch team was hopping, rushing orders, running plates, getting the job done better than any kitchen I'd ever worked before. Me, Miguel, Sam, Ricardo, Yvette, and Lisa had the place hopping. But every few minutes, I fell behind. It wasn't like me.

As assistant head chef at one of New York City's most esteemed eateries, my days were a whirlwind of activity, each service a dance of precision and creativity. I loved every moment—the heat, the pressure, the satisfaction of a perfectly executed dish. A slash of herbed reduction here, a sliver of almond brûlée there. Ice-white dishes painted with every color in the rainbow.

It was a world I controlled with ease, a world far removed from the complications of so-called real life.

What good had real life ever done for me anyway? Not much, that was for sure. It had been almost two months since I ran away from home for a break and three months since my breakup, and I had been doing well enough that Carrie had stopped giving me shit about moping around.

But the vacation had been an escape from real life, not an embrace of it.

I'd found an old bottle of Leo's cologne in the back of my medicine cabinet the other day, and it didn't even faze me. I just tossed it out and kept trucking. It shouldn't have been so easy to let him go after two years. We should have been more attached to each other than that, shouldn't we?

But as Carrie said, I had to stop should-ing. "Should is someone else's expectation," she liked to say. It would have been annoying that she was always right, but at least I had her in my corner. Besides, I had always had a quick turn-around time for relationships. But Leo had been the longest one I'd ever had, so I expected something more than nothing.

In the middle of the lunch rush, I bent over a meticulous plating of our smoked sausage and white balsamic glaze special, a wave of nausea hit me so suddenly that I had to pause and steady myself against the stainless steel counter.

The scent of garlic and seared meat hit like a punch to the gut, turning my stomach inside out. Even the sweet tang of balsamic glaze felt like it clawed at my throat.

The smells of the kitchen, usually so appetizing, were suddenly overpowering.

"Everything okay, Ella?" Carrie's voice cut through the

noise, tinged with concern. She had an uncanny ability to notice whenever something was amiss, even from the front of the house. Her red pixie cut made her easy to spot in the busy kitchen. She wore all black—everyone at Suivante did —and a worried expression.

"Just a bit off, I think," I managed to say, forcing a smile as I straightened up and resumed my task.

Carrie watched me for a moment longer, and her brows knit together in concern. Professional or personal, I never knew with her. The two overlapped in every kitchen I had worked before, and here, the lines were blurred further by our friendship. "You know, you've been 'off' quite a bit lately," she said, her tone light but probing. "Are you sure there isn't a mini-Ella floating around in there?"

"A what?"

"Are you pregnant? You'd tell me, right?"

I laughed once hard and rolled my eyes. "Oh, sure, that's exactly it."

"Hey, you're the one who said she hooked up on vacation. I'm just checking in."

I shook my head. "There's no chance. I'm on the shot, remember?"

"Right, right. I forgot. Maybe it's that bug that's going around."

"I'll be fine. Probably just turned around too fast."

"Carrie," Emily called out from the door. "Someone wants to speak to the owner." The hostess was too new to know how to handle customer requests.

"Be right there." She turned to me. "You're sure you're good?"

"We have crackers and ginger ale. I'll be fine. Go on."

She bobbed her head and left me in the sweltering kitchen. Why was it so hot back here?

"Miguel, hit the A/C again—"

"Already got it as low as possible, chef."

"All right, I'm taking two in the walk-in." My voice came out thin. Weak. Not me. Two minutes down during lunch rush was dangerous—but right now, *so was staying out here.*

The second the cooler door sealed behind me, the cold air hit, but instead of relief, it only sharpened the nausea twisting my gut. The usual crisp scent of greens, citrus, and herbs turned sickening.

The kale smelled like compost. The tomatoes like rot. I blinked, expecting to find mold or wilt—but the bins were pristine. Emerald leaves. Crimson skins. Everything *looked* perfect. So why did my stomach lurch like I'd inhaled something foul?

Carrie's voice came back to me, slithering between the thrum of my heartbeat. *"You've been off quite a bit lately... Are you sure there isn't a mini-Ella floating around in there?"*

I pressed a hand to my abdomen as dread coiled inside me.

No.

It couldn't be.

It's a bug. A flu. Anything but that.

I forced out a breath, but it came shaky and shallow. The vegetables blurred, a cold sweat trickling down my spine.

And yet, somewhere deep down, a quiet voice whispered the truth I wasn't ready to hear.

I cannot be pregnant. It's not possible. I'm on the shot. It's just a flu or something. It has to be.

I tried to comfort myself with thoughts of the shot. My every three-month appointment system had never failed me. I was religious about it. I checked my phone to check when my last crossed out appointment was six months ago.

I had missed the next appointment because it was scheduled the day after I'd been dumped. But I had been on the shot for years. There was no way that one missed shot set me up for a mistake, right?

The rest of the day passed in a blur of forced normalcy. I focused on my work, on the familiar tasks of chopping, sautéing, and seasoning, letting the routine numb my spiraling thoughts. I did everything I could to avoid thinking about the smells and sights and heat, sometimes swiping the fresh mint from the bar to gnaw on. It helped my stomach more than the crackers and ginger ale. But nothing soothed my nerves.

The seed Carrie had planted grew, watered by my rising suspicions and the undeniable symptoms I could no longer ignore.

After my shift, I nearly ran to the nearest pharmacy. I thought about hitting the corner store by my apartment, but Mrs. Bing would have asked too many questions I wasn't ready to answer. She had run that shop for over thirty years and knew everyone and all the gossip in the neighborhood. If I had bought a pregnancy test there, I would have had a congratulations basket on my doorstep by tomorrow. As much as I loved my neighborhood, I also loved my privacy.

Back in the solitude of my apartment, I locked the bathroom door behind me like it might somehow shield me from the answer I already suspected. The apartment felt too quiet. Too small. The only sound was the crinkle of the test wrapper as my shaky hands ripped it open.

I followed the instructions with clinical precision, heart hammering as if I were about to plate a dish for Michelin inspectors.

Minutes stretched like hours.

When the result appeared, it felt like the air thickened around me.

Positive.

The results stared up at me from that tiny plastic window—merciless, undeniable.

"No, no, no," I whispered, the words tasting bitter as they left my lips.

For a second, I felt weightless—like the floor had dropped out from under me. The room tilted, but I caught the edge of the sink, nails biting into porcelain as I clung to the only steady thing in sight.

But panic was a luxury I didn't allow myself. Logistics—that was where I lived.

Where I survived.

Outside of creativity, every chef must handle logistics like a pro. Those were the main elements of the job.

So, I considered schedules, finances, maternity leave—all the practicalities of managing an unexpected pregnancy while running a kitchen. Not the implications. Not the reality of what I was contemplating. Only the logistics were allowed to sink in.

But as the evening wore on and the apartment grew quiet, the ugly reality of my situation began to sink in. This wasn't just a logistical challenge.

It was a life-changing event.

The father was Dominic, a man whose brief but profound impact on my life had left me reeling. I thought about reaching out to him somehow, but the complications were too great.

I paced my apartment as the city lights flickered outside my window. Before I could stop myself, I pulled out my phone. Opened the search bar.

Dominic Mortoli.

The name alone made my pulse race. I stared at it for a long beat, thumb hovering.

What was I even doing? Googling him? Looking for... what? His phone number? A way to break this news that neither of us were ready for?

My thumb hovered over the search button, but my heart was already slamming against my ribs. *He deserves to know*, a small voice whispered. But louder still was the echo of *This will ruin everything.*

I locked my phone and shoved it under a pillow before I could act on impulse.*Later. Maybe. But not now.*

Carrie's husband worked at the same hospital as Dom, and my connection to him was a delicate thread woven with potential repercussions I couldn't risk.

Moreover, Leo had told me about his father—a man more devoted to his career than his family. Whether those stories were colored by bitterness or not, the risk of entangling Dom in this, of potentially disrupting his life, was too great. This could push Leo over the edge, too. I couldn't ruin his family by telling him he had more family.

So, telling Dom was out of the question.

I had my own reasons for keeping this from him, too. I

prided myself on my independence, on my ability to manage my own affairs. I wasn't about to give up that control, not even to the father of my child.

I rubbed my stomach, hating how part of me clung to the memory of Dom's hands on my body, how steady he had felt in the middle of my chaos.

I told myself I was doing this to protect everyone—including myself.

Because if I told him, I'd have to face him. Look him in the eye. Admit that one night in paradise left me carrying something far bigger than either of us could've bargained for.

So, no. Telling Dom wasn't an option.

As I lay in bed that night, the decision formed fully in my mind. I would keep the pregnancy. It was a daunting prospect, but at thirty, it could have been my only chance to have a child. I knew I could do it on my own. Handling pressure was what I did best.

Plus, this kid had fought through ten years of birth control shots in my system to be here. I wanted to give them a chance.

I curled up on the couch, staring at the skyline outside my window. Neon lights blinked like they always had, but tonight, they felt colder. Harder. *Harsher.*

This city made me who I was. Gritty. Relentless. A chef who'd climbed from peeling potatoes to running services at one of the best restaurants in Manhattan. Could I really walk away from all that? From everything I'd built with my own two hands?

But then I thought of rushing a newborn through subway crowds. Of split shifts and twelve-hour days. Of trying to raise a child in a city that hadn't exactly been kind to me.

I rubbed my stomach, letting the weight of it all sink in.

The truth was, I couldn't protect a baby here—not the way I wanted to.

Maybe Carrie was right. Maybe *should* wasn't a real plan.

Chicago.

Dom had mentioned it once, offhandedly. Slower pace. More space. A shot at starting over somewhere that didn't chew people up and spit them out for walking too slow.

I had a cousin there, too, though we hadn't spoken in years. Perhaps it was time to fix that.

It wasn't just about logistics anymore. It was about breathing room—for me and this baby.

In the middle of the night, I started exploring Chicago online. The food scene, the apartments, the parks. The school system was top-notch, as was the public transit, for the most part.

I posted on some Chicago message boards, hoping to find out more. Thankfully, people were quick to answer, and I stayed up all night learning what I could. My mere questions became the groundwork for relocation.

For a few days, I reached out discreetly to connections and explored job openings for a chef in the city. It would be a fresh start, a simpler life for my child, away from the shadows of the Mortoli men and the complexities of New York's culinary scene.

Carrie noticed the shift in my demeanor, and one early morning, called me into her office. "What's going on with you? Flu doesn't make someone haul ass on every task."

I sighed, knowing I had to tell her something. I couldn't hide a pregnancy, and I needed to be able to explain the necessary doctor appointments and other changes. I didn't like lying to Carrie, but considering her connection to Dom, I had no choice.

"Remember when I came back from my vacation?"

"Yeah."

"I went to The Cage—that new club that just opened up."

"We're clubbing again? I thought that was over in our early twenties."

I shrugged. "Just needed to blow off steam. Anyway, um, I hooked up with someone there."

"Good for you, but what's that got to do with how you've been lately—wait. Are you seeing someone new?"

"No. I don't even know his name, actually. And it would seem that he got me pregnant."

Her mouth dropped open. "Are you sure?"

I nodded. "Went to the doctor yesterday to confirm, but yeah."

"And are we happy about this?"

"You know what? I haven't even asked myself that question yet. I've been busy figuring out how to make this work—"

"So, you're keeping it?"

I smiled and nodded. "That's the plan."

A smile slashed across her face as she leaped from her desk and hugged me hard. "That's amazing! I'm so happy for you!"

"Thanks, but it's all still sinking in, so please don't mention it to everyone else."

"Of course not. Your news, not mine." Carrie's smile softened as she searched my face. "You're not superwoman, Ella. You don't always have to do everything solo, you know."

I swallowed hard. "There's more news, actually. I'm leaving for Chicago after the baby gets here."

"What?" she barked.

"It's the best choice for me—for us. I have a cousin there, and you know how my family is—"

"Pretty much nonexistent?"

I nodded. "It's city enough that I can keep pursuing my career, but Midwest enough to have a slower pace and a friendlier vibe. I want my kid to have the best chance to not be a bitter New Yorker."

She laughed. "Yeah, I get that. Whatever you need, Ella. You know I've got your back."

"That is appreciated more than you'll ever know."

I hoped that was the last awkward conversation I'd have to have about the pregnancy so I could focus on the reality of it. There was no more hiding from reality—it was coming whether I wanted it to or not. I might have been Fate's favorite punching bag, but I was not going to let my child be the next one.

I would do right by them, and I'd do it on my own.

Even if it meant never telling him.

Even if it meant breaking my own heart to protect theirs.

Chapter 6

Dom

Friday the 13th had a reputation in the ED, and not a good one.

I wasn't superstitious about most things—broken mirrors, black cats—but this date? It earned my respect. The staff joked about it, but I'd worked enough of them to know they were no joke.

Patients would flood in like clockwork—car crashes, bizarre injuries, and people convinced they were cursed.

Like the guy who'd impaled his thigh on the brittle base of his Christmas tree—the one his wife had been nagging him to put away since January. The wound oozed pine-scented pulp, and it took an hour to dig the splinters out.

Or the woman who got backed over by her own car after hopping out to check her taillights. Somehow, she walked away with a busted foot and a ruined coat.

But 'thirteen guy'? He took the crown. Thirteenth child, born on a Friday the 13th, married a woman who died on the same date. He came in swearing it was his time.

An hour later, he dropped dead in the hallway, like the universe had signed off on the story.

The day came with cases that kept your hands moving before your brain had time to catch up. My shift had been running on black coffee and muscle memory since dawn, and we weren't even halfway through it. Sometimes, that was the only thing standing between life and death, so our coffee pots ran twenty-four hours a day. The muscle memory only came after years of practice.

It had been a brutal winter in the city, and though the calendar promised spring, no one believed it. The bitter cold still clung to the air alongside snowflakes. I expected plenty of interesting winter Friday the 13th injuries. The snow made physics flexible.

Maybe I need another trip to the tropics.

The thought brought a warmth with it that reminded me of squawking seabirds, sandy shores, a parade to end all parades, and a certain poet chef I'd tucked in the back of my mind. It had been eight months since I'd taken that vacation.

Since I'd met Ella.

I didn't think about her all the time anymore, but she was never entirely gone, either. She lingered, a memory with sharp edges. The nights I let my guard down, she crept in—her laughter, the way she'd arched against me in the moonlight, the feeling of her fingers tracing patterns over my skin.

Her softness.

I'd caught myself wondering, more than once, if fate would put us back on that island at the same time. Maybe she had gone back. Maybe she was thinking about me, too.

It was a comforting thought, but one tainted by the memory of the morning after. I wondered whether she regretted leaving me like that, or if that was just standard operating procedure for her. Hookup, get out. It was just a vacation fling, after all.

If it was meant to be, we'd see each other again. That's what I told myself on especially lonely nights. It was easy to feel lonely in winter when the chill settled into your bed to remind you that you were alone. As if I needed a reminder.

While watching the snowstorm through the window, I got paged. Preterm labor. Twins. Mother in distress.

On any given day, I dealt with all kinds of cases. Grandmother fell down the stairs. A dad with a gunshot wound. Cute kid with a broken arm. Each patient had their sob story, and you try to be as professional, yet empathetic as possible. It's impossible to turn your humanity off entirely, though.

Preterm labor with a mother in distress was one of those scenarios that, no matter how many times I faced it, I never got numb to it.

Even still, I responded automatically and tried to slip into that controlled headspace where emotion had no place. But I couldn't quite get there. "Going Vulcan," my daughter Gina called it. My kids gave me a hard time for having that ability, but I never regretted being able to get to that dull headspace. It had saved my mental health more times than I probably knew.

The jog to the ED bay doors was quick—just down the hall. The paramedics rattled off stats as they wheeled her in through the doors. Blood pressure dropping. Tachycardic. Four or five weeks early.

I moved in to assess the patient. And then—

Everything inside me seized.

The hallway shrank, my pulse roaring in my ears.

Ella.

The fragile woman on that gurney wasn't the one who'd teased me over cocktails and kissed me like she'd owned every inch of me. The Ella I remembered had been all heat and hunger, taking everything I gave her—and demanding more.

This Ella was pale. Wrung out. A fighter hanging by a thread.

And *pregnant.*

With twins.

She lay on the stretcher, pale and soaked in sweat, her brown hair a tangled mess against the pillow. Her breathing was labored, her hands gripping the blanket as she fought through another contraction.

Vulnerable.

In pain.

Alone?

My voice shook as I asked, "Anyone with the patient?"

"She came from work."

I blinked, trying to clear her face from the patient's. But it was still her. There was no mistaking her for someone else. This was Ella, and she'd been at work when preterm hit her, which meant she had been on her feet in a restaurant kitchen until now.

Fuck. No wonder she was in preterm labor.

My mind struggled to catch up with my body. It felt like I was watching a movie where the next scene didn't make sense.

Ella, here. Pregnant. With twins.

She was supposed to be a memory. A *what if.* A woman I'd let slip away because I'd believed that if it mattered, life would bring her back to me.

And now she was here. Not on a beach. Not sipping a Halekulani and laughing at my jokes. But on a goddamn gurney, in my ED, fighting to live and to bring two lives into the world.

"Dr. Mortoli?" One of the nurses shot me a questioning look. I realized I had frozen—just for a second, but long enough that someone noticed. Not good.

I cleared my throat, forcing the roaring confusion inside me to settle. "She's in active labor," I said, my voice steady. "We need to get her to Delivery now."

Ella's hazel green eyes fluttered open just for a moment. She gasped, "Dom?"

I gritted my teeth against the ache in my chest. She recognized me. Even through the haze of pain, she knew me. "I'm here," I told her, gripping the railing of the stretcher. "I've got you, Ella. I'm going to take care of everything."

Her eyes closed again as her blood pressure dropped.

We moved fast. If anyone else had been on the floor to help her, I would have pulled myself from the case. I was too close to the patient. Not close. Not exactly. But I was too confused by the patient. Unfortunately, the only other person who could have taken point was Bowan, and I wasn't about to let him touch her.

He was a good doctor. I was better. She needed that.

I focused on the medicine, on the job, because that was what I was supposed to do. It was the only thing that could save her. There was a part of me—something deeper, more instinctive—that rebelled against every rule I had sworn to follow.

This was my case, and no matter what else was true, I wasn't letting anyone else run it.

The twins came fast, tiny but vibrantly alive, their cries thin and determined.

Two girls.

When they screamed in unison, I let out a breath I hadn't realized I'd been holding. I wasn't the only one.

The rest of the staff felt the same way I did about laboring mothers in distress. The NICU team swept in, their movements coordinated as they took the babies to the NICU for further observation and oxygen. Standard procedure.

But there was nothing standard about this case. Not for me, not by a long shot. Ella didn't stir. Her vitals had stabilized, but she was completely unconscious.

I stood there glued to the spot, staring at her, my hands flexing and curling into fists at my sides. The exhaustion on her face, the way her body had fought so hard—it hit me in a way I wasn't ready for.

I am supposed to leave now. I wasn't needed here anymore. But I couldn't make my feet move.

"Dr. Mortoli?"

I forced myself to turn, and it took all the strength I had left.

The OB on-call was watching me carefully. "The patient will be out for a while. She lost a lot of blood, but she's stable."

I nodded like that was news to me. "Right."

He stared at me for another moment, but before he could ask why I was still around, I left.

But I didn't go far. After getting cleaned up, I clocked out for lunch and lingered in the hallway, pretending to check my phone, pretending I had something else to do. She was here.

Ella is here.

Alone.

That was the part of it that confused the hell out of me, even more than her presence itself. If someone like Ella was going to give birth to my kids, it would have taken an army to pry me from her side. And letting her go to work at eight months pregnant, doing what she did? Over my dead fucking body.

Whatever asshole knocked her up is going to answer for not being here, and he better pray he is not that ex-boyfriend of hers. Unprofessional or not, if he shows up here, I'm kicking his ass on principle.

None of this sat right with me. I didn't know why. I didn't know how. But I wasn't going anywhere.

Chapter 7

Ella

Pain.

That was the first thing I felt, wrapping around my ribs and hips like barbed wire. A deep, bone-deep ache that throbbed through every inch of me. Everything hurt—from my throat to the soles of my feet.

For a second, I thought I was dreaming. Then the sharp scent of antiseptic hit me, and the weight of the blankets confirmed this wasn't my bed at home. Or any home.

The memories came like a gut punch. The kitchen. The sharp gush of fluid. Carrie's panicked voice, calling for help. The ambulance. Contractions like a freight train.

And...Dom.

God, had that been real?

I squeezed my eyes shut, but the image wouldn't fade— the sharp lines of his jaw, those commanding dark eyes staring down at me through the fog of pain.

No. Couldn't be him. Couldn't be real.

The stress, the blood loss, the sheer terror of what was

happening—it had to have conjured him out of thin air. A cruel trick from a brain desperate for comfort.

Because if it had been him—

No.

I wouldn't be that unlucky. Out of all the hospitals in this goddamn city, it wouldn't be *his*.

I forced my eyes open, blinking against the dim hospital room light.

And there he was.

Dom.

Seated beside me, elbows on his knees, hands clasped loosely as if he'd been sitting there for hours. Scrubs stretched across his broad shoulders, and his dark brows were pulled tight, studying me like I was a riddle he couldn't solve.

Oh my God. No. No, no, no.

I could barely breathe. Panic prickled under my skin like needles.

My ex-boyfriend's father.

The man I'd slept with.

The man who gave me the two babies now missing from my arms.

It felt like the air got sucked out of the room.

This wasn't just bad luck. This was catastrophic.

What if he saw them? What if they look like him? What if he puts it all together before I can get out of here?

Because he *was* their father. And if anyone would notice the resemblance, it would be him. And what then?

He'd have rights. He could stop me from leaving. Worse —he could demand to be part of their lives.

And even if he didn't want them? Even if he decided

fatherhood wasn't for him at nearly fifty years old? The mere fact that he'd know would ruin everything.

Leo's voice echoed like poison in my head. *"He doesn't do family. He barely did it with us."*

And worse—how the hell was I supposed to look him in the eye?

Leo's father.

The man who had ruined me in all the best ways on that island. The man Leo swore up and down was cold, career-obsessed, emotionally detached.

And yet here he sat, steady and watchful, like he gave a damn.

The forbidden heat under the panic wasn't helping either.

Because beneath the terror was something else.

That impossible pull—the one that hadn't let go since the night in paradise.

God, how could he still look like that? How could the sight of him—even now—make my stomach flutter like it had no clue we were in a disaster zone?

Dom leaned forward, picked up a plastic cup, and gently tipped it toward my lips. "Small sips," he murmured, voice low and steady—*a balm and a razor all at once.*

Then his hand brushed under my head, cradling it as if I were fragile. Too fragile.

The cool water slid down my raw throat, but it barely touched the wildfire beneath my skin.

His touch burned.

It was steady, tender—but it made me feel unsteady, like I was seconds from cracking wide open.

Stay calm. Don't let him see the cracks.

But then his scent hit me.

That subtle, masculine cologne—spicy, woodsy, faintly like him. Like salt air and skin-warmed bourbon. The scent I'd inhaled against his neck the night he ruined me for every other man.

The cool water trickled down my raw throat. This was real. He was real.

My babies.

Panic surged as my hands moved instinctively to my stomach, now sore and empty. My breath hitched, and Dom caught it immediately.

"They're okay," he assured me, his voice steady and firm, cutting through my fear. "They're small, but they're strong, breathing on their own. The NICU team is monitoring them, but everything looks good. Again, they're small for newborns, but considering the circumstances, they're remarkably large. You did good, Ella."

A sharp exhale left me as relief crashed over me, making me momentarily lightheaded. I blinked up at him, trying to process everything. "You...you're really here?" My voice was raspy and hoarse from exhaustion and the intubation tube.

His lips twitched, just slightly. "Yeah, I'm here."

I closed my eyes for a brief second as if that would help me make sense of this. "I thought I imagined you. In the ER."

Dom leaned back in his chair, watching me carefully. "You weren't imagining things. You landed in my hospital."

His hospital. Shit.

Of course. Of course, this had to happen. What are the odds? One hundred percent when it comes to me.

Annoyance flared to life, not at him, but at the cruel

irony of the universe. Carrie had sent me here. She had made the call when I passed out, likely not even thinking twice about it. Just focusing on getting me and the babies the best care possible. Her husband worked here, so naturally, she'd tell the EMTs to take me here.

I knew that. And yet, I wanted to groan in frustration.

Carrie had no idea about Dom. She knew about the "mystery man" from my tropical getaway, but I had deliberately left out any identifying details. If she had known, she never would have sent me here.

Hell, she even sent me to a hospital where my doctor doesn't have privileges. Clearly, the EMTs told her this was a serious emergency. *I can't blame her, but I want to.* But since she didn't know, then Dom still didn't know. And I needed to keep it that way.

"That's...a weird coincidence," I murmured, shifting slightly in bed. Pain radiated through me, but I bit down on it.

His brow furrowed, his head tilting slightly. "Yeah. Some coincidence."

I kept my expression neutral. I had to. Because if I let even a sliver of truth slip through, if I let my emotions get the better of me, I'd be stuck. Trapped in New York. And my girls—my newborn, fragile daughters—would be sucked into the middle of a mess I had spent months planning to avoid. I could not let that happen. Not now, not ever.

I had been so careful. I had saved up, worked extra shifts, and meticulously planned my escape to Chicago. It was supposed to be simple. Get through the birth, leave New York, and start fresh. Clean breaks all around.

A clean break did not include reentering Dom's life.

Introduce newborns into the family that produced Leonardo Mortoli? Not happening. Not only would they have to deal with Leo's drama, but his drama would be amplified by the fact that his new sisters were born to his ex-girlfriend. An ex-girlfriend who was too young to be with his father.

Messy. Too messy.

It would destroy the Mortoli family, tearing them apart from the inside. I couldn't do that to Dom. And just as important, I wanted to do this on my own. *My girls are mine, and I'm getting them out of here.*

The silence stretched between us until it snapped under its own weight. I wanted to scream, Why are you still so goddamn handsome?

Instead, I forced myself to focus on what mattered. "Can I see them?"

Dom nodded. "Soon. The NICU team is making sure they're stable, but they'll either bring them soon, or a nurse will wheel you there to see them."

I swallowed hard, emotion clogging my throat. I wanted to hold them. To *see* them. My body demanded to hold my babies. I felt incomplete without them. But knowing they were okay, that they had made it through, had to be enough for now.

Dom exhaled, running a hand over his face. "You scared the hell out of me, Ella."

Something in my chest twisted, but I kept my expression carefully composed. "I didn't exactly plan this," I muttered, trying for some semblance of levity.

He didn't smile. Instead, he studied me, those dark eyes

filled with something I couldn't quite name. "What happened?"

The question was innocent enough. But my gut clenched because there was too much I couldn't say. I opted for the easiest version of the truth. "I was at work. My water broke suddenly, then there was...blood. I don't remember much after that."

Dom's jaw tightened. I could see his medical brain turning, analyzing, assessing. Something flickered across his expression, but he didn't press. He didn't ask why I hadn't told him I was pregnant. He didn't ask who the father was. He merely nodded.

And that was good. That was perfect. Because as long as he didn't ask, I didn't have to lie. I needed to get out of here. Not immediately—I wasn't physically capable of that yet—but soon.

But then, he shifted slightly in his chair, and my eyes betrayed me.

Even now, post-surgery and drowning in exhaustion, I noticed everything. The strength in his frame, how his scrubs hugged his shoulders and chest, the quiet storm in his gaze. The room shrank to just him. And me.

No. Don't go there.

Still, it hit—the magnetic pull. The heat beneath the panic.

I blamed my hormones for the way my pulse jumped. For the way I felt drawn to him, even after everything that had happened today. Whatever this was, it wasn't *real*. It was just biology. Chemicals and memories and exhaustion playing tricks on me. Nothing more. Nothing meaningful.

He was just my doctor.

Wait—no. Not just.

He hadn't told me he was a doctor.

How the hell had he left that part out?

The pieces didn't add up.

I thought back to Leo's stories—Dom always buried in work, missing birthdays, obsessed with success at all costs. Was this it? The ER grind, the medical empire?

Was this why Leo hated him so much? Had Dom played me on that island? Lied to get me into bed, then vanished back to his double life?

My pulse raced as unease settled over me. I needed space from him. Answers too, but mostly space. Because the man sitting beside me wasn't just a vacation fling anymore— he was a storm, threatening everything I'd built.

"So, you're a medical company owner?"

He huffed a laugh. "You remember that after everything you've been through? Impressive."

"Hard to forget when a man lies to you."

His brows bunched. "I didn't lie to you, Ella." He stood up and slipped a business card from his wallet with Morbinski Incorporated on it. "See?"

"Yeah. I also saw your phony website. Pretty elaborate way to get laid, don't you think?"

"Funny. If I remember right, I didn't mention my company to you until after we'd had sex the first time, so I didn't exactly need it to get laid, did I?"

He had a point. "Then, why even bring up your fake company after?"

"It's a real company, Ella."

"And you work grueling hours in the ER for funsies?"

He exhaled a frustrated breath. "It's a long story. But I

am the owner of Morbinski, and I work here. Why did you leave without saying a word the morning after?"

I closed my eyes and gently shook my head. "Can we not do this right now?"

"I'm sorry. I shouldn't have pushed. Are you feeling worse?"

"Just queasy, I think."

"I'll see about some Zofran. Be right back." He left without another word.

I had no idea what Zofran was, but by the context, I guessed it was for an upset stomach. Now, all I needed was something for my pain and a doctor who didn't make my hormones surge, and I'd be all set.

At least with him out of the room, I could breathe again. Weirdly, though, it felt like he took all the oxygen out of the room when he left.

Chapter 8

Dom

I'd met Ella at her most vibrant—bathed in golden firelight, teasing me over a spilled drink, challenging me with every kiss, her body tangled in mine. She was young and full of life, experimental and adventurous. The woman I met on the island had captivated me with her body as much as her personality.

And now, I was seeing her at her most vulnerable, recovering in a hospital bed after bringing two lives into the world. She was exhausted, pale, bruised from the ordeal of labor, and yet—God help me—she was still the most fascinating woman I had laid eyes on in a long time.

That should have been a problem. Because the last thing I should have been thinking about was how much I wanted her when she had just given birth to another man's children.

I didn't have some birthing fetish or anything like that. My attraction to her was purely due to her. That fiery personality. Her clever mind. As I walked to the nurse's station to find the Zofran, I kept telling myself to give her the pills and walk away.

Her situation was too messy and convoluted for me to stick my nose into her business. I had no right. I had to walk away.

But the attraction was there, deep and insistent, crawling under my skin like an itch I couldn't scratch. A base, gut-deep craving that had never fully gone away. If anything, seeing her now—alive, strong, still so inherently *her*—reignited something inside me I had tried to bury.

There was no cure for this. No treatment short of a lobotomy. Attraction was a hell of an unkillable beast, and I was merely a mortal.

I had a dozen reasons to walk away. I had already stayed too long. I was her doctor, or at least, I *had* been in the emergency phase. There was no medical reason for me to be here. I'd done my job.

I walked back to her room, knocking gently before entering. She beckoned me inside, and just hearing her voice did something to me. Once inside, I just stood there. I didn't move. I couldn't.

She shifted slightly against the pillows, wincing as she adjusted. Her every wince made my gut tighten up. I wanted to take her pain away. My hands twitched at my sides, wanting to reach for her, help steady her—but I kept still, watching her instead.

There was no cure for what I had. But I had one for her.

I passed her the Zofran. "Here, let this dissolve under your tongue. It'll help with the queasiness."

"Thanks." She took the tiny pill and sighed.

I wasn't sure where to begin again. I'd stuck my foot in

my mouth earlier. I had to do better this time. "You look good."

She gave me a wry, tired smile. "Bet you say that to all the girls."

"I'm not lying." I leaned forward, resting my forearms on my knees, letting my gaze travel over her. "You should see some of the guys they wheel out of here after surgery. You look better than all of them. And they didn't have to push out two tiny humans first."

That earned me a quiet chuckle, soft and genuine. The sound did something to me, a low heat curling in my spine. Her brow arched as she weakly smirked. "Flirting with a woman fresh out of surgery? Really, Dom?"

I shrugged and teased, "Forgive me—I failed out of my medical ethics course twice."

She exhaled a small laugh, shaking her head. "What about your common decency course? Did you bomb that, too?"

"Well, in my defense, I lost most of that the first time I kissed you."

She stilled at that, her fingers twitching against the hospital blanket. For a split second, I thought I had pushed too hard, but then she surprised me.

"That's funny," she murmured, a subtle vulnerability slipping into her tone. "I lost mine the moment I met you."

Something tightened in my chest. I was in trouble.

I shifted slightly in my chair, watching her closely. "So... you've been doing this on your own?"

She nodded slowly. "Yeah. Nothing new about that."

There was something in the way she said it—dry, but edged with truth. *I'm alone. I've always been alone.* A pull

74

of emotion tugged in my chest. I didn't want a lonely life for Ella. Or anyone, for that matter.

I knew what it was like to be alone. After my wife had died, I was alone for a long time. I had my kids to worry about, but that was very different from having a partner. The loneliness didn't hit me until three years after Jodie's death.

Someone stole a kiss under the mistletoe at a company Christmas party, and the moment she did, I leaned back in shock. It didn't mean anything to her, but that wasn't why I had pulled away. The last person who had kissed me was Jodie, so feeling a pair of lips on me felt foreign. Wrong.

I didn't know how to handle it, so I made an excuse and rushed out of the party. Somehow, the kiss had made me feel all the loneliness I'd bottled away for years. The weight of that threatened to crush me.

After the stolen kiss, though, I knew I had to start dating, or I'd be alone forever. While the idea of being alone was fine, the pain of loneliness was too much to bear. There was a big difference between being alone and being lonely, and I was the latter. If my kids had been young when I went through that emotional turmoil, I would have been a rotten parent.

Ella had no business being alone.

I hesitated, feeling the shape of my next question before I asked it. "The father—he's not involved?"

A flicker of something crossed her face, something unreadable. Her left hand tightened, but she took a practiced breath before she said, "No. And he won't be." She didn't elaborate.

And I didn't push. It was clear she didn't want to talk

about him. Maybe it was messy. Maybe he was a mistake. Maybe he had bailed. I didn't know. All I knew was that she looked relieved I hadn't pried.

Before I could speak, my pager went off. I glanced at it. Bowan. I snorted derisively and tucked it back into my pocket. That bastard wasn't going to tear me out of here for anything. "So, no trips back to the island?"

She exhaled a soft chuckle. "No. I've been working my ass off to save for this. Kids are expensive."

"Yeah. Pity, though," I mused, stretching slightly in my seat. "I was thinking of going back soon." I let my eyes lock onto hers. "But it won't be as much fun without you."

Her lips parted slightly in surprise, her fingers fidgeting with the hospital blanket. She let out a nervous, breathy laugh, and I realized once again, *too late,* that I was hitting on a woman who had just gone through hell.

Shit.

I cleared my throat, shaking my head. "Sorry. That was...inappropriate."

She snorted softly. "A little."

"I don't know what's wrong with me," I admitted, running a hand through my hair. "You just had twins, and here I am, acting like—"

"Dom," she interrupted, a small smirk playing on her lips. "It's nice to be appreciated."

That shut me up.

I let out a low breath, meeting her gaze. "I *do* appreciate you. And I have since that night. You left me some incredible memories."

She didn't say anything at first. Just watched me, her

expression unreadable. Then, finally, she spoke. "Why are you still thinking about that night?"

I held her gaze. "I never stopped thinking about it. I don't think I could if I tried."

Something flickered in her eyes—something wary. If she was happy to hear that, I couldn't tell. Not from her lip biting, not from the spike in her blood pressure on the machine. Her voice was little more than a ghost. "Oh."

That wasn't the encouragement I needed to hear, but I wasn't about to stop myself from saying what had been on my mind since I realized it was her on the stretcher. The words fell out of me, and I wasn't able to stop them.

"I've never connected with someone the way I did with you that night on the island..." I couldn't turn back now. I had to finish the thought, no matter the consequences. "It wasn't just... good, Ella. It wasn't just a one-night thing to me. It *meant* something."

Her fingers clenched around the blanket again.

"And you vanished the next day without a word. I don't mean to harp on this—"

"And yet?"

I sighed. "And yet, it has confused me for the better part of a year. Tell me what I did wrong that night. Did I hurt you, did I say something—"

She shook her head, interrupting me. "You didn't do anything wrong. You were wonderful."

"I didn't push you too far with the thing on the balcony?"

Her perfect lips twitched at that. "No. I liked it."

"Then what was it?"

She took a breath to speak, but then stopped herself. A

line formed down her brow as she thought about what to say.

Which meant she was conjuring a lie. To spare my feelings? To obfuscate some other detail I hadn't thought of? I wasn't sure. But I wanted answers. "The truth doesn't usually require so much forethought."

"I didn't know what to say to you, Dom," she murmured. "I've never—" She exhaled, shaking her head. "It scared me."

"What we did?"

"The connection. Between us. I'm not...I've never felt that before."

"You're not the only one."

She let out a soft, self-deprecating laugh. "What are we doing?"

"Talking," I said simply. "Catching up."

She looked at me, her expression softer now. Sadder for some reason. "It was a long time ago, Dom."

"Doesn't feel like it."

Silence settled between us like an invisible wall I wanted to tear down with my bare hands. I saw it in her eyes—the conflict, the same push-and-pull I was feeling. I wondered if the spark still burned in her the way it did in me.

But now was not the time or place. I had to tread lightly here, given her medical condition. This was a fragile, unnamed thing. I'd already been inappropriate—who flirts with a woman who just gave birth to someone else's kids?

Evidently, I did.

I had to be better than that, or she'd think the worst of me. "Your family? Anyone around to help?"

She exhaled, shaking her head. "No. I've always been on my own." A small, sad smile ghosted over her lips. "Except for my cousin. But we hardly have a relationship. So, I guess...now I have a family."

Her hands settled over her stomach, over the space where her babies had once been, and something inside me clenched. She had done this alone. Was still *doing* this alone. And yet, the way she said it...n*ow I have a family*...

She looked at peace with it.

Before I could say anything else, the door opened, and a NICU nurse stepped inside, wheeling a chair. "Miss Green?"

Ella's face lit up, and my breath caught in my chest. "Yes?"

"We can take you to see them now."

She gave me a quick glance, her expression unreadable.

I stepped back, clearing space for the wheelchair. I didn't want to leave, but I had to. A debate raged in my head about going with her, but that would have raised too many flags throughout the hospital. It was bad enough that I was in here when the nurse entered.

As Ella was carefully helped into the wheelchair, I watched her, my fingers flexing at my sides. I wanted to help her into the chair. I wanted to be the one to push her to the NICU.

I wanted her.

This wasn't the end.

It couldn't be.

I had let her slip away once before. I wouldn't make that mistake again.

Chapter 9

Ella

The wheels of the hospital chair hummed against the linoleum floors as the nurse pushed me down the quiet corridor toward the NICU. My fingers curled weakly in my lap, nails digging into the fabric of the blanket draped over me, as if anchoring myself to something tangible would stop the storm raging inside me.

Dom wasn't here. And I was relieved. I couldn't deal with his prying anymore. If I slipped up, even just a little bit, I'd ruin my plans for my daughters. The longer I was around him, the more chances I had to ruin things.

It was good that he was gone.

At least, that's what I told myself.

That the night on the island had altered me forever. That he wasn't just someone I had shared a passionate moment with—he was *their* father. Hell, that wasn't even the worst part.

I had almost admitted the worst part to his face. The night on the island had left me shaken up, too. I had never experienced a connection like that. Not during my wild nights in culinary school when everyone hooked up with everyone else. Not with boyfriends in my past. I didn't even know sex could be that good, or that I could feel that way, let alone with someone I didn't know.

The truth clawed at my throat, desperate to be set free, but I had to swallow it back down. I had to be strong. Because if Dom found out, everything would change.

I could not handle another change thrown at me.

But then a sickening question oozed into my brain. Would he hate me for keeping them from him? My heart clenched painfully, but I forced my breathing to stay even. I couldn't afford to think like that.

I had made my decision. I had to put my babies first. Not whatever stupid thing my heart wanted. Not some dream of what could have been. Telling Dom would ruin everything.

It would ruin *him*.

He had a reputation and a respected career—two, really, between working at this hospital and owning some medical company. He had a life that didn't have room for an unexpected scandal. He also had a son who already had complicated feelings about him.

If word got out that he had unknowingly fathered twins with his son's ex?

His world would crumble.

And what would it do to my girls?

They deserved stability. Not a fractured family. Not a potential courtroom battle over custody. Not a father who might only be in their lives out of duty rather than love.

I refused to put them through that. I refused to be a bad mom like mine.

People always ask chefs things like, who taught you to cook? I usually smiled and said my grandmother and spun some story about a loving memory of warm chocolate chip cookies and crocheted doilies.

There was no point in telling them that I taught myself how to cook because my mom was never home long enough to feed me. That she was too busy running scams or gambling to help me with homework or make sure we had groceries. That I learned how to steal to keep from starving.

I had grown up without love or support, and I swore I would never let my daughters feel that kind of loneliness. That they would never know hunger. I would be enough for them.

I *had* to be.

So why was my mind still stuck on Dom, on the way he had looked at me before leaving?

He had wanted to stay. I could feel it.

As the nurse wheeled me down the hall toward the NICU, she asked, "All right, Miss Green, ready to meet your little girls?"

I let out a breathy sigh, shaking my head. "As ready as I'll ever be."

Goodbye, Dom.

Goodbye to the man whose touch still haunted me, to the man who had changed everything with one night. Goodbye to the what-ifs, to the stupid dreams I'd let linger in the corners of my mind.

I let the grief swallow me. Silent and deep.

But the second the nurse opened the NICU doors, grief took a backseat.

. . .

The world shrank to the soft hum of machines and the two impossibly tiny beings in front of me.

My daughters.

My breath caught. My heart stuttered. They were perfect.

The incubators cast a warm, gentle glow around their tiny bodies. Their little fists curled at their sides, and tufts of dark curls peeked out from beneath their hats. Their faces were scrunched in delicate frowns, like they were already displeased with this big, bright world.

My throat closed around a sob. I reached instinctively, as if the distance between us was unbearable.

"They're beautiful," the nurse whispered. "Would you like to hold one?"

I could only nod.

The moment my daughter was placed against my chest, the world reset. The chaos, the fear, the ache for Dom—all of it evaporated.

Her tiny body melted into me. Fragile but fierce. I felt her breathing sync with mine, like her soul already knew me.

"Oh God," I choked out, tears falling freely. "Hi, baby. Hi."

She let out a tiny mewl, curling closer.

"I—I was thinking of naming them now."

The nurse smiled warmly. "That's a wonderful idea."

I kissed the soft fuzz atop her head. "Marissa Claire."

Tears slipped down my cheeks as I looked at my other daughter, still resting in the incubator. "And that's Summer Paloma."

The names settled over me like a promise.

Marissa. Summer. My girls. My family.

They were my lifeline, my second chance. I would give them everything I'd never had.

I pressed my lips to Marissa's head again, letting her warmth seep into my bones. "You'll never go hungry. You'll never feel unloved. I swear."

The storm inside me softened, replaced by sunshine. A quiet, pure joy.

For the first time since finding out I was pregnant, I felt certain.

The road ahead would be tough, but I could handle it.

I was tougher than the road.

Chapter 10

Dom

The hospital corridors felt quieter after I left Ella's room, but inside my head, there was nothing but noise. Flashbacks to the island mixed with Ella on my operating table. Her moans of pleasure blended into the moans of pain she made before anesthesiology arrived. The trust in her eyes as I thrust into her melded with the look on her face when she realized I was with her in the ED. She had been on the verge of death, but the moment she knew I was with her, she had calmed down.

The ultimate trust.

Seeing her again had shaken me. There was no other word for it. I had always thought if I ran into her in the city, we'd have a laugh, a drink, and tumble into my bed. Never thought she'd be on my operating table.

I should have been able to walk away, leave her to recover, focus on my next case, and do anything I was supposed to be doing—but I couldn't. The need to stay, to know more, to be near her, to breathe her in, gnawed at me.

I had spent months telling myself she was a memory, a

perfect mirage that had existed only on that island. For a while, I had told myself she wasn't real. Anything to take the edge off.

Briefly, I even considered hiring a private investigator to track her down somehow. How many assistant chefs named Ella were in a city as big as New York?

Probably a lot. But it was all I had to go on.

The idea of tracking her down, as appealing as it was, was too close to stalker territory, and that would only have expanded the distance between us if she had ever found out what I'd done. I had no intention of letting that happen. After I gave up on that dream, I knew I'd never see her again.

And yet, there she was, very real, in my hospital, with two newborns.

I was too distracted, too tangled in my own thoughts, and I nearly ran straight into the last person I wanted to see.

"Watch where you're walking, Mortoli," a smug voice said, dripping with fake civility.

I gritted my teeth and looked up to find Seth Bowan standing in front of me, arms crossed, a smirk plastered across his annoyingly punchable face.

Seth was one of those guys who had a way of getting under your skin. He wasn't a bad doctor—not by a long shot. That was the problem. He was competent, sharp, and ambitious as hell. We were in the same field, similar ages, similar credentials. The only difference was, he was an ass about it.

"Didn't take you for the type to avoid pages," Seth said, tilting his head in mock curiosity.

"I was busy."

Seth let out a slow, exaggerated sigh. "Sure, whatever

you say. I wanted an update on one of your patients—Ella Green."

How the hell does he know her name? Something inside me prepared for a fight. I didn't want to hear her name out of his mouth ever again. I kept my face impassive. "You're not on her case. What do you need an update for?"

"Sounded like an interesting patient. Status?"

"I'm pretty sure you know sharing patient information is a HIPAA violation."

"Fine." Seth scoffed, rolling his eyes. "The truth is, she works for my wife."

That caught my attention.

"Carrie sent her here," he continued. "She wanted to make sure Ella got the best care. Since I wasn't in the ED when she came, I didn't have the case. So, I told her I'd check in, but you're making that unnecessarily difficult. Anything notable?"

My lips curled into a slow, amused smile. "As I said, that would be a HIPAA violation." I clapped him on the shoulder as I stepped past him and pasted a grim smirk on my face. "And I know you wouldn't want me to get in trouble, just as much as I wouldn't want to have to report you for asking that kind of thing."

Seth let out a sharp exhale through his nose, clearly irritated. "Fine. Be difficult."

But I barely heard him. My mind was turning over a new detail.

Ella works for Carrie Bowan at Suivante.

I'd heard of it, of course—everyone in the city had. It was one of the most sought-after reservations in the tristate area, on the way to a Michelin star. A restaurant that thrived on experimentation, known for its risk-taking menu, where dining was more than eating—it was an experience.

And Ella worked there. That wasn't just impressive—it was *her*. It made sense. She had that same daring energy, that same ability to turn the ordinary into something extraordinary. She wasn't just some girl who was game for anything—being game for anything was how she lived. She was a risk taker, a woman who liked adventure.

Someone who could keep up with me.

The realization sat with me as I made my way toward the hospital's koi pond. I needed air, needed to clear my head before I lost control entirely. The garden was quiet this time of day, the gentle trickle of water from the fountain cutting through the din of the city beyond. I sat on the bench near the pond, watching the koi swirl beneath the surface in the evening light. They came, looking for a donation.

"Sorry, kids, I'm all out. No free dinner today."

After a minute, they gave up begging from me to do whatever it was koi did when people weren't around. That was good. I needed to focus. Ella was a distraction, and I couldn't afford more distractions. I had too much on my plate. My kids, my company and my career at the hospital.

Even with my ambition burning in my chest, my mind still drifted to *her*.

To the way she had looked at me, scared, but not backing down. Not scared of me—but of what there could be. To the way my name had slipped from her lips when she saw me, full of exhaustion and something close to relief.

I told myself I wasn't that guy. Before I had met her, I wasn't the type to get fixated, to let something—or *someone*

—distract me from my goals. The only person who had ever distracted me was Jodie Thompson. My late wife.

Jodie had been a detour from my path to med school. My parents hated her at first because they knew she would be enough to tear me away from what I had to do. For a time, she was.

Eventually, though, I got back on my path and did more with my time in medical school than my parents ever thought I could. All of that was thanks to Jodie. She was my rock. After she left us, there were others I dated to kill time, to help me network, or merely to have a nice weekend with.

But this wasn't some passing interest. This was different. I hadn't felt anything like this in years.

"Dr. Mortoli!"

I turned to see Roxanne Weiss, one of the hospital's lead administrators, walking toward me. With her tailored suit, pristine posture, and clipped tone, Roxanne was every bit the hospital executive—sharp, calculating, and always five steps ahead.

I greeted her, shifting into my more professional persona. "Something I can do for you?"

She smiled, but it was the type of smile that meant business. It never reached her eyes. "Actually, yes. I just had an interesting conversation about a certain administrator role opening up. I understand you've been interested?"

I kept my expression even. "I have."

The administrator role had been on my radar for over a year. I had worked my ass off for it, made the right connections, played the long game. Moving into administration wasn't just about power—it was about *control*.

In my current position, I couldn't stop the bullet from

being shot at someone—I could only patch them up and hope for the best. Administrators had influence, though, and influence was the biggest asset in policy changes. In the ED, chaos was part of the job. You reacted, you adjusted, you fought to save the patients in front of you. A noble cause. But administration? That was where decisions were made. That was where the hospital and the community's futures were shaped.

In the ED, you saved a life. In the administration, you saved *lives*.

I wanted that.

I had spent too much of my life feeling like I was catching up, like I was a step behind, trying to balance everything at once. The competitive edge had always been there, the hunger for something *more*. It wasn't about beating Seth—it was about proving that I was the best. That I was the one who should be establishing protocol, not just following it.

Roxanne had noticed which meant my hard work was paying off. I had been taking on more leadership responsibilities, handling the more difficult cases, and proving I was a surgeon with administrative potential. They already knew about my company, which was a significant feather in my cap, but they had to see me put in the work for the hospital.

But if Seth got the position, I'd put sugar in his gas tank.

"Interesting," she continued. "Seth Bowan has his eye on it as well. Do you know much about his family situation?"

I had options. I could paint Seth as a man distracted and make him sound like an unfit candidate, or I could shoot myself in the foot and be honest. For a moment, I seriously considered lying.

But if I was going to get the job, I wanted to earn it, not get the position through trickery. I wanted to beat Seth fair and square so there was no doubt about who was the better doctor. "As far as I know, it's just him and his wife. They both work long hours, no time for a family."

"What does she do?"

"She owns Suivante."

Roxanne arched a brow. "Well, if he really wants the position, he should get me reservations." It took a moment for a smile to break over her face. "A joke."

I smiled. "Ah."

"His home life is stable? No divorce on the horizon?"

"I've heard him complain about not seeing her as much as he'd like to, but that's all he ever says on the matter."

Roxanne nodded approvingly. "That's good to know. When it comes to our workload, a tumultuous home life is less than ideal."

"Certainly. Administrators are too busy to deal with distractions." Like I was at the moment.

"That and, well, we try to avoid bringing in administrators on the brink of divorce or parents with young children. It's not a good fit for either party. The hours are brutal, and it's impossible to be a fully present parent or running off to the divorce lawyer every five seconds and a fully committed administrator. The job requires one's full attention."

"It's not an easy job, and that's why it's so appealing."

"You like a challenge?"

I nodded once. "An easy life is for other people. I want to work."

"That's good. This job requires eighty to a hundred hours a week, which is why we weed out people with too much going on at home," she said bluntly. "It's too much unless you want to be an absentee parent or a bad spouse. And frankly, we try not to put people in that position." She paused. That's why it's good that your kids are grown."

"Leonardo and Gina are great and, thankfully, well beyond needing their father to care for them." Mostly.

She studied me for a moment, her gaze sharp. "It's a tough job, Dominic. Are you sure you can handle it?"

"I'm more than qualified. And I'm more than ready."

Roxanne gave a small, satisfied nod. "Good to hear. I'll be in touch."

I watched her walk away, feeling a familiar rush of competitiveness stir inside me. The position was mine.

I had spent my whole career preparing for it without even realizing it. My inner competitiveness meant I was never satisfied with being *good enough*. I had to be the best. I had sacrificed weekends, holidays, time with my family. I had spent years proving I was the best in the ED. I was the surgeon people called when things got bad. This was the next step, the *only* step that made sense.

But now, there was another hunger gnawing at me.

Ella. I knew where she worked now. And I wasn't done with her yet.

Chapter 11

Ella

The past few days were a blur of feedings, diaper blowouts, and stealing scraps of sleep between the twins' chaotic schedules. Everyone said twins synced up.

Liars.

Since leaving the hospital, I'd discovered more lies. Leak-proof diapers? Spill-proof lids? Sleep hacks that guaranteed rest? Total crap.

I'd told myself bringing them home would feel like running dinner service during a rush—fast, intense, thrilling.

It wasn't.

It was exhausting and terrifying. How did I convince myself I could do this alone? Was it confidence or just plain stupidity? Either way, it didn't matter. Because this chaos? This was everything. Marissa and Summer were my everything.

I'd prepped my apartment down to the last duckie detail, arranged their nursery a hundred times, and mapped out every possible contingency. None of it prepared me for the sheer tidal wave of love that hit every time I looked at them. One glance at their tiny faces and I'd get choked up, full to bursting in the best, messiest way.

Still, it was hard.

I was still healing—still wrecked. No one tells you how brutal just going to the bathroom will be after birth. The cramps, the sore boobs, the bone-deep exhaustion? A whole new level of wrecked.

And as much as I adored my girls, I missed myself.

Cooking had always been my anchor, my fire. Now, the only thing I "cooked" came from my own breasts. And burp cloths were my new wardrobe staple. Meals? A rotation of half-eaten sandwiches between naps. My life no longer revolved around plating scallops at Suivante but around tiny, perfect babies and counting how many hours they slept.

Thank God for Carrie.

She had been my rock since the second I was discharged from the hospital, shuffling me and the babies home with an efficiency that only she could manage. She had coordinated a food delivery from the restaurant—because as much as I loved to cook, I barely had time to shower, let alone make a meal. Those had been my first real meals since the hospital.

She had even taken charge of bedtime for the night, helping me wrangle my newborns into their bassinets while I sat on the edge of the bed, still adjusting to the reality that this was my life now.

Once the girls were finally down, Carrie reappeared in the doorway, arms crossed, her smile firm. "Well," she said, lowering herself onto the couch beside me, "that only took an hour longer than it should have."

I let out a tired laugh. "They *do* seem to enjoy making me work for it."

Carrie grinned. "Can't imagine where they get that from."

I smirked, nudging her with my foot. "Don't start."

She leaned back against the cushions, stretching her arms over her head. "So, are you feeling like a real mom yet?"

"More like an underpaid dairy cow."

Carrie snorted. "Well, I'd offer you a raise, but you're technically on leave."

My heart clenched at that. "How's everything at the restaurant?"

Carrie's face lit up. "Chaotic as always. We had a vendor screw up a fish order yesterday, so I had to talk Jean off a ledge. He was two seconds away from going full *French rage* and storming into their warehouse with a cleaver."

I sighed wistfully. Jean's rants were legendary—a mix of French curse words, broken turns of phrase in English, a sprinkling of German, and a dash of Japanese. The man had been around the world with the Peace Corps, decided it was too nice, and went to culinary school, where he was disappointed by the laidback nature of other chefs. When he came to Suivante, he demanded rigid order in the kitchen.

I missed Jean and his rants and the way he'd throw a knife into the wall when he was annoyed. It always freaked out the new hires. Good times.

I whined, "No chance I can do the job with those two greedy girls strapped one to a boob, right?"

"You *will* be back," she reminded me, nudging me gently. "It just takes time."

"I know," I said, but my chest ached at the uncertainty in my own voice. "It just feels...different now."

Carrie studied me for a moment before asking, "Still thinking about Chicago?"

I hesitated, rubbing my fingers along the hem of my sleeve. "It's on hold. After everything that happened...I don't know. Nearly dying tends to make you rethink your choices."

"It really was that close, wasn't it?"

"If I hadn't gotten to the hospital when I did..." *If Dom hadn't been my surgeon...* "I'm not sure if I'd be around for my girls. Or if they would have made it..."

She patted my leg. "Don't even think about it. Everyone is here and healthy. That's what you need to focus on now. Not the what-ifs of it all, you hear me?"

I nodded and tried to let her words reassure me, but the thought had crept into the back of my mind and taken up residence. The nurses had thought I was asleep at one point and talked about how lucky I was. That if I'd lost another pint of blood before getting there, we wouldn't have made it.

I let out a slow breath, nodding. The idea of leaving the city still felt like the right move, but something inside me had shifted. The urgency to run away from home had faded. "I'm not sure if Chicago will ever happen after everything."

"Have a little faith in yourself, Ella. If you want it, you'll make it happen. I know you. There's nothing you can't make happen." Before Carrie could say anything else, there was a knock at the door. "Expecting someone?"

I shook my head and stood, moving carefully as I made my way to the door. These days, I always had to walk gingerly, or I might tear a stitch.

When I opened the door, though, there was no one there—just a massive gift basket on my welcome mat taking up part of the hallway, wrapped in pink cellophane and tied with an elegant gold bow. The thing was as tall as me.

Carrie let out a low whistle. "Damn. They really are that huge."

I knelt and ran my fingers over the attached envelope. *Who the hell would have done this?* I flashed a curious smile at her. "Is this from you?"

"I'm generous, but I'm not that generous. That's the Platinum Lollipop Welcome Basket Extraordinaire. My sister-in-law got the Platinum Lollipop Welcome Basket *Remarkable* from her husband and complained she didn't get this one, even though the Remarkable basket was named right. It was stuff like this one, but about half the size. Nothing's ever good enough for Margo." She rolled her eyes, then refocused them on the monster in front of us. "How the hell do we get this through the door?"

"I think we drag it." With that, she dragged and I got out and shoved the thing into my apartment. It was more awkward than heavy, thankfully.

Once I closed the door, she asked, "Who would have sent it?"

"I'm not sure. I'll check the card." I ripped the envelope with all the excitement of a kid on Christmas. Whoever did this, I owed them a big thank you. There was champagne in there. The good stuff. The card was thick and stiff, clearly a pricy one. It had a silver baby rattle on the front.

When I flicked it open, everything stopped.

Dom.

Dom had sent this.

A lump formed in my throat. I didn't know what to think. Why would he do this? After our talk in the hospital, I hadn't seen him again. I was too focused on the babies to think about him, but even more than that, I had to put him out of my mind, or I'd break down and tell him everything.

Why send me an oversized baby basket?

"Who's name is on the card?" Carrie asked, shaking me from the thought.

"The nurses sent it," I blurted out the lie. "They doted on the girls the entire time we were there. And me. They said I was one of their best patients, and the girls were even better. I figured they said that to all the patients. But I guess they wanted to spoil them."

"That's sweet of them."

I nodded quickly, heart hammering as I untied the bow, peeling away the wrapping. Inside among the champagne bottles was a collection of baby essentials—organic cotton onesies, soft blankets, tiny socks, and plush toys. French-milled chamomile soaps. Two of everything, bare minimum. There were bottles of baby shampoo, delicate lavender-scented lotions, even a small, hand-knitted hat in each of my daughters' names.

But at the very bottom, buried beneath all the thoughtful gifts, was something that made my breath catch.

A pink plastic mermaid.

The same mermaid that had once hung from the rim of my cocktail on the island.

I had forgotten all about it.

But he hadn't.

He had *kept it*.

My fingers trembled as I closed around the tiny figurine, my chest tightening.

Beneath it was a small card with his number scrawled across it.

His phone number.

I stared at it, unsure what to do.

"What else is in there?" Carrie asked, peering over.

I quickly slid the mermaid and the card into my palm and tucked them into my sweater pocket. I forced a smile. "Just more blankets." I grabbed one and held it up.

She nodded approvingly. "The nurses went all out. I'll have to tell my other friends to have babies at Seth's hospital."

"Right. Seth's hospital." The most dangerous place in the world for me happened to be the place that saved me and my daughters. *Conflicted* was not a strong enough word for how I felt about that place.

Later, after Carrie had left and the apartment had gone quiet, I sat alone in the dim light of my living room, staring at the cheap plastic mermaid in my hand.

I was still in contact with some of the restaurants in Chicago to keep my options open. Dom's number felt like a weight in my pocket. I wanted to dial it. I wanted to tell him everything and let the chips fall where they may. But I also wanted Chicago for my girls.

There was no debating it really. I wanted to be the best mom I could, which meant I couldn't afford to be hung up on some guy I had one night with almost nine months ago. No matter how he made me feel.

But as I turned the tiny plastic mermaid over between my fingers, my thoughts shifted. Back to the island. Back to who I was that night. Before babies, before knowing who Dom was, before things became real.

That was the odd thing about vacation sex. It was amazing, in part, because you knew it was temporary. Flings had an air of magic to them. This liminal thing barely existed in reality yet gave life so much meaning.

Thoughts of Chicago had faded. I was wondering about Dom.

The one who got away.

I fingered the edge of the card with his number on it. So many possibilities on such a small piece of paper.

A cry broke out in the other room, and I was on my feet before I knew what I was doing. By the time I reached the bassinets, I remembered why I needed Chicago in the first place.

No matter what I thought about Dom, my girls had to come first.

Chapter 12

Dom

The drive up to Briarcliff Manor was always a welcome reprieve from the relentless pace of Manhattan. As much as I thrived in the chaos of the hospital and the city, there was something about the country home—set high along the Hudson River, surrounded by acres of greenery—that gave me room to breathe.

It was too much house for me these days, and every once in a while, I had the urge to sell it. But I could never bring myself to do that. Too many memories. I had a few homes—this country house, my apartment in the city, another apartment in Chicago for when I had to handle Morbinski business, a cottage in Oregon, and a cabin in Aspen. It was too many, but each one held a special meaning to me.

The house itself, with its ivy-covered stone facade and wide terraces overlooking the water, had been something I'd worked toward for years. When Morbinski stock went public, it was the first thing I bought. The country home was grand without being ostentatious and quiet without being lonesome. It was the perfect getaway from the city.

Even in winter, it was lovely. I arrived before the kids to set things up, opening the windows in all six bedrooms briefly for fresh air and then closing them shortly after to prevent the entire house from freezing. The city was always warmer than Briarcliff Manor, and no one wanted to spend time in a frostbitten house. I set up standing heaters in the solarium so we could enjoy brunch with a view of nature.

It was my favorite part of the house, surrounded by red dogwood bushes and yellow-flowering Chinese witch hazel. Their early blooms were the hint of spring that I needed. Renewal and rejuvenation were on the horizon, and I intended to make the most of the season.

The city made it too easy to fall into despair. Gray-on-gray violence, Leonardo had called it. He was right—between the gray sky, gray buildings, and gray sidewalks and roads, the city lacked color. Leave it to my artist son to pick up on those things.

Though it may have been due to how they affected him.

His habits worsened every winter. More drinking, more pills, more benders, less self-care. I hated how Seasonal Affective Disorder hit him, but I hated more how people rolled their eyes at the term. When someone had depression, SAD was harder on them than most.

I thought perhaps brunch in the solarium would brighten his mood. He needed to be in nature, not locked away in a gray city. That was why I had done my best to keep him out of prison. That place would destroy him. He needed color, vibrancy, joy. So, I cashed in favors when needed to prevent his habits from being his end.

Gina had promised to bring brunch, as she usually did. She was the glue between me and Leo, and I knew it meant something to her to see us in the same room, even if our conversations tended to veer dangerously close to verbal sparring matches. I swore I'd be on my best behavior, and reportedly, so did he.

These twice-monthly brunches were a standing request of hers to help keep the family together. Often, we were too busy to drive out to the house, but I had felt the need this weekend. Things felt more grounded here, even if, as a family, we weren't the most grounded people around.

After Jodie passed, my daughter took it upon herself to ensure some sort of cohesion between us. She didn't need to —I was the parent, not her. But she was right that Leonardo and I needed to work on things, and he wouldn't come to these brunches if it were at my behest.

When they arrived, I was surprised to see them in her car together. Normally, my son's arrival was an hour or so after the requested time. Now and then, he didn't bother to show up at all. But I tried not to bring that up when I greeted them. "Come in, come in, hurry before the cold comes with you."

Leonardo carried two large insulated bags from a diner in Manhattan, and Gina carted in an enormous to-go box of coffee. After they set brunch down, I had a look at them.

My kids were more grown up every week, and I was both proud of that fact and depressed by it as well, because it meant I was older, too. Leo would have looked like me at his age, if it weren't for our completely different circumstances. He was thirty, with dark brown hair going prematurely gray at the temples. But it was a floppy-topped mess of curls with the sides buzzed. He had my eyes, but his mother's dimpled chin. And he was too skinny.

But the thing that stood out the most were the dark circles under his eyes.

Not sleeping again.

Sometimes, he went on benders that lasted weeks, and the dark circles were the telltale sign. Other times, he worked on a project long into the late night for months, and the circles told that story. If I asked how he was sleeping, he'd brush it off as work-related stress. So, I learned to stop asking. I could never get a straight answer from my son.

At his age, I had a family, had built a highly successful company from the ground up, and was a doctor. He had a loft and a career as an artist that didn't make any money. It was less a career and more of a hobby, as far as I was concerned, but we'd had that argument too many times, and I would not bring that up to ruin my daughter's family brunch.

Gina, on the other hand, was bright-eyed and bushy-tailed as always. She had her mother's long red curls and my eyes, but her taste in wardrobe was a mystery. She was always wearing the latest and strangest haute couture. Beneath her coat today was a series of black ribbons stitched together that might be called a dress, and her shoes...I was certain she'd find her way into my ED by wearing those spiked things.

As she glanced around, she said, "Dad, this place really could use a freshening up."

"You're welcome to take a stab at it."

"I just might."

She never would, and we all knew it. Neither of the kids wanted to change a thing about our Briarcliff Manor home. It was exactly as Jodie had left it. Sometimes, I wondered whether redecorating would give us some closure. But that was a topic for another time.

After setting up the table in the solarium with all the goodies they had brought, I poured mimosas for us, and we got to the business of a lazy Sunday brunch.

"So, tell me, Leonardo, what is your new project about?"

He downed his entire mimosa before answering. "Neglect."

And with one word, he took the mood down by ten notches. I didn't see it but heard Gina's spiked heel click against the floor, and Leonardo winced.

Now, I know why she had worn them to family brunch. I braced myself for my son's vitriol and said, "Neglect? Sounds depressing."

He shot her a glance. "It's winter. Winter is depressing."

"It doesn't have to be," she said, smiling. "You could get out there and enjoy the snow, you know."

The harshness in his eyes faded. "Only you enjoy the snow, Reggie."

His childhood nickname for Regina always got her goat. "You said you'd be nice today. Don't make me use my enforcers."

"Sorry, yeah, didn't mean it. Just keep those damn heels to yourself." He muttered under his breath, "Reggie."

Another click.

"Ow! You bitch!"

She merely smiled at him. "And don't you forget it."

105

I pointed at his mimosa. "You know, if you drank less of that, you might be less of a smartass."

"If I drank *more* of this, I might find your advice welcome," Leo shot back, grinning.

Gina rolled her eyes, but she was smiling. "Okay, children, let's all play nice today."

I shook my head, but I didn't push it. This was how things were with Leonardo. He was sarcastic, biting, always testing the line between casual and antagonistic. His jabs at her were playful. He never wanted to hurt Gina's feelings. When it came to me, his responses were varied. One moment, it might be a teasing jab. The next might be a cut to the bone. He made an effort, though—only for Gina's sake.

"I forgot how good the food is at Mel's," Gina sighed, reaching for a croissant.

"You *own* an apartment in the city," I pointed out. "You could go there more often."

"Yeah, but brunch isn't as fun without you two," she teased.

Leo scoffed. "Yeah, because Dad and I are *so* entertaining."

"You are," Gina said, grinning as she buttered her croissant. "You just don't realize it."

Leo smirked. "If I had known this brunch was going to be about showering me with compliments, I would have worn something nicer."

His hair looked like it had been washed last week sometime and his clothes weren't pressed. His appearance was disrespectful and aimed at me. He knew I preferred them to dress well for our brunches.

106

I couldn't hold my tongue. "Please," I said, cutting into my T-bone. "You probably rolled out of bed five minutes before she picked you up."

"Fifteen," Leo corrected. "I'm responsible *now*, remember?"

"Oh? And what does 'responsible' look like these days?"

Leo leaned back, popping a grape into his mouth. "Wearing a watch. Keeping plants alive. Occasionally making dinner instead of ordering takeout."

Gina snorted. "That *is* an improvement."

"You see?" Leo gestured to her. "I am *thriving*."

I shook my head, but a small smirk tugged at my lips. "Right. *Thriving*."

He just shrugged. "You laugh, but my apartment *does* have a living basil plant. I've had it for over a month, and it's still alive. Be impressed."

I rolled my eyes, but Gina gasped dramatically. "Leo, is this your way of telling us you're going to open a restaurant?"

Leonardo deadpanned, "Yeah. It's called One Bachelor and a Basil Plant. It's vegan."

Gina burst out laughing, and even I chuckled, shaking my head.

The conversation drifted through work, relationships— or lack thereof—and general complaints about New York real estate. With Gina's budding interior design company growing, she had lots of opinions on the matter.

Then, somewhere between our second round of coffee and Gina stealing the last croissant, she sighed dramatically. "I should lay off of these things. I'm still recovering. Last week, I thought I was dying."

I glanced at her, frowning. "What?"

She waved a hand. "I was sick for, like, three days. Stomach bug. It was awful."

Leo smirked. "Sure you're not pregnant?"

Gina rolled her eyes. "Haven't gotten laid since last summer, so unless this is some kind of medical miracle, I think I'm safe."

Leo let out a loud laugh, while I took a slow sip of my coffee, doing my best to keep my expression neutral. Because it had been since last summer for me, too. I hadn't been with anyone since Ella.

I almost said so out loud—one of those fleeting thoughts that could have slipped past my filter. But I caught myself in time because the last thing I wanted to do was traumatize my children with my sex life. Anytime I had mentioned things like dating or someone staying over, they cringed like they'd need therapy.

Still, my mind caught on that thought. *Last summer.*

My grip on my coffee mug tightened as I thought. Ella's twins had been born preterm. If she had carried them to full term, she would have delivered a month from now, give or take.

I did the math in my head. And then I did it again. My stomach sank.

No. *No.*

It wasn't possible. She would have *told* me. Wouldn't she?

I swallowed hard, my brain racing ahead, lining up timelines and medical probabilities. I was a doctor. I knew the numbers. I knew the way pregnancy worked, the window of conception, the way a preterm birth knocked around the expected due date.

And it lined up. It lined up *too well*.

I barely heard Gina and Leo bickering beside me, my mind somewhere else entirely.

Because suddenly, the world felt like it had shifted, and I wasn't ready.

Chapter 13

Ella

I was drowning.

Not in water, but in everything else—exhaustion, spit-up, and a cycle of laundry, feedings, burpings, rocking, and begging for sleep.

I was drowning in the fear that I was already screwing it all up.

The twins were thriving, according to their pediatrician. Me? Not so much.

"Have you slept?" she asked.

I snorted. "When would I do that? It's just me."

"That's exactly why you have to," she said gently. "They need you at your best."

"Great," I sighed. "More guilt."

"If that's what gets you to rest, I'll take it."

She wasn't wrong. But hearing it didn't make it easier.

My apartment used to be as sharp and organized as my kitchen line—precise, spotless, efficient. Now it looked like a tornado had torn through a baby store. Toys they couldn't even use yet littered the floor, cups of cold coffee hid in random corners, and my laundry mocked me from every surface.

I was a mess too. Sore. Stretched. A human dairy farm with a bun so tangled I might need to buzz it off. No spreadsheet or checklist could have prepped me for this bone-deep exhaustion or the crushing guilt.

How could I be burned out already? They were everything to me. My entire world.

But even so, I needed air.

A shower that lasted longer than thirty seconds. A breath where I felt like me again. And that want, that human need? It gnawed at me with every diaper, every sleepless night.

Carrie had stopped by earlier with food and a reminder. "We'll need you back at Suivante soon," she said softly.

I missed it—the heat of the kitchen, the chaos, the adrenaline. Being needed for more than just milk and diapers.

But the thought of leaving my babies with anyone else made me sick.

I had prepped for this. Planned for it. A nanny. A daycare, eventually.

Yet now?

The idea of anyone else holding them felt like a betrayal.

It was too soon.

I wasn't ready.

A sharp knock on the door pulled me out of my downward spiral. I hesitated before making my way over, peeking through the peephole.

Mrs. Waverly. My elderly neighbor from across the hall, carrying a small basket wrapped in a checkered cloth.

No, no, no.

I couldn't do one of her rambling monologues today. No lessons from the past, thank you very much. I'd be as polite about it as possible, but I had no patience left for adults. It was reserved for my girls.

I pulled open the door, forcing myself to smile. "Hi, Mrs. Waverly."

"Oh, sweetheart," she said immediately, taking in my disheveled state with her milky brown eyes. I had always envied her curls, even though they were ice white. They were perfect, as if she had spent hours in rollers each day. She was slight, maybe five feet tall, and if she owned pants, I didn't know it. Every day, she wore a dress that looked hand sewn and beautiful. Her voice was normally very soft, but today, it felt like a hug. "You poor thing. You look *done in.*"

I let out a weak laugh. "Then I look as good as I feel."

"Well," she said, stepping inside and lifting the basket toward me. "These might help."

I took it carefully, peeling back the cloth to reveal a neat stack of glorious homemade biscuits.

"They're for lactation," she explained. "Made them myself. I used to make these for my daughter when she had my grandson. Lots of good oats, a bit of brewer's yeast, buttermilk for tang, and honey for sweetness. They'll help with your energy, too. You're not eating enough. I can see it on your face."

Before Mrs. Waverly, no one had ever doted on me. I still wasn't used to it. I stared down at them, something thick forming in my throat. I blinked hard, trying not to cry. "That is...*so* kind."

She patted my arm. "I know how rough it is. The early days are the hardest, but you'll get through it. You're strong like me."

I inhaled shakily, nodding. For a brief moment, I thought about asking her for help.

She *loved* babies. She had raised her own, had been a grandmother and a great-grandmother for decades. She was kind, patient, thoughtful.

I could ask her. I could—no. No, I couldn't. She was in her eighties. She didn't look it, and she was as spry as anyone fifty-year-old, but I knew better than to trust that.

What if something happened? What if she tripped? What if she dozed off while watching them? The what-ifs slammed into me, stifling out the idea before I could entertain it any further.

It wasn't an option. I would have to hire someone. A professional. The thought made my stomach churn.

How did people do this? How did single mothers—how did *any* mothers—go back to work and leave their babies with *strangers*? How did you trust anyone enough to hand over the most fragile, most precious thing you had ever known?

"I should let you rest."

Hearing her kind voice brought me back to the moment. I'd mentally wandered off at some point, and it took her voice to shake me out of it. "Sorry—I think I missed something."

"Don't you worry about that." Mrs. Waverly smiled, giving my arm another soft squeeze. "If you need anything,

Ella, you know where I am. I'm always home, and I'm happy to help."

If I thought I could leave my girls with her and her age wouldn't have been a factor, I might have taken her up on the offer, just so I could shower or have a nap. But the reality was, I wouldn't enjoy any of it. I'd be ready and waiting to jump in the second I heard Marissa's melodic wail or Summer's rapid-fire cough she did when she really wanted attention.

No rest for the wicked.

I nodded, swallowing around the lump in my throat. "Thank you. Really."

After she left, I set the biscuits down on the counter, pressing my hands flat against the cool surface. The biscuits smelled like heaven, but I felt like hell. I was in over my head. I had *thought* I was prepared. I had thought I was tough enough, *strong* enough, to do this alone.

I slid down onto the kitchen floor, knees pulled to my chest, and let myself fall apart. There on the floor, I wondered if I'd ever stop crying. But a crackle from the baby monitor made me jump to my feet. It always crackled right before the girls—

Yep. There's the crying.

I ran into the nursery and found the pair crying in unison. *Guess they know how overwhelmed I am, too. Solidarity is a bitch.*

Chapter 14

Dom

I had always been good at math. Med school required it—dosages, statistics, biostats, even the dreaded calculus. I aced them all.

So, I knew how to calculate a due date, and after working out the math on Ella's, I couldn't think of anything else.

For days, I had done nothing but run the numbers in my head, over and over, as if the outcome might somehow change. But it didn't. It never did. The timeline was too perfect.

The twins were early, but not too early. Backtracking their conception pointed straight to that week on the island with Ella.

And now, nothing else mattered. I had to know.

I sat at my hospital office desk, fingers drumming, coffee cold at my elbow, walls closing in.

What else could I do?

I had already reached out—sent a basket, every luxury a

new mom might need. I needed her to know I was thinking of her. Maybe, selfishly, I needed her to think of me.

I had included the plastic mermaid in the basket because I wanted to remind her of what we had. To feel what I felt—that it hadn't just been some meaningless one-night stand. But the truth was, I didn't know what I felt. You don't develop feelings for a person in one night. That's not how this works.

I wasn't a hopeless romantic. Love at first sight didn't exist—not really. That was chemistry. Lust. A trick of biology.

But Ella? She left a mark. A need that hadn't faded.

I wasn't used to being left behind. Women didn't slip out of my bed without a word. They lingered, hoping for another night, another chance. Ella vanished before the sheets cooled, and that shouldn't have gotten under my skin.

But it did.

And if this obsession had been just about pride, I would have forgotten her by now.

I grabbed my phone, my fingers moving before I could second-guess myself again.

Dom: *Hey, Ella. Just checking in. How are you?*

I stared at the screen, my pulse hammering. It wasn't ten minutes before three dots appeared. Then they vanished. Then they came back.

Ella: *Hey. I'm okay. Tired, but good.*

I exhaled sharply. She didn't sound distant. That was *something.* I took a chance.

Dom: *I'd like to see you. Can we meet up?*

There was a longer pause this time. Then—

Ella: *I'm not leaving my apartment anytime soon, so if you want to see me, you'll have to come to me.*

My chest tightened. An invitation. At least things were moving in the right direction.

Dom: *6 good?*

Ella: *See you then.*

The rest of my workday felt like a weight had been lifted. I moved through surgeries on autopilot—still doing my best, but my mind was elsewhere. No one seemed to notice, so I must have been doing well enough. By the end of my shift, the streets of New York blurred past me as I walked, my body moving on autopilot.

My mind wasn't in this office. It was back on that island. Back on her.

I could still see her—sun-kissed skin glowing under the tiki torches, hair wild from the ocean breeze, laughter sharp and intoxicating. She was untamed, messy, perfect.

I remembered how she melted against me. The way she gasped when I slid inside her, nails carving into my shoulders, begging for more without a single word.

I still tasted her—salt, bourbon, fruit, and something purely Ella. I could still hear the low, desperate sounds she made as I pushed her to the edge, the crash of waves filling the room as I buried myself deeper inside her.

I wanted her like I hadn't wanted anyone in years.

And I wasn't done wanting her.

I hadn't thought about protection that night. Not once. I was clean, tested regularly, and I'd assumed she was covered. That's how it usually went—with women my age, women who handled their own birth control or were past worrying about it.

But Ella was younger. I'd been reckless.

I muttered a sharp curse, the sting of it hitting me fresh.

Still... would I have done a damn thing differently? Even knowing what I know now?

No.

Not for a second.

But now, I had to deal with the fallout.

Could I handle raising kids again? At my age?

I'd loved it the first time. But back then, I was younger. I had energy to burn and a wife who managed the home so I could dominate my career.

Now? Everything was different.

I had grown kids. One, a ray of sunshine. The other, Leonardo—a man-child still playing at adulthood.

And just as I was poised to take on a job role that would own my time, my focus... did I really want to swap board-rooms for bottle feedings? Executive decisions for midnight meltdowns?

More importantly—could I still do it?

Patience wasn't exactly my strong suit anymore. I needed sleep. I'd earned the right to need sleep. When Leonardo was born, I was practically a kid myself, running on adrenaline and bad coffee. And Jodie's parents picked up the slack when we couldn't.

This time? There wouldn't be a village.

It would be me.

I didn't have answers yet—but I would get them.

I needed the truth before I made any moves. Logic said there was a chance the twins weren't mine. Maybe she met someone else at the resort. Maybe some guy on the flight home. Hell, maybe she crawled back to that bastard ex of hers.

All possible. But I didn't know if I wanted them to be true.

If she had slept with someone else, if someone else was the biological father, then I was off the hook. And I didn't know if I wanted to be off the hook.

The only thing I knew for sure was how to play it.

She'd open the door, probably tired, but beautiful in that way only new mothers could be—soft, radiant, and stronger than hell. She'd let me inside, and I'd meet the girls —see them up close for the first time. After helping her settle them down for the night, we'd open the wine I brought and talk.

Reminisce about that night. Feel that pull again.

And if luck was on my side, I'd end the night buried inside her.

Finally, I'd ask the question that had been eating me alive, and she'd tell me the answer that could shake my world.

When I reached her building, I hesitated for only a second before knocking. The door opened a moment later, and—

Jesus.

She looked *wrecked.*

She had dark circles under her eyes and her hair was piled into a messy bun, strands falling loose. Pajama pants hung low on her hips, the fabric wrinkled and stained.

And despite all of that—despite the exhaustion written across every inch of her face and leaking out of every pore— she was still the most beautiful woman I had seen in years.

For a second, I forgot what I had come here to say. My brain was nothing but oatmeal.

She just stared at me. Silent. Frozen. Like I'd knocked the wind out of her without even touching her.

Her hazel eyes darted across my face, searching for something—mercy, maybe, or a way out—but finding none.

The color drained from her cheeks, leaving her pale but still maddeningly beautiful, radiant in a way that only mothers were. A fresh glow beneath the fatigue, the kind that made my gut twist and my chest burn.

The air stretched between us, taut as a wire, vibrating with everything we weren't saying.

"Are they mine?" The words ripped out of me, raw and unforgiving, shattering my careful plan.

No easing in.

No waiting.

Just the brutal truth clawing its way to the surface.

Ella froze, her breath hitching like I'd sucker-punched her. Her eyes widened, wild and glassy, and her knuckles turned white where they gripped the doorframe. She stumbled back a step, like the floor itself had shifted beneath her. An invitation? A silent confession?

I followed her inside, shutting the door with a click that echoed like a gunshot in the suffocating silence. Bracing for the storm I knew was coming.

Chapter 15

Ella

I t hit me like a gut punch.

Not the question. The relief.

It was sharp and terrifying, the kind of relief that makes your stomach drop on a rollercoaster. The walls I'd built around myself—the ones that had kept me safe, that I thought were made of steel—cracked at the seams. For the first time in weeks, I could take a full breath.

And it felt like knives in my chest.

Because now it was out there.

He knew something was off, and there was no stuffing this back into the shadows.

Dom stood like a storm in the doorway, broad, commanding, every inch of him vibrating with restrained power. I couldn't look away, but I also couldn't step closer. My heart pounded in my ears, drowning out the hum of the city outside.

His dark eyes pinned me in place, sharp and unrelenting, waiting for the verdict. He wasn't giving me room to dance around it or push him out.

He was here, and he wasn't leaving without the truth.

I was trembling, knuckles white as I clenched my fists at my sides. I wanted to be strong. I wanted to be defiant. But all I felt was tired. So damn tired.

And the words slid from me in a voice that barely sounded like mine.

"They're yours."

Soft. Ragged. Irrevocable.

The second they left my lips, the air between us shifted. Tighter. Hotter. Like we were standing at the edge of a cliff and there was no going back.

For a moment, Dom didn't move. Didn't even blink.

The silence stretched, thick and suffocating, as if the room itself held its breath.

Then, slow and deliberate, he stepped toward me. And I braced myself for anger, for doubt, for accusations. But instead, he exhaled. Not harshly. Not sharply. Just a slow, measured breath, as if the weight of the words had been heavy, but not unexpected.

My heart hammered in my throat, wild and unsteady. His scent—clean soap, faint coffee, and something distinctly him—wrapped around me. The sheer size of him, the quiet power in his frame, made me feel cornered in the most electric way.

His eyes never left mine, dark and unreadable.

And when he finally spoke, his voice was a low, rough vow that sent a shiver racing down my spine.

"I'm not letting you out of my sight again."

Something inside me flared hot. Defiance. Sharp and molten, like I was nineteen again, daring anyone to cage me.

I squared my shoulders, tilting my chin up. "You don't get to tell me what to do, Dom. Not now, not ever."

His lips curved—not quite a smile, more like a shadow of one. Controlled. Calm. But there was something softer buried beneath the steel of his gaze. "That's not what I meant."

"Then say what you mean," I snapped.

He dragged a hand through his hair, then let it fall to his side, clenching briefly. "I mean..." His voice dropped lower, rougher. "I'm not walking away. I'm going to be in their lives. And if you let me... I want to be in yours, too."

I froze.

I'd been ready for a fight. For custody threats or cold logic or some legal ultimatum. But this? The simple, honest vulnerability in his words knocked the breath from my lungs.

Me. He wanted me.

And I wasn't ready for that.

My stomach twisted, the guilt gnawing like glass under my ribs. Leo. His son. The secret I'd buried so deep it felt like poison now.

I pressed my lips together, swallowing down the sob that clawed at my throat. He had no idea what he was really asking. No idea about the fracture already running through the ground beneath us. How could we be anything—anything real—if I couldn't bring myself to tell him the whole truth?

I wanted to scream, *You don't know the half of it.*

But fear slammed down like a lid, trapping the confession behind it. Fear of breaking him. Of breaking us before we even began. Of setting fire to every fragile thing holding this moment together.

Yet standing here, with Dom watching me like I was something precious he wasn't ready to lose, I felt my resolve splintering. My daughters deserved better. They deserved their father.

I had never known mine, and I wouldn't be the reason they went without.

I forced a breath past the knot in my chest and whispered, "Okay."

One word. One promise. And it shook the ground beneath me.

He nodded. Relief, or maybe shock, rippled across his features. Then he exhaled hard, raking a hand through his hair. "Why didn't you tell me?"

"Because—" My voice caught. "I was scared. I didn't think you'd want to know."

He stared at me, brows knitting together. "Why would you think that?"

Bitterness spiked in my chest. I remembered all the trash my ex—*his son*—had spewed, claiming Dom was a cold, distant father who'd always chosen work over family. But I couldn't tell Dom that. Not without dropping the bigger bombshell that his son was my ex-boyfriend.

"I had...reasons," I said finally, voice wavering.

Dom nodded slowly, like that was all he needed. "Can I see them?"

My heart stumbled. But I found myself nodding. "This way."

The apartment shrank around us as I led him down the

narrow hallway. Dom's presence changed the air itself—made it denser, more charged. The faint scent of baby powder clung to everything, layered over warm laundry and the untouched biscuits cooling on the counter.

He didn't comment on the clutter or chaos. He just observed, silent and steady, as if absorbing the life I'd built here.

When we reached the nursery, Dom hesitated on the threshold. His breath caught, audible even in the quiet.

The room was small but soft—muted pastels on the walls, two cribs side by side beneath the warm halo of the overhead light. The rocking chair in the corner, toys strewn like breadcrumbs on the floor, and the faint smell of lavender and newness made it feel like a safe harbor.

Dom stepped in, and the space felt even smaller. His height dwarfed the nursery, but the look in his eyes wasn't domineering—it was awe.

"They're..." His voice faltered. "They're so small."

I swallowed the lump rising in my throat. "They've grown a lot since the hospital."

He exhaled, shaky, like he'd been punched in the gut. Then he reached out, fingers grazing the crib rail with a care that didn't match his rough edges. "Which one is which?"

I shifted closer, almost brushing his arm. "That's Marissa." I pointed to the left crib where a tiny tuft of dark hair poked out from the blanket. "And Summer's the one who's probably about to wake up and demand attention."

He repeated their names quietly, like a prayer. Like he was committing them to memory and wouldn't dare forget.

. . .

My heart clenched at the tenderness in his voice. *Leo said he was cold, but look at him now.* Guilt stabbed me again. *Leo.* Dom's own son, my ex-boyfriend, the reason I'd almost convinced myself not to let Dom in. The secret pressed like a heavy weight on my chest, but I couldn't tell him now. Not when he looked at our daughters with such wonder.

"Marissa...Summer," he murmured again, voice thick. He leaned closer to Marissa's crib, eyes shining with unshed tears. My throat tightened at the sight.

Summer's tiny fists flailed. Marissa stirred but stayed drowsy, eyelids fluttering. Dom's jaw tension eased a fraction at the sight of them, as if just breathing the same air as his daughters grounded him.

I gently lifted Summer from her crib, cradling her to my chest. She let out another soft cry, then blinked up at me. Her dark eyes, so much like his, made my heart twist.

Dom inhaled sharply. He was silent for a long moment, just *looking*.

I watched as his chest rose and fell, as his hands flexed at his sides like he didn't know what to do with them. And then, with slow, careful movements, he crouched down, bringing himself eye-level with Marissa.

His daughter.

Something changed in his face. I had seen Dom in many different ways—cocky, commanding, teasing, distant. But I had never seen this.

This was pure, unguarded awe.

"They're beautiful," he murmured.

A lump formed in my throat. "Yeah. They are."

Dom stood beside me, close enough that I felt his warmth. "Can I?" he asked, holding out his arms.

Wordlessly, I transferred Summer into his waiting grasp. Her cries ebbed, replaced by curious little whimpers as Dom rocked her gently, brushing a fingertip across her cheek. Marissa shifted in her crib but stayed mostly asleep.

The tension in the room shifted, from fraught to quietly intimate. I watched Dom with our daughter, my throat tight. He'd told me he wanted to be here for them, for us. Seeing him handle Summer with such tenderness affirmed that promise more than any words ever could.

"I have baby daughters," he said softly, almost like he was saying it to himself.

A single tear slipped down my cheek before I could stop it. I wiped it away quickly, but I knew he saw.

We both stood like that, lulled by the hush of the nursery, until Summer's eyelids began to droop. Dom smiled at her, that soft, almost disbelieving smile I loved, then carefully settled her back into the crib. She let out a tiny sigh and nestled into the blanket.

My heart felt too big for my chest, and at that moment, he turned to me, and neither of us spoke. I should have stepped away. I *should* have put distance between us. But I didn't.

Instead, I let him reach for me. His fingers skimmed along my cheek, brushing away the stray strands of hair that had fallen from my haphazard bun. His touch was warm, steady. My name rolled off his tongue like it was something precious. "Ella."

I knew what was coming. I saw it in his eyes before he even moved. I should have stopped him. But I didn't.

His lips met mine, slow and sure, sending warmth spiraling through my exhausted body. It wasn't rushed. It wasn't hungry. It was something deeper, something deliberate. Something *real*.

I felt the tension in him, the restraint, the need coiled just beneath the surface. I stiffened for half a second—fear coiling in my stomach—then exhaled, letting the warmth of his kiss wash over me.

It was nothing like the frantic, impulsive heat we'd shared by the ocean months ago. This was sweeter, tinged with uncertainty and gratitude. For a few precious heartbeats, I let myself melt into it, savoring the comfort, the promise.

Then reality crashed back. I pulled away, pressing a hand to his chest. My breath came in shaky bursts, my mind swirling with guilt and longing. "I'm sorry," I blurted, cheeks flushing. "I'm just...I'm kinda overwhelmed right now."

He froze, concern darting across his face. "Right, I'm sorry, I didn't mean to—"

"It's okay," I assured him quickly, feeling my emotions seesaw between wanting him closer and needing distance. "I just—I have so much in my head, Dom." My gaze dropped. *I'm lying to you about your son.*

He nodded, though I saw the strain in his eyes. He wanted more—more closeness, more certainty. But he respected my boundary, stepping back. "I get it."

My heart twisted at the sight of him controlling himself, that fervent desire banked in the lines of his jaw. I quickly smiled, trying not to cry or beg for more. Whatever was going on, I didn't trust myself to speak. Smiling was far safer.

He took a slow step back, giving me space. But the look in his eyes told me everything. This wasn't over. Not even close.

Chapter 16

Dom

The alarm never got the chance.

I was already awake, staring at the ceiling, chest tight with the familiar pull of anxiety.

I didn't want to be here. Not in this quiet apartment. Not alone.

I wanted to be across town, where two tiny daughters were probably stirring for their first milk, and where Ella—tired but resilient—was starting her day.

But I wasn't there. I was here, alone, because...well... Ella and I hadn't agreed on anything.

My career was also important. The hospital administrator job was hanging in front of me like bait, and any sign of distraction would give Bowan the edge.

Still, as I stepped into the shower and cranked the water hot enough to sting, the images followed me. Ella's tired smile. Marissa's tight grip on my pinky. Summer's soft breathing against my chest.

I clenched my jaw and let the heat bite into my skin.

Focus. Handle today.

The rest could wait.

By the time I stepped out, the mirror was nothing but fog. I swiped it clear with one hand and stared myself down. The silver at my temples had been there for years, a sharp contrast to the dark strands still holding on. My body was still solid—broad shoulders, a chest that could handle a fight or a full shift on my feet. But the eyes staring back at me?

They'd seen a lot. Done a lot.

And now, they were asking the same question I couldn't shake.

Am I really ready to be a dad again?

The wind clawed at my tie as I crossed the parking lot. Inside, the hospital hit me like muscle memory—fluorescent lights, antiseptic air, controlled chaos.

"Morning, Dr. Mortoli." A nurse handed me a chart as I scanned the triage board. Gunshot wound. Stroke. Panic attack. Business as usual.

I dove in, head down, moving from bay to bay, treating, diagnosing, keeping everything professional. But every quiet second, my mind drifted to that apartment across town. To two newborns and the woman fighting through the fog alone.

By noon, hunger slammed into me. I ducked into the lounge, unwrapped a protein bar, but appetite wasn't in the cards. Not today.

Because no matter how hard I tried to lock it away, the memory of Ella was right there.

The kiss.

Soft, hesitant at first. Then deeper. Real. The way her breath had caught, the way her fingers had curled into my shirt. It wasn't just heat. It was need. Hunger. The same as mine.

The taste of her was still on my lips, distracting me every damn second.

I was in the middle of unwrapping the bar when a nurse flagged me down. "Dr. Mortoli, we need you in bay four."

I sighed and tossed the bar onto the counter, hurrying to bay four, where a post-op patient was having complications.

Even now, as I scanned the vitals, my mind wandered back to the weight of Ella against me. The way she'd trembled, like part of her still wanted me—despite the walls she kept building.

And just like that, I was wrecked all over again.

I needed to get my head on straight. I had work to do, patients depending on me, and a rival waiting to eat me alive.

But all I could think about was going back to that apartment. Back to her.

My mind lagged a fraction of a second behind. That fraction was all it took.

"Dr. Mortoli, you there?" a voice asked.

I blinked back to reality. "Hmm? What?"

"Wrong dosage." A nurse smiled as he reminded me.

Fuck. Horror shot through me. It wasn't a lethal error, but it was an error all the same. If I hadn't been corrected, the patient could have suffered serious side effects.

Heat washed over my face, a blend of embarrassment and fury at myself. If Seth had seen that...

It took another hour to stabilize that patient. When I finally stepped away, my heart was pounding. I retreated to my office and sank into the chair, running a trembling hand through my hair. My tie felt like a noose.

I hadn't made a mistake like that in years. Years. I prided myself on clarity under pressure and on never letting my personal life bleed into my performance. But here I was, screwing up because I couldn't stop worrying about two tiny humans who needed me.

And Ella.

The door opened without a knock, and I straightened, expecting a resident with questions.

Instead, it was Seth Bowan. He closed the door behind him, crossing his arms. "You got a minute?"

I tensed, not trusting the quasi-polite tone. "If this is about the department meeting, I'll be there."

He shook his head, stepping closer. "No, it's about the near-miss in bay four."

My jaw clenched. How the hell did he know about that? Didn't matter. Maybe the nurse told him, or maybe someone else did. Regardless, he knew.

I cleared my throat. "It's handled."

"Barely," he retorted. "Dominic. That was sloppy. You're lucky a nurse caught it."

"I'm aware."

He studied me for a beat, eyes narrowed. "I'm not here to gloat. But you should know, if the admin board gets wind that you're messing up basic dosage—"

"I said I'm aware," I growled, cutting him off. "I don't need you to lecture me."

Seth grimaced. "Fine. Don't make me win the admin role because you screwed up the basics. When I win, I want you clear-headed so you know I beat you at your best. I want my win to haunt you for the rest of your life, so get your head in the game."

With that, he turned on his heel and left, leaving me with my fists clenched at my sides, fury and guilt storming in my chest.

The rest of the shift, I moved like I was defusing bombs —no risks, no slip-ups. But the damage was done. Doubt was already creeping in. By the time my shift ended, my nerves were frayed.

As I was about to leave, my phone buzzed. Gina's name flashed on the screen. Dread and relief tangled in my gut.

"Hey, sweetheart," I said, trying to keep my tone light.

"Dad! Just checking in. Are we still good for brunch on Sunday?"

I let out a measured breath. "Yes, absolutely. But it has to be at my apartment this time."

She made a disappointed sound. "How come? I miss the house. I was thinking of bringing some swatches for us to go over."

Damn. "I'm on call this weekend," I lied. "Can't leave the city, just in case."

"It's not that far, and you used to drive up there all the time."

"I know," I said, forcing a chuckle. "But I really can't leave the city right now. It's complicated."

"Everything's always complicated with your work." She sighed, making me feel worse. "But I get it. It's work. Work always comes first."

Something I'd told her since childhood. Something I hoped to never tell the twins. "Yeah. I'm sorry—"

"It's fine, but I'm bringing extra pastries. Oh, and Leo's

been complaining about your coffee machine at the apartment. Want me to bring a new one?"

I winced at the mention of Leo. "Sounds good. Looking forward to it."

There was a pause, like she expected me to say something more. And I almost did. The words bobbed on my tongue, thick with significance. *You have twin sisters.*

We said our goodbyes, and when the call ended, I was left staring at the black screen, feeling like a coward.

I dropped the phone in my pocket, the weight of my secrets pressing heavily on my chest.

Chapter 17

Ella

I hadn't realized how suffocating a New York winter could be until I spent the end of it locked inside with two premature newborns. I loved my daughters, but the four walls were closing in. So when I woke to a sunny sky and fifty degrees outside, I nearly cheered.

"All right, girls," I announced, glancing between the two bassinets. "We're going out for a day on the town, and I don't care if the city crumbles. We are going to have some fun in the sun."

Marissa stared me down like she didn't believe me. Summer cooed, which I took as approval.

No one tells you that half of new-mom panic is trying to decode baby signals. Hungry, tired, wet—same noises, same faces. At least now, I knew Marissa liked to scream and Summer babbled like she was born to be a talk show host.

I wrestled them into jackets, which they hated with every fiber of their tiny beings, and by the time I finished packing the stroller and diaper bag, I was sweating like I'd prepped for Everest.

But the second we stepped outside, it was worth it.

Sunlight kissed my face, warm and bright after months of gray. "Welcome to the world, ladies," I whispered, pushing them down the sidewalk. "By five, you'll own this city."

Chicago felt like a distant idea lately. Maybe I'd feel differently once I was back at work with space to think, but right now, my only mission was fresh air for the girls and caffeine for me.

The neighborhood was pure lower Manhattan— bustling, a little cramped, but charming in its chaos. I aimed for the small park up ahead, flanked by a corner café with outdoor seating. The perfect combo: sunlight, people-watching, and maybe a minute to breathe.

I snagged a table just outside the café door, parking the stroller so the twins had a clear view of me. My feet were killing me, but freedom tasted better than pain. When the server stopped by, I ordered a decaf cappuccino with a grin that probably read as unhinged. She didn't question it.

Sunlight warmed my face, the breeze teasing loose strands of hair, and for the first time in weeks, I felt human again.

I let my gaze drift to the park across the street, where a dad boosted his daughter onto a jungle gym, both of them laughing under the clear sky.

The sight tugged at something inside me.

Dom.

Watching scenes like that used to gut me—equal parts awe and jealousy for the little girl inside me who never knew her father. Therapy helped, but some wounds don't close; they just fade from angry red to faint scars you pretend aren't there.

But seeing Dom with Summer? That had done something. The way his entire face softened, like she was his entire world. Or the breath he'd caught when leaning over Marissa's bassinet, his awe plain as day. He was hooked—no question.

Part of me melted just thinking about it. My heart flipping like I was sixteen again.

And yet, another part of me stayed locked tight, colder. The part that whispered the truth I couldn't outrun.

He's Leo's father, Ella.

For the millionth time, I wondered if I was just delaying the inevitable.

No matter how sweet the moment, that reality loomed. And every second I stayed silent, the harder it became to tell him the truth.

My cappuccino arrived, and I took a glorious first sip. Heaven. Well, about as heavenly as life got these days, considering my existence revolved around diapers and a dash of existential dread.

As I swirled the coffee in my cup, my phone buzzed. Carrie's name flashed across the screen. I answered as fast as I could without spilling my cup of bliss. "Hey!"

"Hey, Mama," Carrie teased, her voice crackling with warmth. "How are my favorite twins? And how are *you*?"

I watched Marissa's tiny foot kick at the blanket while Summer seemed to be dozing off. "We're good. I'm risking a walk in the sunshine."

Carrie let out a soft laugh. "That's what I like to hear. So, listen, I hate to be a workaholic tyrant, but I wanted to check in about your return. You mentioned maybe coming back by the end of the month?"

I'd known this conversation was coming. Carrie had been unbelievably kind with my leave—especially given the drama of my preterm labor. The preterm aspect threw things into chaos at the restaurant, I was sure of that. "Yeah," I said, fiddling with my coffee sleeve. "End of the month should still be fine, *if* I can find a nanny."

She hesitated, concern bleeding through the line. "I can give you more time if you need it. Suivante will survive, I promise."

For a split second, I considered taking her up on it. But the restaurant was like oxygen to me—I missed the kitchen, the rush of prepping for service, the dance of plates and staff. And I didn't want to exploit Carrie's generosity. "No, it's okay. I can't hide forever, right? Besides, I need to feel like *me* again. I miss me."

"We miss you, too. Hell, even in our visits, I haven't heard you swear once. What's up with that? You're not turning all perfect mom on me, are you?"

I snorted a laugh and part of my cappuccino. After blotting and making sure I didn't waste a drop of my life-affirming coffee, I realized she was right. I'd been almost G-rated lately. *Weird.* "Oh fuck no. Can't really say why. Tired, I guess."

"If you say so," she teased. "But if I see you in makeup or high heels—"

"Then my body was taken over by aliens and you should run and save yourself."

Carrie laughed that way that I missed. "Will do. Just keep me posted on the nanny thing, okay?"

"You got it." I set my phone down, heart thudding.

A nanny.

The word alone made me queasy. The idea of leaving my babies—my tiny preemies—in someone else's care felt like handing my soul to a stranger.

But what other choice did I have? Dom had his own chaos, and I wasn't about to rely on him full-time, especially not when we were...*what* were we, exactly?

I sipped my coffee again, letting out a breath. *We're nothing.* We shared a past night of passion, a shocking revelation, and a pair of newborns.

And a hell of a lot of unanswered questions.

Yet, my hormones apparently decided to stage a rebellion, because just thinking about Dom's dark eyes and that slow, devastating smile made me want to slam my cappuccino and sprint across town to see him.

The twins dozed, their tiny cheeks glowing pink in the sunlight. So peaceful. So perfect. So mine. And his.

That truth jabbed at me—sharper than I expected. I'd carried them, birthed them, but Dom? He was already hooked. Already ready to fight for them. And as much as I'd planned to do this alone, part of me liked that he wanted in. More than liked it.

But then the darker thought crept in. What happens when he finds out who you are to Leo?

I shoved it aside. Not today. One storm at a time.

I sipped the last of my coffee, sighed, and packed up. The twins were starting to stir—tiny fists wriggling free of their blankets.

"Alright, ladies," I murmured, tucking them in tighter.

"Sun time's over. Let's make it home before you launch a rebellion."

I cast one last look at the dad in the park—the way he scooped up his giggling toddler like it was the easiest thing in the world. A pang of longing hit, but I rolled my shoulders back. My path wasn't easy. It never had been.

But it was mine.

And if Dom wanted to walk it with me? Maybe—just maybe—I'd let him try. Once I survived going back to work. Once I figured out how to protect my girls. Once I decided what the hell to do with this ticking-time-bomb of a secret burning a hole in my chest.

Chapter 18

Dom

I hadn't seen Ella or the girls since that night.

Since the kiss.

The memory of her mouth, soft and hungry against mine, haunted me. Every curve of her body was etched into my head, a temptation I couldn't shake. This morning, when I woke up hard as a rock, the only thing on my mind was her.

Her lips. Her body under mine. The way she gasped my name like she wanted more.

I took care of it with my fist, fast and rough, biting back her name. Not my proudest moment, but it got the job done.

When I got to the hospital, I told myself that my release would help me focus. That maybe I could finally clear the fog from my head.

"Dr. Mortoli, incoming!" one of the triage nurses shouted. "Male, mid-forties, GSW to the abdomen, BP dropping. ETA two minutes."

In a practiced motion, I grabbed gloves, a gown, and protective eyewear, because blood can shoot out from anywhere with a gunshot wound. My adrenaline surged. This was the part of the job that used to calm me—a high-stakes puzzle with a life on the line.

Back when I was a young doctor with a very young family, I both hated and loved coming to work. Sure, I felt needed at home, but it was nothing like the emergency department. When Leo accidentally spilled juice, there was no urge to rush and clean it or to get upset over it. I never reacted the way Jodie thought I should, and it took a long time for her to understand why.

My perspective was different from hers. Rushing was saved for burn victims, not juice. Being upset over the juice seemed silly compared to tending a kid with a dog bite. For a long time, she took it personally, feeling like she was the only parent in the house.

Looking back on it now, in some ways, she was.

The doors slammed open as EMTs rushed in, pushing a gurney. "Forty-three-year-old male, single gunshot wound to the lower left quadrant," one of them barked. "BP's eighty over fifty, pulse one-forty, in and out of consciousness!"

The patient's skin was waxy, eyes unfocused, pain etched into every line of his face. The problem was, he wasn't screaming. Not good. I pushed everything else from my mind. *Focus.*

"Bay four," I ordered, voice clipped.

We wheeled the gurney past two other trauma bays that were already full—someone who had been in a bar fight in one, a multi-vehicle collision victim in another. Lights blinked overhead, fluorescent and harsh, reflecting the tension thrumming through every hallway.

I stepped up to the head of the gurney. "Sir, can you hear me?"

A gurgled moan was the only response. His eyes rolled back. Great.

"The bullet's probably lodged near the bowel," I muttered. "We need an immediate scan, or—"

"Scan will take too long," a voice cut in.

I glanced to my right and saw the last person I wanted to see. Dr. Seth Bowan. He was already snapping on gloves, jaw set in that smug determination I'd come to hate. "We open him up here," Seth insisted. "He's crashing."

I gritted my teeth. "We need imaging, Bowan. We're not going in blind."

A nurse wiped sweat from the patient's brow, eyes darting between us. The tension was thick enough to choke on. *Time is of the essence.*

Seth turned on me, fire in his eyes. "He's going to bleed out if we waste precious minutes. I'm calling it."

"You're not in charge here," I snapped back, but my protest rang hollow. The patient's vitals were plunging dangerously low, monitors blaring shrill warnings. There was no time for bullshit.

Before I could argue further, Seth grabbed a scalpel from the tray. "Prep for an emergency laparotomy," he barked to the nurse. Then he looked at me, challenge gleaming in his gaze.

My hands curled into fists. *Dammit.* If we stood here debating, the patient would die. "Fine," I ground out. "But we do this my way."

"No," Seth growled, "we do it the right way. Stand aside."

He moved in, and I tried to hold back the urge to shove him aside. This was an ED, not an OR, meaning we lacked the usual setup and the space to move. We had some surgical tools and a chance to patch up a catastrophic bleed, but it was hardly ideal. We needed speed, coordination, a steady hand, and solid leadership.

The patient let out a wet groan that turned to a choke. I positioned the suction, ignoring the storm of anger in my chest. I barked, "Nurse, get me more suction. He's aspirating."

Fluids gushed onto the sterile drapes, and I felt my stomach roil. That almost never happened anymore. If Seth screwed up…

He made the incision with practiced efficiency, but I could see the tension in his posture. Blood immediately welled up, thick and dark.

"Clamp!" he shouted, and a nurse passed it to him. Seth's hands darted into the open wound, searching for the bleeding vessel. "I see it."

I leaned in, adrenaline thrumming, scanning for an opening to step in. "Careful—"

"I know," Seth hissed.

Then everything happened in a flash. He shifted, and a fresh torrent of blood spurted, slicking his gloves and staining the drapes a deep crimson. Monitors beeped erratically.

"Clamp that artery!" I yelled, panic spiking. "He's crashing!"

Seth fumbled for a split second—just a blink, but enough time for my heart to lurch in my chest. The monitors screeched warnings, the nurse rattling off the patient's plummeting stats. Seventy over forty. Pulse weakening.

Finally, Seth pinned the bleeder with the clamp. The flow of blood slowed, the patient's vitals stabilizing just a touch. The entire team sagged in relief, but my blood boiled.

"That was reckless," I bit out, voice low so only Seth could hear.

He glared up at me over his mask, sweat dripping down his temple. "I saved his life."

"The imaging would have shown a clearer path," I snapped, controlling my volume with an iron will. "He almost bled out because you rushed it."

"You want to blame someone, blame yourself for hesitating," Seth spat back, his knuckles white around the clamp.

I opened my mouth to retort, but a nurse cleared her throat, eyes flicking nervously between us. The patient was still in danger if we didn't finish up.

Seth turned back to the wound, finishing the immediate patch job. The commotion settled into a tense hush as the rest of the team worked to close. My stomach churned at the coppery smell of blood.

As soon as the patient was stable enough for transport, we ran him to the OR, where a full surgical team would take over. Seth peeled off his gloves, meeting my gaze with a glare that screamed *don't you dare*.

I dropped my voice, though anger pulsed behind every syllable. "That is not going unreported."

Seth tore off his mask, his lip curling. "Do whatever you want, Dominic. The fact remains—I saved his life, and you stood there, stalling."

146

Seth brushed past me, leaving nothing but tension in his wake. My pulse hammered, rage simmering under my skin. He'd regret this.

Half an hour later, I was still pacing my office, adrenaline refusing to fade. Images flashed—blood, the crash cart, Seth's smug grin.

That reckless bastard.

I rubbed my eyes, bone-tired. I'd had my fair share of clashes over the years, but fewer now that I outranked half the staff. Still, every argument pissed me off.

This wasn't about ego. It was about survival. Seth had gambled with a patient's life, and I wanted to put my fist through a wall.

But then I thought of my daughters. Would they be proud of a dad who lost it?

I unclenched my fists and let the rage burn out.

For now.

Why am I even doing this anymore?

The question cut deep. I used to know exactly why—the thrill of saving lives, the pursuit of a top role in administration.

But everything had changed since I learned about the twins. The hospital no longer felt like my whole world. Ella and the girls were out there, and I was stuck in these fluorescent corridors, playing a power game with a man I despised.

My phone buzzed with a text from the hospital admin, something about a scheduling conflict. I ignored it. I couldn't deal with more politics right now. I needed an anchor.

And that anchor was Ella.

I didn't want her to feel like the only parent at home. I

didn't want her to feel alone in this. And right now, I didn't want to feel alone, either.

I glanced at the clock. Two hours left. Screw it. I was done. I never left mid-shift, but today? Today I couldn't breathe.

I grabbed my coat, stuffed my phone in my pocket, and stormed out. No guilt. No second-guessing. Just raw fury. Staff stared but kept their mouths shut, probably sensing I'd snap.

In the Uber, traffic crawled, and my mind replayed it all —the blood, the panic, Seth's smug face. We'd been forced to co-lead tonight, a pairing nobody wanted. Maybe admin had set us up to see who was best under pressure. That seemed like the sort of mindfuck they'd use to dig into who was the better man for the job.

It wasn't Seth Bowan.

That man is going to cost someone their life someday. And I'll make sure the board knows it. I'll testify, if it comes down to it.

But even that vow felt hollow, overshadowed by the need gnawing at my gut. The hospital mattered less and less with every passing block. I pictured Ella's apartment, the small living room filled with baby gear, the twins' bassinets in their pastel bedroom. I needed to see them—needed it like I needed air.

I didn't call or text. Couldn't risk hearing "not now" or "I'm too tired." Logic told me to wait. Emotion dragged me there anyway.

Traffic crawled. I nearly tore the door off the cab when we stopped. My pulse was still jacked as I hit the stairs, taking them two at a time.

When I reached her door, my chest tightened. That worn welcome mat, chipped paint—it all screamed stop. But I was already knocking.

I knocked. Then I knocked again, barely waiting two seconds between.

For a beat, there was silence. Fear slithered up my spine —maybe she wasn't home, or maybe she was ignoring me.

Then I heard the soft shuffle on the other side.

The door cracked open, revealing Ella's face. Her hair was loose around her shoulders, eyes reflecting a tiredness I recognized in myself, but a flicker of surprise danced there too.

She took one look at me—my disheveled state, my clenched jaw—and her eyes went round. "Dom?"

I opened my mouth to explain, to apologize for barging in. But the words stuck in my throat. Instead, I just let out a breath I hadn't realized I was holding, the anger and stress of the day flooding out in that single exhale.

And then, the door was wide open, inviting me into the warmth of her apartment beyond. A sanctuary.

Chapter 19

Ella

I barely processed the shock of Dom at my door before the sight of him hit me harder.

He looked wrecked. Like a skyscraper hit by a wrecking ball but somehow still standing. His dark eyes met mine, heavy with something I couldn't place. I stepped aside without a word, my throat tight. "Everything okay?"

His shoulders sagged, just a little. "I... needed to see you. And them."

The words pierced straight through me. I should have asked more—what happened, why now—but he looked battle-worn.

"Come on," I murmured, softer now. "I was just about to start bedtime."

His gaze flicked to the bassinets, where Marissa and Summer were stirring, as if they sensed a new presence. The lines of stress on Dom's face eased minutely, and he nodded. "I'd like that."

We worked together in a quiet, unspoken rhythm.

Marissa fussed first, so I scooped her up while Dom tended to Summer.

We got them into their sleep sacks—those soft, zippered cocoons that made them look like swaddled little peanuts—and Dom's fingertips brushed mine as we adjusted the fabric around Marissa's tiny arms.

"She trusts you," he murmured, watching me closely.

"She trusts us," I corrected softly.

Dom's smile was fleeting but warm, his dark eyes flickering between me and Summer as he lifted her gently into the crook of his arm.

We fed them side by side on the nursery floor, bottles balanced in our hands, the glow from the dim lamp casting soft shadows. Summer's tiny fingers latched around Dom's thumb while Marissa blinked up at me, half-asleep, her lashes fanned against flushed cheeks.

Dom let out a quiet laugh under his breath as Summer gave a little sigh of contentment, milk-drunk and blissful.

The air between us was heavy but tender. Like somehow, without saying it, we both knew this was the most natural thing in the world.

Once their bottles were empty, we moved in sync, easing them into their cribs. Summer's fingers clung to Dom's shirt until the last second, and Marissa let out one last soft sigh before curling into herself like a sleepy kitten.

Dom and I stood side by side for a moment, just watching them settle.

He chuckled quietly. "Guess we did a good job."

For a second, we just stood there in the soft hush of the nursery, neither of us moving, both of us reluctant to disturb the peace. The girls slept soundly, their tiny chests rising and falling in perfect rhythm, their faces bathed in the soft glow from the nightlight.

I looked over to see Dom lingering, his hand hovering protectively near Marissa's cheek. The expression on his face—torn, relieved, grateful, so deeply in love with his girls —hit me with a force I hadn't expected.

"Thank you," he whispered, so quietly I almost didn't hear.

"For what?"

He swallowed, his dark eyes meeting mine. "Letting me be invade your home. For tonight. For this." He nodded to the girls.

The knot in my throat tightened. I wanted to say, *you're their father, of course you belong here.* But the words wouldn't come. Instead, I just nodded and placed a light hand on his arm. "Let's have some tea."

He wordlessly nodded and followed me to the kitchen, where I made tea in silence, wondering what was on his mind. In the living room, I nearly asked about his day again, but Dom spoke first, voice low and haunted.

"Work was...bad. There was a case in the ED. A patient nearly bled out because—someone else made the wrong call. I was this close to watching him die on my table."

He ran a hand through his hair, pacing the small space. My heart twisted at the frustration etched into every line of his posture.

"I couldn't stop thinking—why am I doing this? Putting myself through the chaos and risking people's lives, when all I really want is to be here, with—" He glanced at me, eyes flicking to the bassinets in the other room. "With them. And you."

A lump rose in my throat, and my chest felt too tight. His honesty made me ache. This was a man who took pride in being calm, collected, in control. Yet here he was, spilling raw vulnerability.

"They're why you do it," I said softly. "So you can give them the best, right?"

He exhaled, a bitter laugh escaping his lips. "That's what I've always told myself. That it's all for my family. But...I'm not sure anymore."

We sat there in silence for a beat, the hum of the city outside the only noise. Then, as if drawn by some magnetic force, we both closed the distance. My hand found his chest, the steady hammer of his heart racing under my palm.

In that moment, it struck me that this—*this*—was more intimate than anything we'd done on that tropical island. We were in my cramped apartment, with newborns asleep in the next room, and I felt *closer* to Dom than I ever had to anyone.

He looked down at me, shadows playing across his face. "Ella..."

I rose up, and he met me halfway, our lips colliding in a kiss that felt like a quiet exhale after too much tension. The taste of him washed away the longing of the day. I slid my arms around his neck, fingers tangling in his hair.

We broke apart, breath mingling in the hush.

His voice was a low rumble. "I want you so bad. But, Ella, if this is too much for you, or too soon—"

But I shook my head. "It's not."

"Are you sure?" he murmured.

The answer lodged in my chest was a resounding *yes*. I'd spent so long battling my own fears, secrets, and insecurities. But right now, seeing his pain and knowing he had come here for solace, it made me feel so much more important to him than just some girl he happened to impregnate. It made me feel like I *wasn't* the biggest mistake of his life, I was someone he counted on, and more than any of that, *I wanted him.*

"I'm sure," I whispered, taking his hand and leading him to my bedroom.

In this space, everything felt different. With the girls quietly sleeping in the nursery, Dom and I sank onto the bed, hearts pounding. His mouth covered mine again, the kiss deeper, more urgent. I gasped at the contact, my body remembering that electric connection we'd shared on the island.

Clothes found their way to the floor, and he trailed kisses along my throat, making my breath catch. A moment later, his hand skimmed my waist. I tugged him closer, reveling in the press of his body.

Every sense seemed heightened—the muffled hum of traffic through the window, the rasp of his breath as he whispered my name. Each second bound me tighter to this man I barely understood, yet needed more than I'd ever admit out loud.

When he entered me, the sensation tore a gasp from my lips. It wasn't the frantic, reckless desire of that first time on the island. This was something deeper—an undercurrent of shared vulnerabilities, new parenthood, and raw need. Our bodies moved in a rhythm that felt almost like inevitability, a dance we'd started months ago and were only just now finishing.

My fingers dug into his back, and his forehead dropped

to my shoulder, stifling a groan. I cradled the back of his head, pressing him against me there to hold him close. Despite everything—my secrets, his conflicts—I felt safe. This felt right, as though it was exactly where we belonged. In this moment, we were just two people clinging to each other against the chaos outside.

He kissed my collarbone and moved down further until he slid out of me. He nibbled his way over my chest, my boobs, my ribs and stomach, until he reached his destination.

When he spread me wide, I gasped from the sheer over-whelming sensation, and from the first press of his mouth against me, I bucked and gasped, digging my fingers into his silvery hair. My core tightened and pulsed, stealing my breath. He devoured me until I burst on his tongue.

The moment he knew I was done, he rolled me over and pressed in from behind slowly as he planted lazy kisses and bites on my shoulders and neck. His groans filled my ears, and I memorized each one.

His cock dug against the right spot again and again, making me shake like a leaf. I felt his whole body go rigid, even as he worked through me. He murmured, "That's it, baby, just like that."

My voice went weak. "I'm gonna—"

"With me."

We cried out together, hands pawing, teeth gnashing, curses peppering the air. When the wave finally subsided, I nestled against his chest, feeling his heart thud against my cheek. We lay there in the dim light, the only sound our uneven breathing. My eyes fluttered shut, exhaustion mingling with a fragile kind of joy.

He brushed a kiss across my temple, and I breathed in the scent of him, a mix of hospital antiseptic and the raw sweat of our intimacy. I told myself I'd only rest for a minute, but as my mind drifted, one final thought tugged at me:

How long can this last before everything comes crashing down?

Chapter 20

Dom

I woke to a mouthwatering view—Ella, sprawled half on top of me, tangled in the sheets. Bare, golden skin kissed by the early morning light. The curve of her ass, the soft weight of her full, round breasts pressing against my chest, had my cock instantly hard. How could it not be? Every inch of her body was temptation wrapped in warm, sleepy softness.

I ran a hand down her bare back, fingers skimming her spine, slow and deliberate.

"You're staring," she murmured against my chest, voice still hoarse with sleep.

"I earned the right," I rumbled, eyes shamelessly drinking her in. "I plan on staring every damn morning."

Her lips curled into a smirk against my skin. "Possessive much?"

I shifted under her, letting her feel exactly how hard I was, thick and ready, pressing right against the soft inside of her thigh. "No," I growled. "Just making sure you know what you do to me."

She let out a breathy, satisfied sigh. "Message received."

I grinned, brushing her hair back to get a clearer look at her face. "Good, because I'm planning on making you mine, Ella."

Her brows lifted, but her eyes held that same spark from the night before. "Oh, are you now?"

"Mhm," I traced up her thigh with my fingertips, coming deliciously close to between her legs. "You. The girls. All of it."

She let out a soft laugh, breath hitching as I trailed kisses along her shoulder. "You don't scare easy, do you?"

"Try me." I nipped at her neck, feeling the goosebumps rise under my mouth. "I want real. Not another night. Not some passing fling."

Her breath caught, her nails lightly scraping my chest. "Dom..."

I pulled back just enough to meet her gaze, my voice dropping to a low growl. "Say yes."

She chewed her lip, debating, eyes flicking to my mouth and then down between us. I caught it. So did the part of me pressing against her thigh.

"You gonna make me beg, sweetheart?" I teased, voice rough with hunger.

She arched a brow. "Maybe."

I let my hand drift higher. My fingers found her already wet and eager, slick heat welcoming me. I teased her, circling slowly, then slid a finger inside, deep and easy.

Her breath hitched, hips rocking into my hand as she clung to me.

"If I drag you beneath me and make you moan my

name," I murmured darkly against her ear, "you'll be begging to say yes before you even remember the question."

Her breath came faster, pupils dilating. "You're cocky."

"No," I murmured, nipping at her earlobe. "I just know what you sound like when you fall apart for me."

A shaky breath escaped her. "God, you're trouble."

I slid a second finger inside her, stretching her just enough to make her gasp against my mouth. "So, is that a yes?"

Her lips brushed mine, teasing. "Yes."

I groaned, claiming her mouth in a deep, filthy kiss as my fingers worked her deeper, slower. She trembled beneath me, clutching my shoulders as if I were the only thing anchoring her to the bed.

Her breath hitched. "Dom—"

"Shh," I murmured. "Let me show you how serious I am."

She whimpered when I pressed my fingers deeper, feeling how wet and ready she was. I shifted above her, grabbing her thigh and hitching it around my waist. With one slow, long, deliberate thrust, I slid inside her, feeling every inch of her around my cock, tight and hot.

She arched beneath me, nails digging into my back as she moaned, head falling back against the pillows. "God, you feel—"

Knock. Knock. Knock.

We froze, panting, eyes wide.

I dropped my head to her chest with a frustrated groan. "Are you kidding me?"

Another round of knocks followed, this time more insistent, accompanied by a muffled voice, "Ella? You there? It's me, Carrie!"

In the next room, the twins' cries exploded like an alarm bell.

Ella's eyes went wide. "Oh, shit—it's Carrie."

Carrie. Seth Bowan's wife. Ice shot through my veins. If she saw me here—shirtless, fresh from Ella's bed—the fallout would be catastrophic. Ella had been my patient. There was no way to make our being together okay in any professional sense of the word. The promotion would be Seth's without a doubt.

"I have to hide," I muttered, already reaching for my pants.

But Ella caught my arm, eyes pleading. "Yes, but—just go. Closet. Now."

I paused, reading the panic on her face. This wasn't just about my job. She was terrified of something else entirely.

"Ella, what—"

"Please, Dom. I'll explain later."

I didn't have time to argue. Another knock rattled the door. Carrie's voice followed, chipper and way too close. "Ella? You in there?"

I swore under my breath and grabbed my shirt, ducking into the tiny closet as Ella scrambled to tie her robe.

In the dark, crammed between coats and a pile of baby supplies, I pressed my back to the wall, heart hammering.

Outside, Ella opened the door, voice all sunshine and nerves. "Carrie! What a surprise."

I clenched my jaw, listening to the twins wail—and to the creeping realization that I wasn't just hiding me from Seth.

Ella was hiding me from Carrie, too.

Carrie's voice floated through the apartment. "Sorry to drop in—I brought you some groceries and pastries. Figured you could use a treat."

Shit. She's staying.

A sharp cry from the nursery snapped me into action. Marissa. I grabbed the first thing I saw—a pink tank top of Ella's—and yanked it over my head, rushing to the babies.

Marissa's tiny face was scrunched, her lungs impressive. I scooped her up, bouncing gently. "Hey, sweetheart," I murmured, forcing calm into my voice.

Through the cracked door, I caught snippets of Carrie chatting, oblivious to the storm brewing behind the nursery wall.

Then— "Mind if I peek at the girls?"

My blood iced.

Ella stalled. Carrie pressed, softer, "I'll be quiet."

No time. I set Marissa down, whispered an apology, and ducked into the cramped closet, pulling the door shut just as footsteps creaked closer.

The darkness closed in around me—baby laundry, spare blankets, and my own disbelief.

Forty-eight years old, crouched in my daughters' closet, hiding like a damn teenager. This is insane.

But then again, losing the promotion to Seth? Worse.

Carrie, just outside the door to the nursery asked, "How are you feeling? Still sore everywhere?"

Ella chuckled nervously. "Um not really, but this morning might be an exception."

"I've heard it comes and goes."

If only she knew how Ella got sore...though, if this goes on any longer, I will be, too.

Between her husband last night, and Carrie this morning, I started to think anyone named Bowan was determined not to do the right thing. My lats had started to cramp up from the weird position I was in.

I ground my teeth, forcing myself to stay silent when all I wanted to do was curse and stretch. The pain built, though, not heeding my order to stop.

From my narrow view, I caught sight of Ella as she stepped into the doorway, Carrie right behind her. The other woman craned her neck, scanning the room, eyes lighting up at the sight of the twins. I couldn't see her face fully, but I recognized the voice—she was all warm chatter, the tone of someone who adored babies and wasn't leaving until she got her fill.

I recalled one of the hospital functions—a gala, I think—where she cooed over somebody's baby. Seth, tipsy on one too many gimlets, confessed she had always wanted one, but settled for the restaurant because she didn't think she'd be a good mother.

I didn't know if that was how she felt about it, or if he was just drunk, but seeing half her face now, I imagined he was right.

"There they are," Carrie whispered. "Oh, Ella, look at them. Have they grown since the last time I saw them?"

Ella chuckled nervously, moving to pick up Marissa. "Feels like they have. They're eating like horses."

Carrie cooed, leaning in to stroke Summer's soft hair. "Aww, still asleep. Good girl."

I pressed myself further against the closet's back wall,

every muscle taut. If Carrie turned even slightly, she might see me through the crack. My stomach twisted with the tension of it all—the bizarre image of me, a grown man, father of these twins, hiding in a closet like some guilty teenager.

Not that she knew I was their father.

And it had to stay that way.

Chapter 21

Ella

I never realized how absurdly small my nursery was until Carrie stood there, humming at my daughters while Dom—the six-foot-something, broad-shouldered, former-island-fling-now-secret-baby-daddy—hid like some kind of overgrown ninja.

Carrie beamed down at the twins, completely oblivious. "Wow, it's so calm in here. Last time, I thought I was walking into a horror movie with all the screaming."

I forced a breathy laugh, tugging my robe tighter around me. "Yeah... they're mellow today."

Meanwhile, I could practically feel Dom's presence radiating from somewhere behind me. The closet. Definitely the closet. He was in there, probably folded in half like a piece of badly packed luggage.

And all I could think was: Why the hell had he said that he needed to hide?

This was *Dom*—Mr. Alpha, Mr. Commanding, Mr. "Let me pin you to the wall and ruin you in the best way."

Yet now? He was playing hide-and-seek behind a row of onesies.

Why did it matter so much to him to keep this secret from Seth? Was it just about work? Or was there something else he wasn't telling me?

I kept my face neutral as sweat trickled down my back. Carrie might not notice Dom's cologne, but I could smell him. Warm and masculine and very much trapped behind that door.

Stay calm. Play it cool.

Carrie reached down and stroked Summer's tiny hand, sighing like this was the most peaceful scene she'd witnessed all month.

Yeah, peaceful—if you didn't count the giant elephant of a man hiding three feet away from us.

"Let me help you put the groceries away," she said, tucking a stray lock of hair behind her ear. "Just the basics— milk, eggs, bread, some fruit. I thought you might appreciate not having to drag the twins out to the store."

"Oh my God, yes," I said, a little too eagerly. "You are officially my favorite person today."

I scooped her arm in mine and nearly power-walked to the kitchen like it was the finish line of a marathon. Anywhere away from the nursery—and the six-foot-some-thing stress ball in the nursery closet.

"Everything okay?" Carrie asked, falling in step beside me.

"Yep!" I chirped, slapping a carton of eggs onto the counter like I was performing a cooking show for toddlers. "Totally fine. Just excited to put groceries away. Like a real adult. With a functioning brain and no secrets in her nursery."

Okay, I didn't say that last part out loud. But I was definitely thinking it.

She chuckled. "I swear, you're the only person I know who finds joy in organizing a fridge."

"You know me," I said, forcing a breezy smile as I yanked open the fridge door. "Refrigeration is my happy place."

And right now, it was far preferable to the room where the father of my children was crouched like a sexy game of hide-and-seek. If I didn't get Carrie out of here soon, we were going to run out of groceries and lies.

I paused and managed a tight but genuine smile. "Thank you, Carrie. You have no idea how helpful that is. I feel like I'm juggling chainsaws most days, and the idea of grocery shopping with two preemies is terrifying."

She laughed softly, and for a moment, the tension in my shoulders eased. Carrie had always been a comforting presence—she was my boss, yes, but also one of my closest friends. We'd bonded over the frantic intensity of running Suivante and I'd always admired her ability to handle chaos with grace.

Which only made me feel worse for lying to her.

I'd told Carrie bits and pieces—enough to keep her from asking too many questions—but never the full truth. I had never told her that the father of my daughters was the same man currently hiding in my closet. Never told her that I'd met him before, not just as a patient, but at a bar on a tropical island.

The guilt pressed against my chest like a weight. Carrie had been there for me in ways few others had. And I was keeping her in the dark about the biggest thing in my life.

But now? With Dom hiding, with sweat prickling the back of my neck, now was definitely not the time to come clean. I couldn't very well blurt it out over a grocery bag and two sleeping babies. *Oh hey, by the way, the father of my twins? Surprise! He's your husband's colleague.*

Yeah. No.

But eventually, I'd have to tell her. The longer I waited, the worse it would be.

Just... not today.

"And how about you?" Carrie asked, her voice drawing me back into the moment. She reached out, resting a comforting hand on my arm. "Are you managing? Any luck finding a nanny?"

I drew in a shaky breath, grateful for the small question that didn't require me to reveal Dom's presence. "No luck yet," I admitted. "I've interviewed a couple of people, but none of them felt right. I can't exactly explain it—it's just a gut thing."

She nodded in sympathy. "I get it. Letting a stranger take care of your babies is huge. But remember, once you do find someone, you can come back to Suivante." Her eyes lit up with gentle enthusiasm. "We miss you in the kitchen, especially Giuseppe. You're the only one who can keep up with his rapid-fire Italian. I'm at a loss."

I don't want to chat, I want you to leave, a traitorous voice screamed inside me. *Because the man I love is stuck in a closet and I have a million questions to ask him.*

The realization stunned me. *Love?* When had I started using that word, even in my own mind?

Carrie must have seen something flicker in my expression because her brow furrowed slightly. "Ella? You okay?"

"Uh, yeah." I scrambled to keep my voice steady. "Just tired. You know how it is—feeding, burping, changing. It never ends."

She squeezed my arm once more. "I hear you. Well, I won't keep you too long. I'll just finish up here, then head out. But seriously, call me if you need anything, yeah?"

My heart clogged with conflicting emotions. I was relieved she was leaving but also felt a fresh wave of guilt at wanting her gone. "I really appreciate it, Carrie. I mean it."

She touched my shoulder lightly in a brief, affectionate gesture. "Anytime, Mama. All right, I'll see myself out." She paused, eyes flicking past me to the hallway. "Unless I should say goodbye to the girls again? They were so peaceful, I don't want to wake them if they're letting you have a good morning."

Blood pounded in my ears. "That's for the best. They're being good, and I don't want to jinx it."

She offered a final wave, and then the door clicked shut. The latch's sound echoed in my frazzled nerves, and I exhaled a shuddering breath, slumping against the nearest counter. *She's gone.* Finally.

I closed my eyes, letting the silence settle around me like a warm bath. Maybe now I could retrieve the father of my children from wherever he'd wedged himself.

And then— thud.

A loud, unmistakable crash echoed from the nursery.

I froze. That was not a baby noise.

Another beat of silence. Then a muffled, "Shit."

I groaned, dragging a hand down my face.

That could only have been Dom rolling out of the closet.

Chapter 22

Dom

Closets were not made for grown men.

Especially not six-foot-two doctors with broad shoulders and a mild claustrophobia problem.

I hit the nursery floor with a grunt, one leg twisted awkwardly in what I suspected was a receiving blanket, my elbow jamming painfully into a bin of pacifiers. Dignity? Gone. Airflow? Questionable. My ego? Bruised in multiple places.

I stared at the ceiling, trying to convince myself that I hadn't just spent fifteen minutes folded like a lawn chair in a space the size of a carry-on suitcase.

I groaned, peeling the blanket off my leg and sitting up slowly. The nursery smelled like lavender lotion and baby wipes. It was silent. The girls were still asleep. Peaceful. Unlike me, who was sweating through a pink tank top that was very much not mine.

Ella appeared in the doorway a second later, arms crossed, mouth twitching as she fought back a laugh.

"You good?" she asked, one brow arching.

I ran a hand through my hair. "Define good."

She shook her head, stepping into the room and closing the door behind her. "You fell out of the closet."

"I'm aware."

She leaned against the crib, clearly enjoying herself. "That was a dramatic exit."

I couldn't help but grin back. God, she was beautiful. Even rumpled in her robe, hair wild and cheeks flushed from the stress of our little comedy of errors, she looked like the best part of my day.

"Did Carrie suspect anything?" I asked, quieter now, as I adjusted the blanket that had somehow attached itself to my ass.

"No," she said, still smiling. "But we need to talk."

My grin faded, just a little. "That's never a good sentence."

She gave me a look. "Don't worry, I'm not about to kick you out or say we made a huge mistake. But I need to know what that was back there."

My grin faded. "Yeah," I said, pushing to my feet. "I figured you would."

Her mouth twitched. "You panicked and dove into a closet like we were teenagers sneaking around."

I rubbed the back of my neck. "Right."

"Dom..." she softened, stepping forward, her robe brushing against my bare arm. "I get it. Seth's your coworker. Carrie's his wife. You want to keep your personal life out of the hospital gossip mill."

I nodded once. "That's part of it."

"But it felt like more than that."

I swallowed hard. "We're up for the same promotion. We are not friends."

She shrugged. "What's that got to do with you hiding?"

"You were my patient, Ella. If they find out—"

Her lips parted. "Oh," she whispered, eyes widening as it sank in.

I exhaled hard, dragging a hand through my hair. "Seth and I have hated each other for years. But this? If word gets out that I was with someone I treated in the ER—someone who gave birth to my children the night I was on shift—he'll bury me. No admin job, no credibility, nothing. My entire reputation would be shot."

She was quiet for a beat, just watching me. The teasing edge had vanished, replaced by something deeper—concern, maybe guilt.

"I wasn't thinking about the hospital," she murmured. "I was just thinking... we were hiding you from my best friend."

I tilted my head, watching her. "Is that why you wanted me to hide in the closet? To keep me from Carrie?"

She opened her mouth, then shut it again. For a second, I thought she might lie, but instead she glanced toward the sleeping babies and lowered her voice. "Can we talk somewhere else? I don't want to wake them."

I nodded, following her as she padded quietly out of the nursery and into the living room. The soft light from the kitchen spilled over her shoulders, casting everything in a hazy warmth. She dropped onto the couch with a tired sigh, pulling her robe tighter. I sat beside her, waiting.

She rubbed her hands over her knees, as if buying time. "I never told Carrie you were their father," she admitted, voice low. "When I got pregnant, I just... kept it vague. She knew I'd met someone on vacation, but I didn't say who."

I frowned. "Why?"

She hesitated, chewing on her lip, eyes flicking toward the window like the answer might be written in the city skyline. "Because I was embarrassed," she said finally. "About the whole thing. A one-night stand with an older man I barely knew... it didn't exactly sound like the setup to a happily-ever-after."

I let the words hang there, my jaw tightening—not at her, but at how small she looked saying it, like she expected me to judge her for it.

"Ella," I said, leaning in, my voice low and steady. "You don't ever have to be embarrassed about me. Or about them. We're not some mistake that needs hiding."

Her eyes flicked back to mine, uncertain. But she didn't look away.

She tucked a knee beneath her and turned to face me fully, her eyes searching mine. "So... are you willing to let Seth know? Because if I tell Carrie, he's going to find out. There's no way around that."

I sat back slightly, the question hitting harder than I expected. My jaw clenched as I looked away for a beat, running a hand down my face. "Not yet."

Her brows drew together. "Not ever? Or... just not now?"

I met her gaze again. "Just give me a little more time. I'm this close to locking in the administrator role. If Seth finds out I had a personal relationship with a patient—no matter how complicated the situation was—it'll be over. He'll use it to bury me."

She was quiet for a moment, chewing her bottom lip like she was trying to bite down a dozen thoughts.

"Is the promotion really that important?" she asked softly.

I didn't hesitate. "Yes. Especially now."

She blinked, caught off guard by how quickly I answered.

I leaned in, brushing my fingers over hers. "It's not about the money. You know I don't need this job for that."

Her brows lifted slightly, but she didn't speak.

"This promotion... it's about proving I still have something to offer. That I'm not done. That I can still lead, still build something meaningful. I've built companies, teams, and systems—but this hospital? It's personal. I've given twenty years of my life to it. And now, with the girls here, with you... I want to show them what it means to fight for something that matters. I want to make them proud."

Her eyes softened. "So this is about legacy."

I nodded. "Exactly. It's not about the title. It's about who I get to be—for them."

Ella smiled softly at my words, that little dimple of hers showing. It felt like the air shifted—lighter, less tense.

Then I added, "Also, I heard you and Carrie talking about a nanny."

Her brow arched. "You were eavesdropping now, too?"

"I was trapped in a goddamn closet. I didn't exactly have a choice." I gave her a crooked grin. "But it's a good idea."

Her lips quirked. "You think I should hire a stranger to watch the twins?"

"I think," I said, moving in closer, "we need a night out.

Just you and me. Somewhere no one knows us. Somewhere we're not parents or coworkers or secrets. Just... two people who really want to see where this goes."

She looked at me for a long moment. "A real date?"

"A real date," I confirmed. "No hospital scrubs. No baby monitors. Just us. Maybe even some bad lighting and overpriced cocktails."

Ella laughed, the sound like a balm after everything we'd been through. "I don't even know if I remember how to flirt."

I pulled her on top of my lap, my mouth brushing the shell of her ear. "Lucky for you, I do."

She shivered, just slightly, and tilted her face up to mine. "Dom..."

"I never got to finish what I started this morning," I murmured, letting my hand drift to the knot of her robe. "You said yes, remember?"

Her breath hitched. "I remember."

My mouth found hers, slow at first, deepening as her hands slid up my chest. The robe slipped open, and my hand found her waist, pulling her flush against me. God, the feel of her body still made me dizzy. She melted into me, and I was already hard again, ready to lose myself in her.

Straddling my lap, her robe parted just enough to drive me insane. Our mouths moved in sync—hungry, unfiltered, the kiss deepening until I was dizzy with need. My hands slid up her thighs, slow and teasing, and then one found its way between them.

She gasped as my fingers brushed over her slick heat.

I found her clit and circled it, slow at first, then firmer, just the way I remembered she liked. Her hips rolled instinctively, chasing the friction.

Ella let her head fall back with a moan, lips parted, hair tumbling wild over her shoulders.

"God, Dom," she whispered, voice wrecked and breathy.

I growled softly, tightening my grip around her waist, wanting—needing—to feel her come apart in my arms all over again.

Then—

The piercing wail of one very awake baby cut through the air.

We both froze.

Ella let out a frustrated laugh, forehead dropping to my shoulder. "Every. Time." She laughed, pressing a quick kiss to my temple before turning toward the nursery.

"Yeah," I muttered, adjusting myself with a sigh. "But damn, it was worth the attempt."

Chapter 23

Ella

Nanny interviews weren't supposed to be this stressful. Then again, I never pictured myself as a single mom to twins—let alone interviewing high-end nannies that Dom insisted on paying for.

I sat on my battered couch, phone on speaker, scrolling through polished résumés that looked more like LinkedIn profiles than childcare applications.

"You're really sure about this?" I muttered, eyeing one candidate with a PhD in early childhood development and a client list that read like a Manhattan social registry. "She's impressive. And expensive."

Dom's voice crackled through the line, calm and confident. "Let me handle the cost. I want you to feel good about whoever's with our girls."

I blew out a breath, frustration simmering. "I'm not used to people paying my bills."

"I know," he said. "But this isn't a bill. It's support. And you need it."

I glanced over at the twins, asleep in their bassinets. I

hated how right he was. "Fine. I'll meet them. But I reserve the right to be skeptical."

He chuckled. "You're always skeptical."

"Text you after," I said, ending the call and rubbing my temples. Deep breath. I wasn't quitting Suivante. Which meant I had to find someone I trusted with the most important job in the world.

Even if I hated every second of it.

Thirty minutes later, I sat at my kitchen table—baby bottles everywhere—facing three hyper-qualified nannies who smelled like money and competence. They rattled off answers about safety, feeding schedules, and twin care like seasoned CEOs.

Meanwhile, I sat in a milk-stained T-shirt and a messy bun, trying not to sweat through the interview.

"So," I said, closing my notes. "That's it?"

Amanda, the oldest, smiled. "Your girls will be in excellent hands."

"Right. I'll talk to Dom and let you know."

They left with perfect posture and polite nods, and I collapsed into my chair like I'd just run a marathon. I glanced at Marissa stirring in her bassinet and sighed. "No idea if I'm ready for this. But here we go."

By the next day, Amanda was hired. She had the warmest energy of the bunch—even if she still scared me a little. Dom handled the deposit. The contract hit my inbox.

She arrived for a trial shift looking like she could run a Montessori empire. I hovered while she breezed through bottle prep like she'd lived here for years. My stomach churned. Amanda looked calm. I looked... not.

"You'll see them again soon, Ms. Green," Amanda said

kindly, after the tenth time I repeated instructions. "They'll be fine. Enjoy your time."

"Sure," I said, heart pounding. Time? I'm just going to the restaurant to prep. But it felt like a colossal leap. Still, I stuffed down my motherly panic, grabbed my bag, and headed out.

Dom texted me en route:

You got this, chef. Amanda's top-notch.

Me: *Yeah, but I feel like a shitty mom.*

Dom: *They're in safe hands. You deserve to get to do your job.*

I breathed in, letting his confidence buoy me.

Fine, I'll trust your fancy nanny.

Monday was the perfect day for stepping back into Suivante, that chaotic dance of knives, sauce, and a staff that functioned like a machine. A machine that felt like a memory that didn't belong to me.

I walked into the kitchen itself, scanning the stainless-steel counters, the stacked produce crates. People bustled, but not in the frantic way of a dinner service. Mondays were for shipments, cleaning, reorganizing. The restaurant was closed Mondays, so it was the slowest day we had.

Standing there awestruck, I didn't know where to begin. Abruptly, Carrie ushered a thickly built blonde woman into the kitchen, catching my attention with a quick wave. "Ella," she said, beckoning me over. "Meet Grace Winstead. Everyone calls her Winner."

At first glance, Grace's imposing stature—broad shoulders and a firmly planted stance—screamed confidence. A few strands of hair escaped her tight bun, framing a face that seemed both approachable and razor-sharp in equal measure. Her eyes flicked around the busy counters, taking in the clamor of pots and pans with a calm, assessing gleam. I caught a hint of challenge there, like she was sizing up not just the workspace, but me as well.

Grace chuckled softly when Carrie mentioned her nickname, a sound that held just a touch of mischief. "I do my best to earn the name," she said, flashing me a wry smile. "But nobody's perfect."

Carrie laughed. "Says the woman who finally made Mrs. Oberndorf happy."

It was like hearing a record scratch. "What?"

Carrie's head bobbed proudly, and Grace—*Winner*—explained, "She's like any other society woman. Give them something they've never had, and they'll love you for it."

My head swiveled to the new kid on the block. I'd thought pleasing Mrs. Oberndorf was akin to finding truffles on Mars. That woman had been coming to Suivante since it opened, and every single time, she found something to complain about. We didn't understand why she kept coming back, so we decided she merely enjoyed complaining.

I asked, "What did you—"

"Salisbury steak!" Carrie said, still laughing. "That old bat thought it was this exotic thing, not 1960's TV dinner filler." She turned to Grace. "Not that yours was that quality—"

But Grace humbly waved her off. "It was the Salisbury steak my mother used to make us. Nothing too crazy."

"I guess I'll have to try your Salisbury steak some time."

She smiled, nodded, and assumed her work, leaving me

and Carrie in the dust. I had to ask, "Who is she, really? Does she have blackmail on Oberndorf?"

Carrie shook her head. "I'm telling you, Ella, I've never seen that woman smile. I thought she was born without smiling muscles. But that night, she smiled at Winner. She's been a polite good tipper ever since."

"No fork throwing?"

"None."

"Huh." I didn't know what to make of that. "Well, I better get into the swing of things."

"Once you're comfortable again, we'll figure out what to do with Winner."

"What do you mean?"

She explained, watching Grace work, "I'd hired her on temporarily, but I don't know. She meshes really well here."

I didn't like the sound of that. "Well, I'm back, so she doesn't have to stay on."

"We'll see," Carrie said. "Chat later. I've got a meeting with distributors." She left me standing there.

As I dove deeper into the kitchen, a few bussers and dishwashers gave me nods of acknowledgement, each too busy with their duties to say more than that. But Jean-Paul raised a ladle in greeting. "Welcome back, chef. You good?"

I forced a half-smile. "Never better," I lied, mind drifting to the twins. "What'd I miss?"

He jerked his chin toward the prep station. "Winner's over there, reorganizing. She's got ideas about organization, the menu..." His lip curled in a disapproving sneer.

Fucking perfect.

"I'll handle it," I said, ignoring the tension in my gut. At least Jean Paul was on my side about Grace.

181

Sure enough, she was at the far counter, carefully labeling containers of fresh herbs and talking with some line cooks. "Chef," she greeted me, that confident smirk never leaving her lips. "Welcome back."

"I see you're making yourself comfortable around here."

"Just trying to help," she replied lightly. "Carrie said if I prove myself, I might stick around."

My mouth twisted, but I forced a wry grin. "Well, don't get too comfortable."

"A girl can dream, right?"

I let out a short, forced laugh, ignoring the spike of stress. "You've got shipments to sort. Don't let me keep you."

She flashed a grin. "Sure thing, *chef.*"

I exhaled sharply. My phone buzzed in my pocket—no doubt Dom or the nanny. My hand lurched, for it, almost dropping the thing into a pile of fresh basil. I slid it out, seeing only Dom's text:

How's day one with the nanny?

Me: *So far, so good. No meltdown texts. Just my meltdown.*

His reply came quick:

Dom: *You'll be fine. I believe in you.*

A faint smile tugged my lips, tension easing. But the day slogged by in a haze of sorting produce, reorganizing the pantry, and triple-checking that Winner didn't overshadow my authority. Meanwhile, guilt gnawed at me for leaving the twins, even for a few hours.

What if they need me? What if the nanny's all show and no real care?

But each time I checked my phone, no messages of

doom popped up. By midafternoon, I'd gotten so used to hearing the rest of the staff calling Grace by her nickname, I found myself doing the same.

I double-checked inventory with a pencil jammed behind my ear, cursing under my breath when I realized we'd run low on tapioca flour. "Son of a bitch, I told them to keep it stocked. Now we gotta scramble."

"Everything cool, Chef?" came Winner's bright voice behind me.

"Fine," I said sharply. "Just a missing tapioca flour."

She arched a brow. "Carrie said we can do without it until next shipment. We have alternatives."

My temper flared at her cavalier tone. "I know how to run my own damn kitchen. Just go handle your station."

"Sure thing, boss."

With a surly glare, I returned to my notes. The rest of the staff gave me a wide berth. *Good.* I wasn't in the mood for small talk.

Finally, the short shift that felt like it had been lifetimes-long came to a close. We'd processed all shipments, the place was tidy, and Carrie called me into her office to debrief. I tried to listen, but my mind drifted to Dom, to the twins, to the nanny, to the big secret I still kept from Dom about Leo.

After a while, I dragged myself out of the restaurant, the city's evening bustle welcoming me back.

Back at my apartment building, my nerves twisted as I climbed the stairs. Being at Suivante had made me think about how Leo and I met—he had been a part of a large party, all of them drunk or tweaking, celebrating a sale of one of his pieces. He was cocky, and that was all it took for me to give him my number.

What an idiot I was.

But that memory today pressed the need to tell Dom everything. I couldn't hide this forever, and sooner was better than later for everyone involved.

I still didn't want to tell him, though. He'd hate me forever, and I couldn't blame him for that. But he was a good man. He wouldn't take that out on the girls. This would crush only me and him.

I shook off the grim thought and opened the front door. An evening hush greeted me—plus the faint whir of a fan.

"Ms. Green," Amanda, the nanny, greeted me with a warm smile, gently rocking Summer in her arms. "Everything went smoothly. No issues at all."

They were fine, but I wanted to cry. I cleared my throat before saying a heartfelt, "Thank you."

She handed me a report of diaper changes, feedings— God, so official—and I realized Dom's money had bought the best. *I hate feeling indebted, but I'd be lying if I said this wasn't a lifesaver.*

With the twins settled, Amanda headed home, leaving me in the quiet. My shoulders sagged. No meltdown from them.

Just one for me.

I was failing as a mom and failing at work and failing at romance.

I collapsed onto the couch, phone in hand. I typed a quick message:

Babies are good. Nanny's a pro. I'm exhausted, and I owe you a big conversation soon.

Dom: *I'm here whenever you're ready. We'll talk on the date if that's okay.*

My heart hammered. *Sounds good.*

I stood, crossing to the window, arms folded. Outside, the city buzzed with life, neon signs flickering. My reflection stared back—tired. I looked bone tired.

Sighing, I raked a hand through my hair. "Screw it," I muttered. "If I can handle a new nanny and a mouthy temp, I can handle telling Dom about Leo."

Chapter 24

Dom

The hostess barely glanced at me when I walked in —which was exactly how I wanted it. No last names, no handshakes, no special treatment. Just a quiet nod and a "this way, sir," as she led me through the low-lit dining room toward a secluded table in the back.

Ella had insisted we meet here instead of arriving together—just in case. Her words, not mine. The nanny had the twins at home for a trial evening shift, and this was supposed to be our night.

Our first real date. One night to pretend we were just two normal people, out for good food and better company. No secrets. No lies. No baby monitors. Just us.

But she was late and I was getting worried she wouldn't show. I downed my whiskey to calm my nerves but nothing could have prepared me for the moment she finally did walk in.

She was radiant.

Curves wrapped in silky black fabric that hugged her hips like a second skin. A neckline that teased just enough cleavage to make my mouth go dry. Her hair was pinned up, loose tendrils falling around her face, and her lips were stained a deep red that made me want to ruin her makeup in the backseat of my car.

I stood immediately, drinking her in like a man dying of thirst. "Jesus, Ella."

She blushed, but her eyes sparkled. "Is that a good Jesus or a too-much-cleavage Jesus?"

I stepped around the table and reached for her coat. "It's a how-am-I-supposed-to-make-it-through-dinner-looking-at-you Jesus."

She rolled her eyes but smiled as I slid the coat from her shoulders, revealing the full curve of her ass as she turned. My cock stirred. Of course it did. I guided her to her seat with a hand on the small of her back, letting it dip slightly lower than polite.

The host handed us menus and poured the wine I'd pre-selected, then said with a warm smile, "It's always lovely to see a father and daughter out with each other."

"Date," I snapped, a little too fast.

A beat of silence.

Ella snorted. She actually snorted. "Wow, that's one for the scrapbook."

The host paled. "I—I'm so sorry, sir."

I forced a tight smile. "It's fine. Let's just...start with the wine, yeah?"

He retreated like his shoes were on fire. Ella bit her lip, holding in laughter.

"You think that's funny?" I asked, leaning in, brushing her thigh under the table with my fingers. "You like being mistaken for my daughter?"

She leaned forward, her voice low and wicked. "I like watching you squirm."

"Careful, baby," I murmured in her ear, letting my palm slide higher on her thigh. "I'm one wrong look away from dragging you into the bathroom and reminding you exactly who you belong to."

She licked her lips. Her legs parted, just slightly.

Yeah. I had her.

But something in her gaze flickered. Just for a second. Like her thoughts had drifted somewhere heavier than the heat between us.

I kept the conversation light, feeding her the most expensive bites on the menu, watching her cheeks flush when I whispered things she'd earned with that dress. But beneath the banter, something in her was wound tight.

"What?" I asked finally, brushing her knuckles with my thumb. "You're somewhere else."

She shook her head, smiling like it was nothing. "I just... I said I wanted to talk about something tonight, remember?"

I nodded, but before I could ask more, she slid back her chair.

"Let me run to the bathroom first," she said, rising.

I didn't answer—just watched her go.

Her hips swayed with every step. The curve of her ass in that dress was a goddamn threat.

I waited ten seconds. Maybe twelve. Then tossed my napkin on the table and followed.

The hallway to the bathrooms was dim and deserted. I caught her just as she was slipping into the women's restroom.

"Dom," she hissed, wide-eyed, backing up a step. "You can't—"

But I was already inside, locking the door behind me.

"I don't care," I growled.

She blinked at me, breath catching as I stalked toward her. "Dom—"

"You show up looking like that, and expect me to sit through dessert without touching you?" My voice was low, rough, and I backed her up until her spine met the wall.

"You're insane," she whispered.

"I've been hard since you walked in."

She shuddered when I kissed her, mouth hot and open under mine. My hands roamed—thigh, waist, ass—then slid up the slit of her dress, dragging it high enough to bare the lace tops of her stockings.

Her gasp lit me up.

"Say the word and I'll stop," I murmured, lips grazing her throat. "Otherwise, I'm going to make you come with my fingers right here against this wall."

Her nails dug into my biceps. Her eyes fluttered shut. "God, Dom..."

I pressed a hand between her thighs—already wet. The moment I slipped one finger inside her, she bit back a moan that sounded like my name. Her hips rolled toward me, need making her reckless.

"Not here," she panted, pulling my wrist.

I stilled, jaw clenched. My fingers still deep inside her.

She opened her eyes, wild and desperate. "Not here. But later?"

I nodded, slowly pulling back, pressing one last filthy kiss to her lips.

We returned to the table flushed, breathless, pretending nothing had happened—like I didn't just have my fingers inside her, like she wasn't still trembling when I pulled out her chair.

Ella picked up her wine glass with shaky fingers. Her lipstick was smudged, pupils still blown, and she looked wrecked in the most delicious way.

But then I saw it again—that flicker.

Whatever had her distracted earlier wasn't gone. If anything, it had gotten worse.

Her fork moved food around her plate, untouched. She kept glancing at the candle between us, like it held the answers.

I reached across the table, took her hand. "Ella."

She looked up. And I knew something was coming.

"I was going to wait," she whispered. "Until after dinner. Or maybe tomorrow. Or maybe... never."

I sat up straighter. My stomach tightened. "What is it?"

She pulled in a breath like she was about to jump off a cliff.

Three.

Two.

One.

"I used to date Leo," she said softly.

The words didn't land all at once.

Leo?

The name echoed in my head like a dropped tray in a quiet ER.

Leo... my Leo?

My son?

No.

I stared at her, trying to blink it away, trying to reshape reality. "What did you just say?"

She swallowed. "Before the island. We were together..."

Every muscle in my body locked.

Leo. My goddamn son. The one I'd raised, the one I was constantly at war with, the one I never quite knew how to reach. He had dated Ella?

I saw flashes of her on top of me. Her breathy moans. Her soft, flushed skin. The things I'd done to her body. The things she'd let me do.

And Leo had—

My stomach turned.

I pushed back in my chair, unable to breathe.

"You... dated Leo?" I said again, needing to hear it, to make sure I wasn't hallucinating. "My son?"

Time didn't slow. It stopped.

I sat there, absolutely frozen.

What the fuck?

I remembered him offhandedly talking about an ex once. Said her name was Mariella, I think.

No. No fucking way.

Mariella. Ella.

"You're that ex?" My voice was a rasp. "Leo's Mariella?"

She winced.

"You knew this. All this time." My hands clenched the table's edge. My jaw clenched so tight it ached. Fury. Betrayal. Confusion. All of it whirled like a storm behind my ribs.

And it made me want to punch something.

"Why the fuck didn't you tell me?" I growled, my voice low but lethal.

She flinched, and part of me hated that, but the rest of me was too full of shock and betrayal to stop.

This wasn't just some awkward coincidence.

This was my son.

This was Ella.

She sat still, like she was bracing for me to explode.

And honestly? I didn't know what I was going to say next.

So I didn't speak.

Not when she whispered my name.

Not when she reached across the table like she could take the words back.

Not when the waiter brought the dessert menu like we weren't both seconds from imploding.

I raised a hand. "Check."

Ella blinked, her face pale now under the flickering candlelight. She opened her mouth, then closed it. Smart. Because if she said the wrong thing right now, I didn't know what I'd do.

My hands shook. I hid them beneath the table.

My thoughts were a cyclone—Leo's voice, Ella's eyes, the image of my girls asleep in their bassinets, soft and pink and perfect. Our girls.

God. What did this mean?

Leo would never forgive this.

Would he even believe I didn't know?

Would I forgive this?

She had let me fall for her. Touch her. Claim her. All while knowing I'd raised the last man she had called, 'boyfriend'.

I paid the bill without looking at the total. Didn't even touch the last sip of wine.

When we stepped outside, the cold air slapped me across the face. Still, I didn't speak. My fists jammed deep into my coat pockets. My jaw locked.

Ella walked beside me, shoulders hunched, her heels clicking against the sidewalk. She didn't reach for me. Didn't speak either.

She didn't need to. I could feel it.

She thought this was the end.

That I'd already walked away.

And maybe I had.

I didn't know yet.

I just knew I couldn't breathe.

Chapter 25

Ella

The cold slapped my skin the second we stepped outside, but I barely felt it.

I was too busy trying to breathe.

Dom walked beside me, silent, stiff, every inch of him locked down like he was trying not to feel anything at all. The same hands that had been on my body less than an hour ago now hid in his pockets like they didn't know what to do with themselves.

And I hated it.

Hated the space that stretched between us like a chasm, hated the way I couldn't read him anymore, hated myself most of all.

I wrapped my coat tighter around me, trying to keep myself from shattering completely. The city lights blurred around us, traffic noise barely registering. All I could hear was my own heartbeat, frantic and desperate, and the pounding thought that I'd ruined everything.

"I didn't know," I said, and my voice cracked the second it left my mouth. "I didn't know who you were. That night."

Dom didn't look at me. His jaw flexed, but his eyes stayed forward, and I pressed on anyway, because silence was worse than yelling. Silence meant he was retreating. Pulling away.

"I swear, I didn't know your last name until the next morning. I woke up and..." My voice trembled, but I pushed through it. "I Googled your company. Just something dumb, like checking out the hot guy I slept with."

I forced a breath. "And then I saw your name on the About page. And realized who you were. And my stomach dropped."

I finally stopped walking, because I couldn't keep moving with all the weight pressing down on me. I turned to him, heart pounding in my throat. "That was the moment I knew. That I'd just slept with...well..." I couldn't bring myself to say the words.

Dom's eyes finally met mine. They were dark. Guarded. I couldn't tell what he was thinking, and it terrified me.

"I panicked," I whispered. "I didn't know what to do, so I left. I told myself it was a one-time thing and I'd handle it. That I wouldn't complicate your life or ruin your relationship with Leo. I didn't want to be the reason things got worse between you."

The tears were dangerously close now. "So I ran. I kept my mouth shut. I made a hundred excuses, but the truth is— I thought I was doing the right thing."

Still, nothing. Just the rise and fall of his chest, sharp and uneven.

"I was willing to do it alone," I said, barely holding it together. "Raise the girls. Be a single mom. Whatever it

195

took. Because I thought it was better than tearing apart your family."

The silence between us settled heavy, thick as wet wool in the chilly night air. I could hear the hum of the city just beyond the curb, a cab horn in the distance, the whisper of wind against the building. But all I could feel was Dom—his presence beside me like a storm barely contained in a man's body.

I kept my arms wrapped tight around myself, clutching the edges of my coat like armor. My breath came out shaky. My confession still hung between us, and I braced for whatever would come next. Yelling. Accusation. Walking away.

But when he finally spoke, his voice wasn't hard.

It was wrecked.

"I should be thinking about why you didn't tell me," he said, not looking at me, his jaw rigid as stone. "That's what I should be stuck on. That you kept this from me."

He paused, chest rising like it hurt to breathe.

"But all I can think about... is that night. On the island. When you told me your ex didn't like touching you. That he didn't want your curves. That he made you feel like too much."

My breath caught. I hadn't expected that. Not now. Not here.

His eyes found mine then—sharp, dark, burning.

"It was Leo, wasn't it?" he asked, his voice low, dangerous. "He was the ex who made you feel that way."

I felt myself nod before I could stop it. The answer pushed past my pride. The shame. The fear.

Dom closed his eyes for half a second, and when he opened them again, something in him had changed. He looked at me like he was seeing everything I'd hidden. Everything I'd tried to carry alone.

"I wanted to find the bastard who made you feel that way," he whispered. "Back then, I didn't know who he was. But I felt it. That rage. The second you said it, I wanted to tear him apart."

Tears burned behind my eyes, but I blinked them back. Because I wasn't the only one breaking.

He stepped closer, his hand lifting—hovering at my jaw, then lowering like he couldn't bear not to touch me. His palm found my waist instead, warm and solid.

"No one gets to make you feel like that again," he said. "Not him. Not anyone."

I opened my mouth, but nothing came out.

I didn't have words for what that did to me. For how the girl who once stood in front of a mirror and wished herself smaller now felt seen. Not just wanted—but defended.

I nodded, throat tight.

And he nodded, too. Like it wasn't a question. Like it was a promise.

I barely had time to breathe before he surged forward—closing the space between us with a force that stole the rest of the oxygen from my lungs. His hands gripped my waist like he couldn't tell if he wanted to anchor me or drag me against him. His jaw was clenched, eyes wild, burning like fire had replaced the calm control he always wore like armor.

"You're mine, Ella."

I blinked up at him, heart ricocheting in my chest.

"I don't care what's between us and the rest of the world," he growled, voice low and rough, like it was clawing its way up from someplace buried deep. "I want you. I want our girls. And I'm not walking away."

He didn't wait for my answer. Just pulled me flush to his chest and wrapped his coat around my shoulders like a shield. His mouth crashed down on mine—hot, unrelenting, like he was making a vow with every bruising kiss. I melted into him, into the heat and hunger and heartbreak of it all.

But even as my lips parted for him, the fear was still there. Lodged in my chest like glass.

I pulled back just enough to look him in the eye. "Dom, I'm your son's ex-girlfriend. Do you even hear what you're saying?"

His hands flexed against my hips. "I hear it."

"I dated Leo. I slept with Leo. Are you even aware of the fallout this could cause? With your career, your reputation, your son—"

"My son," he snapped, cutting me off. "My son is a grown man who walked away from something good and didn't have the sense to know what he lost."

I flinched, but he didn't let go.

"You think I give a shit what people will say about me? What Seth or Carrie or the goddamn hospital board says? No." His hands cupped my face now, and his voice dropped—dangerously low. "I care about you. About our daughters. About this life that snuck up and took me by the throat."

I was breathing too fast. My hands trembled in his coat. "You don't mean that. You're upset. This is adrenaline—"

"I've never been more fucking sure of anything."

I searched his eyes, looking for a sign to confirm if he really meant what he was saying.

"Leo may be my son," he said, voice ragged, "but you... you're my family now."

Tears stung the backs of my eyes. His words hit like a match to kindling, lighting up everything inside me that had been cold and afraid and alone for so long.

I wanted to believe him. I wanted this.

But the stakes were so impossibly high.

I stood there, wrapped in his coat and his arms, stunned into silence.

He meant every word.

I could see it in the rawness of his expression, the shake in his voice, the way his hands hadn't left my body since he'd pulled me close. But even under the heat of his possessive vow, a part of me still trembled. Because words were easy. Reality... wasn't.

His thumb brushed along my cheekbone, catching the tear I hadn't even realized had fallen.

"You really mean it," I whispered, not quite believing it.

"I do."

I nodded slowly, breath catching in my throat. "Okay," I said, voice small. "Okay."

His eyes softened for the first time all night. His forehead pressed to mine. We didn't kiss. We just stood like that —touching, breathing, clinging to something that felt impossible and inevitable all at once.

And still, under all of that, the truth sat heavy in my chest.

Carrie couldn't know. Seth definitely couldn't know.

And Leo... God, would there ever be a right time to tell him?

I'd been prepared to raise the twins alone to avoid

blowing up their family. But now? Now it wasn't just about protecting them. Now it was about us.

Because I wanted this. I wanted Dom. I wanted a family, messy and tangled and real.

But how were we supposed to build something honest... when everything between us was a secret?

My chest squeezed as I looked up at him.

"We're going to have to keep this quiet," I said. "Not just for now. Not just because of the promotion. Because of Leo."

His jaw clenched. "I know."

A bitter laugh escaped my throat. "So that's three. Carrie. Seth. Leo."

I turned my face into his chest, breathing in the scent of his skin, and let the weight of everything we hadn't figured out settle around us like the cold night air.

How the hell were we going to make this work?

Dom's hand rubbed slow circles against my back. We stood there for what felt like forever, caught in that space between hope and fear, between what we wanted and what the world would allow.

Then, his voice rumbled low against the top of my head.

"You know what the worst part of all this is?"

I pulled back just enough to look up at him.

He gave me a crooked, almost-smile. "It ruined our damn date."

A startled laugh escaped me—half gasp, half sob. And somehow, just like that, the tension cracked open.

God help me, I loved this man.

Chapter 26

Dom

"You know, we have the nanny for a few more hours," I said.

Ella glanced at me. "What're you thinking?"

"You've never seen my place."

A smile split across her lips. "I'd like that."

So, instead of straight to her place, we went to mine. I guided Ella toward my Manhattan apartment, her hand clutching mine.

I needed her in my bed the way I needed air.

Once we reached my building, she let out a low whistle as she scanned all the way up to the top of the skyscraper. "Really?"

For an answer, the doorman greeted me and we walked inside. Her eyes went wide at the sight of the lobby, the way every surface gleamed. The elevator shot to the last floor and once we stepped inside, she whispered, "Wow."

It was a reaction that made every penny spent worth it. My penthouse was a testament to years of hard work that had led me here. From the art on the walls and tables to the floor-to-ceiling windows all around, every aspect told the story of what I'd done to get here.

She paused, turning in a slow circle, taking it all in. Her dark hair fell over her shoulders and her dress hugged her curves—curves I'd spent the evening ogling at the restaurant. Now, all I could think was *mine*. The primal possessiveness jolted me, and I let out a ragged breath, trying to rein myself in.

"This is swanky," she murmured, shooting me a teasing grin over her shoulder. "Makes my little apartment look like a college dorm."

I smiled, stepping up behind her, letting my hands settle at her hips. "I like your place, but I've been dying to have you here, alone, with no reason to hide."

Her breath caught, and she twisted to face me, eyes gleaming. "Show me around?"

I curved an arm around her waist, pulling her flush against me. "I will. But I might need to skip the guided tour if you keep pressing yourself against me."

Her lips parted in a half smile, half challenge. "What would we possibly do in the meantime?"

That was all it took. The tension that had crackled between us all night ignited. My mouth captured hers in a hungry kiss, as I tangled my fingers in her hair. She responded instantly, arms slinging around my neck, her body arching against mine.

A low growl escaped my throat as I slid my hands down the curve of her waist, savoring her warmth. She pressed closer, a moan slipping free when my tongue teased hers. The chaos of the day dissolved in the heat of her taste.

I backed her against the nearest wall, hardly aware of my apartment's décor. Her gasp spurred me on, the rustle of fabric as I found the hem of her dress, fingers exploring soft skin beneath. She let out a breathless laugh, grabbing the collar of my shirt.

"You're in a hurry," she teased, eyes dark with want.

I flashed a wry grin. "Ella, I've wanted you for days. Finally uninterrupted." Another kiss, deeper, my hands sliding up her thighs, heart pounding. "And before we found each other again, I wanted you for months. We have a lot of time to make up for."

Her answering smile turned wicked. "Then don't hold back," she whispered, pulling me into another searing kiss that left my head spinning.

We barely made it two steps before I pressed her onto a sleek leather ottoman near the living room. Her dress slid higher as she hooked a leg around my waist, pulling me down to meet her. Every nerve in my body sparked at each point of contact.

The faint hum of the city outside seemed distant, as though we were the only ones in the world. I kissed down the column of her throat, reveling in her soft moans, guiding her hips beneath my palms. The press of her body against mine was intoxicating, a woman made of softness and defiance that had hooked me from the start.

"God, you're perfect," I groaned against her ear, unable to resist tasting the delicate skin there.

She let out a shaky laugh, voice trembling. "If you stop now, I might kill you."

"Not stopping," I promised, lips curving into a triumphant smirk.

The next few minutes blurred into a heated tangle of limbs, kisses, and low murmurs as we discovered just how comfortable that ottoman could be. Her nails raked up my back under my shirt, and I bit back a growl of pleasure. I wanted to consume her, to let go of every ounce of control—but I also wanted to take my time.

Eventually, I scooped her up, ignoring her yelp of surprise. "My bedroom," I rasped, voice uneven. She nodded, eyes hazy with lust, and I carried her down the short hallway, nearly stumbling over a discarded shoe.

"Fancy," she teased between kisses, glancing at the spacious room with its king-size bed and windows offering a panoramic cityscape. "I wouldn't mind waking up to this."

"Plan on it," I growled, depositing her onto the bed's soft expanse.

Clothes fell away—my shirt, her dress, shoes kicked off with a clatter. The lamplight revealed every inch of her body, every curve, every hollow, and I took a second to appreciate the sight, adrenaline pulsing in my veins. She arched on the sheets, eyes molten with need.

Mine.

"Dom," she whispered, beckoning me closer.

I climbed over her, hooking an arm under her back, pressing her against my chest. The slide of skin on skin ignited a fresh wave of heat, and I swallowed a groan at how perfectly she fit against me. How soft her body, how yielding to every movement.

I couldn't hold back any longer. A primal need drove me to touch her, guaranteeing she was ready for me. With my lips on her neck, her nails scoring lines down my shoulders, breathy curses and pleas mingling with the low hum of the city, I thrust deep in one go. We cried out together, ecstasy and curses in equal measure.

We christened the bed with our desperation, bodies moving in tandem, hearts pounding in unison. She gasped my name, and I lost track of coherent thought, drifting on the haze of her warmth, her taste, her *yes*.

Somehow, we ended up with her on top of me. I watched as her tits bounced and her body writhed, all while feeling the most intense pleasure in the world. Ella was perfection. There was no other word for it.

Time slipped, the citylights shifting as we rode out each wave of sensation. I moved behind her, half-kneeling on the bed so we could still be as close as possible to one another. My fingers were on her clit, her hands fisted in the sheets, there was nothing better than this. It wasn't possible.

When her pleasure peaked, I pressed a muffled groan against her neck, her answering cry echoing through the room. In that moment, there was no outside world. No troubles. Nothing but Ella and sheer, raw need.

After she came, she turned around and playfully shoved me onto my back. Before I could speak, her mouth was on me. Hot, wet, soft, and busy. She sucked me deep until I saw stars. My balls tightened, seizing with every stroke of her tongue. I tried to hiss a warning, but I had no breath. I tapped her shoulder, but she swallowed me down further as she put my hand on top of her head.

This woman.

I laced my fingers into her hair, guiding her to my rhythm until I erupted and she drank me down, every last drop. I didn't know what I'd done to deserve her, but I vowed to keep it up.

I pulled her to me for a deep kiss until our kisses threatened to become more. But we were both breathless and needed a break. My chest heaved, her hair tangling across my arm. The windows revealed a glimmer of lights across Manhattan, silent witnesses to our stolen hours of freedom.

Finally, I managed to prop myself on an elbow, brushing stray strands from her face. She gazed up at me, cheeks flushed, eyes shining. A lazy grin tugged at my lips, and I pressed a gentle kiss to her forehead.

"That was..." She trailed off, eyes rolling shut in blissful aftershock.

"Yeah," I murmured, voice still rough, "it was."

We shared a quiet laugh, letting the night air cool our sweaty skin. After a few minutes, she wriggled free from my hold and slipped off the bed, swaying slightly as if drunk on pleasure.

"Where do you think you're going?" I teased, half-rising to follow her.

She shot me a mischievous glance over her shoulder, hair tumbling in disarray. "Thought I'd check out your living room again," she said, arching a brow. "I didn't get a full tour earlier."

A low chuckle rumbled in my chest as I stood, letting the sheet drape around my hips. "Be my guest. But don't blame me if you can't walk tomorrow."

She snorted, eyes dancing with challenge. "Big talk, Dr. Mortoli. Prove it."

A thrill shot through me, lust reigniting. *Hell yes.* I strode after her, adrenaline pumping. She made it to the hallway before I caught her around the waist, guiding her backward until she pressed against the wall with a startled gasp. Our laughter mingled as we devoured each other in hungry kisses, hands roaming, exploring every curve and plane of skin.

The next hour blurred in a haze of frantic desire—my kitchen counter, the sofa, the bathroom sink. Each new surface spurred fresh moans and curses, each new angle a testament to the pent-up tension we'd been carrying. The city beyond the windows felt nonexistent compared to the heat crackling between us.

Eventually, we ended up back in the bedroom, panting and flushed, bodies slick with sweat. I cradled her against my chest, her giggling half-smothered by my neck. *Fuck, I can't get enough.*

She nestled into the pillows, gazing up at me with a wry smile. "I—I can't believe we did that. On our first date."

My pulse still hammered, but I mustered a teasing smirk. "We're not exactly a brand-new couple, you know. I think we're allowed to skip some formalities."

She let out a shaky laugh, trailing her fingers across my chest. "Still. You'll respect me in the morning, right? Even though I jumped you in your fancy apartment?"

I pressed my lips to her forehead. I knew she was teasing, but I had to be clear. "Ella. I'd respect you if we'd done this within five minutes of meeting. You're a damn force of nature, and nothing changes that. I'm proud you're with me."

"Good," she whispered, voice still thick with post-coital emotion. "Because I want this. Us. No regrets."

"Same," I murmured, wrapping an arm around her waist, hauling her close. "You know, we'll have to pay for Amanda all night and tomorrow too?"

She laid her head on my shoulder, tension easing from her frame. "You're insatiable."

"Can you blame me? Have you seen what you look like naked?"

She giggled and still managed to blush somehow. "Same to you."

"Yeah, about that. What's gotten into you?"

She bit her lip, eyes gleaming. "Maybe I just like using your swanky apartment as my personal playground."

"Knock yourself out. As long as you give me time to rehydrate," I teased, trailing a hand down her spine.

Her laughter rang soft and low in the space between us. For a few beats, we just breathed together, the city lights painting shadows on the walls. I felt the edge of responsibility nag at my mind—*the twins, the hospital, Seth, Leo.* But in the hush of my bedroom, with Ella's warmth pressed against me, none of that could intrude.

We might be on the precipice of a hundred challenges, but tonight, we were allowed this stolen, passionate reprieve. My fingers drifted along her arm, a soft caress, and she sighed contentedly, eyes drifting shut.

Chapter 27

Ella

I woke to unfamiliar smooth white sheets and a skyline view that nearly took my breath away. The dawn light filtered in through vast windows, revealing the expanse of Dom's swanky Manhattan apartment.

Apartment? More like a damn palace, I thought, stifling a groan as I stretched. My muscles protested the enthusiastic activities from the night before.

A lazy smile tugged at my lips, recalling how he'd arranged everything—the nanny watching the twins all night so I didn't have to rush home. No crying babies, no bottles, no reason to panic if I wasn't there to soothe them. I missed them, sure, but the novelty of having zero responsibilities for once felt heady and luxurious. Dom and I used that freedom well.

I had the soreness to prove it.

I shifted, blinking away the morning haze, and spotted him in the doorway, leaning against the frame with a cocky expression. He wore only a pair of low-slung pajama pants, and the sight made my pulse skip.

"Morning," he said softly, voice still rough with sleep.

"Morning," I replied, propping myself on an elbow. "You always wake up this early? Or did you never sleep?"

A low chuckle rumbled in his chest. "I slept, eventually. Hard not to, after that workout you gave me."

"You know, if you keep bragging about your stamina, I'll hold you to higher standards."

"Wouldn't dream of disappointing you," he teased. Then, his expression softened as he crossed to the bed, sitting on the edge. "How do you feel about leaving the twins with the nanny all night?"

I pursed my lips, scanning the sleek décor of his bedroom. Everything screamed modern, expensive, and carefully curated, from the minimalist furniture to the abstract art on the walls. It was worlds away from the cozy cluttered chaos of my place.

"Honestly, it's weird," I admitted. "A part of me freaks out thinking they might need me. But the other part is like, 'Hallelujah, a full night of grown-up time'."

He nodded, sympathy in his gaze. "I remember those conflicting emotions. But trust me, they're fine. Amanda's a pro, and you deserve a break."

My heart fluttered at his gentle reassurance. I let out a sigh, pushing a stray lock of hair behind my ear. "Thank you for this weekend. I needed it."

Dom smiled, leaning down to press a soft kiss to my forehead. "Anytime. Coffee?"

"You're a god among men."

He chuckled and fetched me a cup. Rich and satisfying. Like Dom.

Eventually, I swung my legs over the side, letting the plush rug sink beneath my toes. "So," I said, shooting him a playful glance, "what's for breakfast in the land of luxury? You have a private chef, or do I get to rummage through your presumably well-stocked fridge?"

He chuckled. "No private chef, just me. But you're welcome to rummage. I think there's some fruit, maybe eggs." He shrugged, as though unsure what exactly lived in his own fridge.

"Of course, the brilliant Dr. Mortoli can't remember what groceries he has," I teased. Standing, I glanced around for my scattered clothes—evidence of last night's fervor. "Bet you can recall the entire anatomy of the human body, though."

He smirked. "I'd be a lousy surgeon if I couldn't."

I tugged on one of his T-shirts—soft, smelling of him—and followed him through the spacious apartment, taking in the panoramic view of Manhattan. "Still can't believe how big this place is," I muttered, trailing behind him. "Makes my apartment look like a dollhouse."

He paused near the open-concept kitchen, turning with a fond smile. "You said that last night, too, remember?"

I shrugged, feigning nonchalance. "Well, it's still true." The memory of "last night" made my cheeks flare, but I swallowed the flutter in my chest. "So, your medical device company? Is that how you can afford this place?"

Dom's lips twitched, amusement dancing in his eyes. "Still can't believe you thought I was exaggerating when I told you about it on vacation." He opened the fridge, rummaging for ingredients. "But yes, that's how. I built a company around my inventions. Still own the majority of shares, though I barely do more than a quarterly check-in these days."

"So you just...what, decided to keep working the ED for kicks?" I leaned against the marble countertop, crossing my arms.

He shrugged, pulling out a carton of eggs and some vegetables. "Saving lives directly is what keeps me going. If I sat in a boardroom all day, I'd go crazy. The ED is where I thrive."

I watched him with a half-smile, noticing how comfortable he seemed talking about something that would be a bragging point for most. He rummaged for a pan, totally relaxed in his domain, but I see the spark in his eyes when he talked about helping people.

"And you plan to jump ship for administration?" I pressed, arching a brow. "Thought you said the ED was your first love."

"Emergency surgery is. But it's a young man's game, Ella. I'm still at my peak, but eventually, my body will fail. I've seen it happen to other surgeons—they hit the wall. A tremor in their hand, losing focus at a critical moment. They're natural signs of aging, but..." He sighed. "That's my nightmare. So, I'd rather move into an admin role while I'm still ahead, help shape policy and patient care on a larger scale."

"Damn," I murmured, leaning closer. "You're unstoppable, you know that? Medical devices, top surgeon, future hospital exec. Gonna run for president next?"

He let out a laugh that crinkled the corners of his eyes.

"I take back what I said about aging out of surgery. I have a new nightmare."

I snorted a laugh.

He set the pan on the stove, turning on the burner with practiced ease. The faint hiss of gas accompanied the flicker of a flame. "You want scrambled eggs?"

"Sure," I said, a wry grin pulling at my lips. "Guess you can show off your dexterous surgeon's hands cracking eggs."

He smirked, swiftly cracking two eggs with one hand, tossing the shells aside, then whisking them. I watched, impressed despite myself.

"Show off."

"I've got a chef in the house. I have to show off."

We fell into a comfortable rhythm—he cooked, I sipped coffee from his fancy espresso machine, occasionally tossing in a sarcastic remark about how I'd never see him flipping eggs in the ED. He countered with a retort about how he'd never see me do surgery at the restaurant.

Damn goofball.

As he plated the eggs, my mind wandered to the twins. Ordinarily, I'd be consumed with guilt for not being there. But I knew the nanny was fully paid, thanks to Dom, letting me stay the night in a carefree bubble. A pang of longing flared—*I miss them,* but I also relished the mental break.

He set the plates on the sleek kitchen island, pulling up a stool beside me. We ate in companionable silence for a moment, the city's morning buzz drifting through the windows.

This is surreal.

Part of me marveled at how quickly I'd adjusted to a "new normal" with this man, while the other part remembered the unstoppable spark that led us to hooking up on an island in the first place.

After a few bites, I cleared my throat. "So...once you're in administration, you said you'll sell your shares in the device company?"

He nodded, wiping his mouth with a napkin. "Yeah. The time commitment to run that plus the admin role at the hospital would be impossible. I barely have time now."

A sardonic smile tugged at my lips. "I guess that means no more expansions to your penthouse, huh?"

He chuckled, shaking his head. "I think four thousand square feet is enough." Then his tone grew more serious. "But yeah, the company deserves someone who can give it their full attention. And if I'm going to help thousands of patients through hospital leadership, that's where my focus will be."

"You know," I said quietly, "it's kinda crazy how you keep leveling up, all in the name of saving lives."

He paused, studying me. "It's what I love. Sometimes it's grueling, but knowing I made a difference—like with you and the twins—makes it worth it."

My throat tightened, remembering how he'd literally saved us. The lingering gratitude, the sense of safety, it all rolled together, making me feel dangerously vulnerable. I poked at my eggs, forcing a casual tone. "Well, I won't complain. Since your hero complex saved me and my girls, I guess I can let you keep being unstoppable."

"You *let* me, huh?"

I shrugged, fighting a grin. "As a favor."

He laughed and gently smacked my thigh. "You are such a brat sometimes."

"You like it."

He smiled and shrugged, a silent admission.

Eventually, he stacked the dishes in the sink, rinsing them with quick efficiency. I hopped off the stool and wandered into the living room, trailing a hand over the back of his plush sofa. The memory of last night's frantic passion sent a delicious shiver through me.

Dom joined me, wrapping an arm around my waist from behind. His breath tickled my ear. "Penny for your thoughts?"

"Just...thinking how my tiny apartment is going to feel even tinier now," I joked, though a note of truth lingered.

He pressed a soft kiss to my neck. "Space is overrated," he murmured. "Besides, if you had too much room to roam, there'd be nothing holding in your feistiness."

A laugh bubbled up, and I twisted in his arms to face him. "Insult or compliment?"

"Compliment. Always compliment."

"Good," I teased, "because I might bite if it was an insult."

He smirked, leaning down to claim a kiss. My heart fluttered at the tender press of his lips, the lazy swirl of his tongue meeting mine. We broke apart, both of us a bit breathless. He guided me to the massive windows overlooking the city. The morning sun glinted off distant skyscrapers. It felt like we were on top of the world.

In a way, we are.

"I'll have to go check on the twins soon," I said softly, though I made no move to leave his embrace. "But for now..."

"Stay a bit. I'm in no rush, and neither are you."

I allowed myself a small smile, letting my head rest against his chest. "Fine, I'll indulge in this fancy morning a little longer."

He squeezed me gently, and for a while, we just stood there, soaking in the hush of his apartment, the distant hum of the city. My restless mind, always anxious about the girls or my job or the next crisis, felt strangely still.

Chapter 28

Dom

Now that Ella had left for the day, one thought echoed off the walls of my apartment. I paced around my living room, the skyline glittering outside, my stomach twisted with nerves.

I have to tell Leo and Gina everything.

They deserved to know about the twins—and about Ella, the woman I'd chosen. It was like I told her. No more hiding. Even if I knew this could blow up in my face.

Ella left an hour ago, pressing a quick kiss to my cheek, voicing her support. "You handle your kids," she'd said softly, a flicker of worry in her eyes. "I'll handle ours."

I couldn't blame her. The potential fallout with Leo had weighed on us since she confessed he was the asshole ex who'd hurt her. I refused to drag her into a confrontation that might explode.

So it fell to me. I'd invited Leo and Gina for a last-minute brunch, off our usual schedule. Predictably, they asked if I was okay. *I will be,* I told myself grimly, setting out pastries and fresh fruit on the dining table. Now it was set for a conversation that might tear my family apart.

Gina and Leo arrived in a brisk swirl of tension. Gina wore a casual sweater, hair in a messy bun, to-go box of coffee in hand. Leo looked oddly at ease—like he'd woken up on the right side of the bed for once.

Guess I'll ruin that today. Father of the year, folks.

"What's going on, Dad?" Gina asked, scanning my face as she stepped in.

"Yeah, you okay?" Leo added, more neutral than usual. "You never do random brunch calls. Everything is schedules with you."

"I'm fine," I lied, motioning for them to follow me. "But I...have something I need to talk to you two about." My attempt at casualness fell flat, and I saw them both stiffen with apprehension. "Grab some brunch and we'll sit and talk."

We ended up in the dining area, pastries untouched. Gina eyed me warily. Leo stood with arms crossed, brow creased. I forced a steady breath. *Just do it.*

"You're making us nervous, Dad," Gina said. "Just spit it out."

"Like a Band-Aid," Leonardo added.

"If you're eating Band-Aids, you're doing something wrong."

"Dad!" Gina playfully barked and giggled. "Just tell us."

"There's no easy way to say this. Before I say it, I want you to know that none of this was planned—"

"You did something unplanned?" Leonardo cut in, one brow raised. "Since when?"

"Since last summer..." I raked my fingers through my

hair. "I met a woman then, and..." How do I say this while minimizing the mental scarring? "We had a fling."

They exchanged a glance. Gina said, "Well, that's great, but I'm not sure why you're telling us now."

"Unless it's gotten serious." Leonardo's eyes went flat as he folded his arms over his chest.

"It has," I said delicately.

Gina beamed and her voice shot high. "You're seeing someone?"

"I am—"

She smacked Leonardo's shoulder, but his icy gaze didn't change. She asked him, "What's the matter with you? We've been saying he needs to start dating."

He chucked his chin up at me. "There's more. There's always more, isn't there, Dad?"

"There is. The summer fling...she got pregnant."

"What?" Gina whispered in a gasp.

"I have twins," I said bluntly, voice pitched low. "Infant daughters, almost three months old."

For a moment, silence reigned. Gina's jaw dropped. Leo's eyes went wide before his expression hardened. "You got some random summer fling pregnant?"

"I met her on vacation, and things...you know how it goes. I didn't know until recently that she was pregnant."

Gina set her coffee down, shock etched on her face. "Dad, this is...insane. You never said anything—"

"Because I only found out about them a few months ago," I insisted quietly. "And I needed to be sure of everything before talking to you two."

Leonardo's eyes flashed. "So you're a father again, out of nowhere?"

My stomach knotted. "Yes. And there's more. The mother—her name is Ella."

"And?" he prompted.

I braced myself, focusing on him. "She's...your ex. The one who—who left because you body shamed her. Mariella Green."

His face went pale, then dark with fury. "The same Ella I told you about?"

"Yes."

Gina's hand flew to her mouth. "Oh my God."

A thick silence fell. Leonardo stared at me, betrayal stamped on every line of his face. It felt like an eternity before he spoke. His voice went raw. "You're telling me you fathered kids with my ex?"

"It wasn't intentional. We didn't know who the other one was before we hooked up. But I love her now. And the twins—they're everything." I forced a calm note. "I want you both to be part of their lives, if you can handle it."

Gina's gaze darted between us, horrified. "Leo..."

He let out a ragged exhale. "I can't...I can't believe this." Without warning, he spun on his stood up fast enough that his chair fell behind him. He stormed out, the apartment door slamming.

"Dad?" Gina whispered, eyes wide, as if uncertain whether to chase him.

I felt numb, grief rolling in my chest. "Go. I'll be okay."

She hesitated, then squeezed my hand. "I'm so sorry," she breathed. "He'll come around, I'm sure."

I nodded wearily, watching her hurry after him. The brunch I'd prepared sat untouched—pastries growing stale, fruit losing its shine. I sat there, hollow, mind replaying Leo's shock and anger. *At least it's out in the open.*

But the raw ache of his abandonment cut deeper than I'd expected.

Eventually, I cleaned up the table in a daze, tossing pastries in a container, dumping untouched coffee. My phone stayed silent, no calls from either of them. When I finally forced myself to text Gina, she replied that Leonardo had taken off, ignoring her too.

Great.

The emptiness of my apartment pressed on me, the hush more oppressive than comforting. I wanted to call Ella and let her know what happened, but the thought of hearing her voice also stung—she'd want to comfort me, or worse, apologize when she has nothing to apologize for.

I made it as far as the den before the weight of everything struck and forced me to sit on a leather armchair faced a modest fireplace, rarely used because I spent most of my life at the hospital. But now, I needed warmth, something to chase away the chill. I flipped the switch on the gas fireplace, watching the flames flicker to life.

Slumping into the armchair, I raked a hand over my face. *Leo walked out without a word.* Guilt, anger, sorrow—all warred inside me. *I had to do this. The twins are my second chance at fatherhood, and I won't hide them.*

My gaze fell on a glass-fronted cabinet where I kept a few bottles of good scotch for special occasions. This didn't feel like a celebration, but I needed something to blunt the edges of my emotions. With a sigh, I rose, grabbing a tumbler and pouring two fingers of aged scotch. The amber liquid glinted in the firelight.

Sinking back into the chair, I let out a bitter chuckle. "Cheers to honesty," I muttered, taking a sip that burned down my throat. *Fuck, that stings.* But maybe I deserved a little sting.

My phone vibrated once on the side table, and I tensed, hoping it was Leo or Gina. But the screen showed a hospital group text about scheduling changes. *Not now.* I silenced it, focusing on the quiet flicker of flames.

One crisis at a time, Ella had said before. She was right, but tonight I had no illusions about the magnitude of this crisis.

My stomach churned with the weight of it all—my career, my kids, my future with Ella. If I caved, tried to hide them again, I'd lose everything that mattered, and I wouldn't be the man they needed me to be.

Minutes blurred, and the scotch still burned. I forced myself not to pour a second round—wallowing in alcohol wouldn't fix anything. The fire crackled, warm against my skin, reminding me I still had a home, a place to gather the people I loved...if they'd come.

The memory of Gina's worried eyes spurred a flicker of hope—she'd calm Leonardo down eventually, or at least keep him from doing something drastic. And maybe in time, he'd realize I hadn't done this to hurt him.

Or maybe not. The ache in my chest deepened. *I can't control his reaction.*

I closed my eyes, leaning my head back against the chair. In the darkness behind my eyelids, I pictured Ella's face—her feisty grin, the way she calmed the twins, her unwavering stance by my side.

Eventually, I stood, placing the half-drained scotch on

222

the mantel. I turned off the fireplace, letting the room plunge into a dim hush. My phone still sat on the side table, dark. No new messages. Which was good and bad.

The second chance I'd been given with these twins felt bittersweet now, overshadowed by the fear that I'd lost my son. But honesty was the only way forward. I squared my shoulders, heading to my bedroom to gather myself, prepare for another day of navigating hospital demands, fatherhood, and a wounded adult son who might not forgive me.

My chest still ached, but beneath the sorrow was a steady determination. I'd stand by this family—my family—no matter what. Because I owed it to the twins, to Ella, and yes, even to Leonardo, to be the father I should've been all along.

And if that meant a lonely night with a bottle of scotch, so be it.

Chapter 29

Ella

Another Monday, another peaceful day at Suivante. No service meant no customers breathing down my neck, no frantic plating up. Just me, my team, and the chance to get our house in order.

But as I trudged into the restaurant this Monday, my phone buzzed with a short text from Dom.

Dom: *Hope you're good. Taking Gina for coffee, seeing if she's heard from Leonardo. Will text later.*

It wasn't exactly the comforting message I'd hoped for. All I knew about things was that Leo had stormed off the other day after finding out about the twins. Dom was upset, though he tried not to show it. But he'd been suddenly too busy to come by since then. I was pretty sure he was waiting until he calmed down.

A pang of worry pressed into my chest. *If only I could fix that for him.*

I shoved the phone into my back pocket, inhaling the familiar scents of Suivante. Tomato sauce, natural cleaner, a strong whiff of espresso from the bar up front. At Winner's suggestion, Carrie had started a new practice of letting staff come in at ten on Mondays, so the place was quiet except for a few early-arrival line cooks rummaging through crates of produce in the kitchen.

"Morning, Chef," Jean-Paul called, glancing up from a massive box of tomatoes. "We got a double shipment of these guys. Looks like a mix-up at the supplier."

"Great," I mumbled, tucking my hair under a bandana. "We'll figure it out."

He nodded, returning to his sorting. I forced a small smile, ignoring the worry swirling in my gut about Dom and his kids. The hush of the kitchen should've been soothing, but the moment I stepped into the walk-in to assess inventory, a bright, perky voice made my hackles rise.

"Ella!" It was Winner. She stood near the shelves of flour, arms folded, wearing an expression that screamed *I have gossip.*

What fresh hell is this? "Morning, Winner."

She grinned, all teeth. "Heard from Tom, who heard from Harris, that you were at his restaurant for date night last week. *Fancy*, chef."

"Why are you name-dropping people like I'm supposed to know them?" I stiffened, rummaging through a box of parmesan wheels.

She ignored the question. "He mentioned that your date probably qualifies for AARP."

The urge to defend Dom almost made me crack, but that was what she wanted. "Not sure why that's your business."

Winner shrugged, leaning against a metal rack. Her

eyebrows waggled, practically humming with glee. "Something about father-daughter confusion by the server?"

A spark of anger flared in my gut. *Are we really going to do this?* "Yeah, it's a shame they don't train their servers to be less nosy. No one likes when someone butts into their business," I said pointedly.

She chuckled, unbothered. "Okay, Miss Secretive. But I gotta say, hooking up with an old man—that's a power move, if you're looking to be a sugar baby."

My patience snapped as I dumped the parmesan onto a dolly. "Stop acting like you know me or my life and get back to work."

She smirked, raising her hands in mock surrender. "So touchy about your old doctor boyfriend. How does he pronounce that mouthful of a last name? Mortally?"

"Winner, get back to the line," Carrie's no-nonsense tone echoed in the chilly space as she approached us. "Ella, in my office. Now."

My stomach lurched. *Shit.* Winner shot me a smug grin and ducked out, leaving me alone with our boss, whose eyes glittered with something that wasn't friendly.

"Office," Carrie repeated, turning on her heel.

I followed, nerves twisting in my belly. I'd lied to Carrie about Dom for a while, sure, but I'd planned on telling her soon. Winner...she must have told her.

Inside Carrie's office, she closed the door behind me with a click, arms crossed over her chest. The room was small, cluttered with stacked papers and a half-finished cappuccino on the desk, but it felt cavernous under her glare.

"What's up?" I asked, trying for casual, though my voice wavered.

She pinned me with a hard stare. "Mortally? *Mortoli*, right?"

My heart thumped. "You're spying on us in the walk-in?"

"No, I happened by when Winner asked you about a date you never mentioned, so I listened in, and yeah, okay, that sounds like spying. Whatever. Point is, you don't talk to me anymore. Not like you used to. If you're dating Dominic Mortoli, the doctor who saved your life...that crosses all kinds of ethical boundaries for him, right?"

"Okay. And that concerns you because...?"

Her eyes blazed. "It concerns me because no doctor with his reputation would casually date a patient unless he had cause to do that. The only way he'd justify that is if," she swallowed, "if he was the father of your girls."

Fuck. I didn't want to lie to her anymore. It was past time for this to come out. "You're right. He is."

She glanced away, the hurt plain on her face. "You lied to me, Ella. Lied about the father of your kids. You let me think it was some random fling or nonexistent man, but all along it was Dom and you knew it was him, right?"

My cheeks burned hot. "Carrie, I—"

She shook her head, jaw tight. "Everyone's whispering that you have a sugar daddy. *God.* And I've been nothing but supportive, letting you have extra time off, covering your shifts. I thought we were friends."

"We are friends," I insisted, voice shaky. "I just...it was complicated, okay? I didn't want to make things messy with Seth and Dom both in the same hospital department. And I planned to tell you soon, once Dom and I were certain about us."

Her nostrils flared. "Messy? Ella, do you realize how bad this looks for *me*, vouching for you, letting you take extended leave, only to find out from the rumor mill that your baby daddy is some guy from my husband's department? You made me look like an idiot."

"I'm sorry," I whispered. "I didn't mean to blindside you."

She exhaled, raking a hand through her hair. "We used to share everything, or so I thought. Why did I have to hear about your relationship by spying on you in the walk-in?"

Shame crawled up my neck. "I didn't want to complicate things. You and Seth have enough drama with the hospital politics. Dom's going for the same promotion, and Seth hates him. If I told you about us, you'd tell Seth, and—"

"And you didn't think I'd have your back if I knew?"

"You're married to Seth, not me. Of course, I thought you'd tell me."

Her eyes went cold. "He's my husband, but you're my friend. Or at least, you were. What Seth does at work is Seth's business. But you are my business. I don't tell him about my business. You should have trusted me, Ella."

I clenched my fists, frustration mingling with remorse. "It wasn't about not trusting you. It was about not stirring the pot. Dom and I only reconnected after the twins came home. Before that, we were just...it was complicated."

She scowled, pacing behind her desk. "So you haven't been secretly seeing him all this time?"

"No. We only hooked up again months after I gave birth. We're serious now, but it wasn't always that way."

She paused, arms dropping to her sides. "So you're saying you didn't know he was the father until later, or you did, but you just didn't want to share that with me?"

"I knew. But I was scared, Carrie. He's older, he's my ex's father—"

Her lips parted in shock. *"Ex's father?"*

I froze, realizing I'd let that slip. Dom's confrontation with Leo was supposed to remain hush-hush, but now... fuck. "Yes," I mumbled. "Leo, Dom's son, was my last boyfriend before Dom. That's a whole other fiasco. That's why I've been terrified to tell *anyone.*"

Carrie stared, mind clearly blown. "I—holy shit, Ella." Then she sighed, pressing her fingers to her temples. "I had no idea."

"I didn't either, not when we got pregnant. Neither of us knew about our Leo connection when it happened. I only figured it out the morning after, and I bailed on him. We didn't see each other again until I was wheeled into the emergency room."

"Shit," she muttered.

I fought the urge to cry. "You see now why I kept quiet? It's not exactly easy to explain."

She sank into her desk chair, face etched with conflict. "It's huge, Ella. And I still feel...betrayed, I guess. I was your friend, your boss, and I had no clue. People asked me about you, and I had nothing to give them, other than you're a wonderful mom. When this comes out, no one will believe me when I say I didn't know, because they all know we're close. That will break a little of their trust in me. You get that, right? Restaurants run on gossip and trust—"

"Carrie," I said softly, stepping closer. "I'm sorry. Truly.

I never wanted to hurt or embarrass you. But this was something Dom and I had to figure out privately."

"And now you're officially together?"

"Yes. We decided we're done hiding. That's why we went to that restaurant."

She pursed her lips, nodding. "I appreciate you finally telling me, even if it's late. But Ella, this is going to be... complicated. With you two going public, Seth will find out, and he won't be as understanding."

A cold ball formed in my stomach. "Seth and Dom aren't friends anyway. What else can he do?"

"He can try to sabotage the promotion, for one. Or feed rumors to the board about him and a patient hooking up. And if he finds out you're the ex of Dom's son? Jesus, it's a scandal waiting to happen."

"We can't control that. Dom said we're better off being honest."

She rolled her eyes. "Dom might not care about the gossip, but Seth sure does. He's petty, Ella. He might use this as leverage to paint Dom as unethical or a conflict of interest."

A flush of anger lit my cheeks. "That's ridiculous."

"Agreed," Carrie muttered. "But that won't stop Seth if he sees an opportunity. He hates Dom with a passion." She paused, exhaling. "Look, I'm still mad at you for lying, but... I get it. It's a messy situation."

"Thank you. I was scared of losing your friendship. And my job. I know how weird this is."

She softened, leaning back in her chair. "I won't fire you over your personal life, Ella. That's not me. Just—no more secrets, okay? If I have to go to bat for you, I need the truth.

Even if it's ugly." She paused, thinking. "*Especially* when it's ugly."

"No more secrets," I promised. "From now on, you'll know everything."

Carrie sighed, tapping her desk thoughtfully. "We'll keep this quiet from the rest of the staff, though, okay? At least until you're ready to tell them. I can't handle Winner's smug face if she realizes how juicy this gossip is."

"Agreed. She's a pain."

"She is, but she's hell in the kitchen, and I've needed that, so I let some of her shit slide. And she's funny, in her own way." Rubbing her temples, Carrie shot me a pointed look. "Just be careful. If Seth finds out Dom impregnated the ex of his own son..."

My gut twisted. "I know. It could destroy Dom's career. But he's prepared to fight for it."

Carrie's lips thinned, and she gave a slow nod. "Well, for what it's worth, I hope you two make it through this in one piece. You've been through enough."

"Thank you," I repeated, voice trembling. "I'm really sorry I lied to you, Carrie."

She stood, circling around the desk to pull me into a quick, firm hug. "Dammit, Ella, don't make a habit of it."

"I won't," I murmured, hugging her back.

When we separated, she cleared her throat, squaring her shoulders with that brisk authority. "Now, get out of my office. We have a double tomato shipment to deal with."

A half-laugh, half-sob escaped me. "Right. On it, boss."

Leaving Carrie's office, I brushed away the tears that threatened to spill. My phone buzzed in my back pocket, likely another cryptic text from Dom about his kids, but I couldn't handle that right now.

One crisis at a time.

I spotted Winner lurking near the kitchen pass, shooting me a curious glance. I forced a bland smile. "You need something to do, or what?"

"Just checking if you need help, *chef.*"

I ignored her pointed tone, stepping briskly into the kitchen. Jean-Paul waved me over, asking about sauce variations. Fine—work, I could manage. My personal life was a circus, but at least I was in my element here.

As I directed the staff to store tomatoes, re-label containers, and handle the usual Monday chaos, my mind swirled with everything Carrie had said.

Seth might sabotage Dom.

The thought made me bristle. Amid the bustle, my phone buzzed again. Curiosity gnawed, but I held off checking, focusing on finishing the morning tasks. If it was Dom, I'd catch up once I wasn't in front of prying eyes. If it was Winner's next rumor, I'd fling my phone into the fryer. Or at her head.

By noon, the shipments were squared away, and I finally retreated to the alley behind the kitchen for a moment of quiet. Leaning against the brick wall, I pulled out my phone. Sure enough, Dom had texted.

Dom: *No word from Leonardo yet. Gina's worried. Let me know if you're okay.*

My heart squeezed. His kids are being a handful, but he's worried about me. That sweet man.

Me: *I'm fine. Had an awkward talk with Carrie. She knows everything now.*

Dom: *Everything? You okay?*

Me: *Shaky, but we'll manage. Seth might be an issue. But it's out in the open now.*

Dom: *I'm sorry. If I can help, let me know. I'm here.*

Me: *Thanks. One crisis at a time.*

With that, I pocketed my phone, letting out a breath. Carrie was mad, but we'd come to an understanding. Dom was dealing with his own fallout. The staff might gossip, but I had no regrets about claiming Dom openly—except for how it might impact him.

Still, as I headed back inside, I squared my shoulders. *Let them talk.* Carrie had forgiven me. The rest of the staff could whisper all they wanted about my "ancient boyfriend". The only thing that truly mattered was me, Dom, and our girls.

And if that meant handling a few meltdown Mondays, so be it.

Chapter 30

Dom

I'd always prided myself on composure—working in the ED had taught me how to thrive when chaos raged. I loved being the calm, level headed one in a storm. But as I left work this evening, I couldn't deny the tension in my shoulders, the solid set of my jaw. Chaos was taking its toll.

My son still wasn't responding to my messages, and his silence gnawed at me. I'd done what I had to do, telling him about the twins and my relationship with Ella. Honesty was the only way forward. Now, he was holed up in that questionable loft, ignoring every attempt I made.

Fine. If he wouldn't come to me, I'd go to him. I'd raised that boy. I wasn't about to let him spiral without at least making an effort.

Traffic moved sluggishly through the city, the orange glow of streetlights illuminating my thoughts. The way he'd stormed out upon learning the truth of the matter...it stung, but I'd known it could happen.

Better face it now than live a lie. Or worse—have him find out on his own.

I parked at the edge of the run-down lot adjacent to his building. Typical. He insisted on living in a half-gentrified neighborhood, citing "vibe" and "artistic atmosphere", as if that made up for a lack of safety. He had enough in his trust fund to live somewhere better. I was pretty sure he picked this neighborhood to spite me.

I buzzed the metal door at his loft, letting the speaker crackle. No response initially, but I wasn't leaving without seeing him. After the third try, a static-laced voice barked a terse acknowledgment. The door clicked open. *Not exactly a red-carpet invite, but I'll take it.*

Inside, I climbed the rickety stairs, ignoring the stench of stale cigarettes and questionable housekeeping. Tension tightened my gut with each step. His door was half-open, neon light spilling into the corridor. I stepped in, eyes adjusting to the dim interior.

The place was a wreck—beer cans, empty liquor bottles, and the stale odor of a wasted weekend. Some furniture was overturned, or that might have been how he kept things. Crumpled mail sat atop horizontal surfaces with no rhyme or reason. Tall canvases lined the walls. Four of them, each as tall as me, had been painted with various themes and designs. But he'd taken a can of red paint to them, and a slash of crimson ruined the artwork.

Goddamn it, Leonardo.

He sprawled on a battered couch, hair a mess, eyes red-rimmed. A bottle of cheap whiskey perched on the scarred coffee table, full-to-spilling ashtrays scattered around. The sight made my chest tighten, but I kept my expression calm.

This was the kind of chaos that made me lose my calm. "Leonardo."

"Dad," he said, voice slurred. "Didn't expect you to come."

I scanned the chaos, forcing a steady tone. "You buzzed me in, so here I am. You haven't answered my calls. I needed to check on you."

He let out a bitter laugh, fumbling with the whiskey bottle. "Because you're worried, right? About your new babies, your new...everything else. Thought you'd see if your old son's still alive?"

"You're my family," I said flatly. "That hasn't changed."

He swigged from the bottle, dribbling whiskey down his chin. "Oh, sure. Family. Since when, Dad? You're off playing hero doctor, hooking up with my ex, having babies, and only now you remember you have a son."

"Stop with the cheap shots. You know that's not how things are. You're not a child anymore. I'm here because I care."

He sneered, eyes darting away. "Care. Right. Where was that care when Mom was coughing up blood?"

The old accusation, but it landed every time he wielded it. "She hid it from me. By the time I knew, it was too late. You know this."

He lurched upright, unsteady. "You're a doctor. You should've *known*. Mom died because you were never around. You were always at the hospital. You saved strangers but not her. That tells me what you think of family."

"I can't rewrite the past. If I could, I'd have saved your mother a thousand times by now. But I won't apologize for trying to save lives. I have provided for you and Gina as best I could."

"Sure. Vacations, toys, all the latest shit. You gave us *everything*." He barked a mirthless laugh. "Everything except yourself. We needed you, and you vanished. Now you've got new kids—kids with *Mariella*."

"She's the mother of my twins, yes. But that doesn't change who you are to me."

"Why did you have to tell me, anyway?"

"How would you have reacted had you found out on your own?"

He snorted derisively but said nothing. He knew I was right.

I sighed. "And because honesty is the only way to keep a family alive. If you're mother had told me—"

"That's on you!" he barked, pointing at me. "Don't lecture me about honesty when it's your fault she was neglected to death!"

I closed my eyes for a moment. Not to ignore him, but to stop seeing what he had become. A bitter, angry man who hated everyone in the world, including himself.

"Leonardo, you are my son. You will always be my son. I love you—"

He flung the whiskey bottle across the couch, liquid sloshing. "Oh spare me. I told Mariella all about the asshole father who never gave a damn. Guess she's into older men with hero complexes. Good for you, Dad. Round two of fatherhood. But she'll realize I wasn't lying about you soon enough. And then where will you be? A sad old man, all alone."

Pain twined with irritation. "I'm not here to fight about the past, Leo. I'm here to see if you're all right."

He lunged forward, eyes bloodshot, breath reeking of stale liquor. "Go to hell. And take your new babies and my pretty ex with you."

My jaw clenched, but I refused to lose my temper. "I won't leave you in this pit. Drink some water, let's talk."

"I don't need your help or your guilt trips. Go play doting daddy with those brats. I'm done."

A flicker of cold rage pulsed through me at him calling the twins brats, but I reined it in. He was drunk, lashing out. "I won't beg, but I'm not walking away from you either."

"Get out," he repeated, voice cracking. "You should've saved Mom, but you didn't. So don't pretend you can save me."

I knew he was hurting. But that didn't stop the barb from landing. "I did what I could. I'm doing what I can now. Let me help you."

He muttered a curse, turning his back on me, shoulders sagging with either anger or despair. The neon sign cast harsh pink shadows, emphasizing the hollows under his eyes.

"Fine. I'll go. But I'm not abandoning you. If you need me, call. If you don't, I'll still check in."

He didn't answer, just huddled on the couch like a wounded animal. I stared a moment longer, lamenting the gulf between us, then turned on my heel and strode out.

No point in lingering. He's made his choice for tonight.

Outside, night draped the street in murky gloom. I slid into my car, shutting the door with a controlled sigh.

That stung more than I care to admit.

Leonardo's words echoed in my soul. But I refused to yield to self-pity. I'd spent my life forging a path in medicine, providing for my kids, saving countless lives. I gave people what they needed. That was a doctor's duty. If my son needed a scapegoat for his pain, I'd be that scapegoat.

Sometimes, fatherhood demanded we step into the line of fire, risking heartbreak and blame. But I'd do it again and again for my children—both the grown one raging in a dingy loft and the newborns who needed me. This was my second chance at a family, and I wouldn't let them down.

Honesty had come at a stiff price, but I'd pay it, no matter how high.

Chapter 31

Ella

It had been days since Dom's texts felt anything close to normal—days of me staring at my phone, rereading short, tense replies. I knew he'd told his kids about our twins, which was bound to stir the pot. But aside from a few terse mentions of stress, Dom gave away nothing. Each one-word text made me question whether he was slowly drifting away or simply overwhelmed.

By the third night of near-silence, I was reading too much into everything, swinging between anger and worry. I tried focusing on the twins or burying myself in work to ignore the building anxiety. Still, the ache in my chest lingered. I couldn't shake the sense something was wrong.

Then, near midnight, a sharp knock broke the hush of my apartment. I jolted off the couch, glancing at the two bassinets a few feet away. Still asleep.

My phone lay face-down on the coffee table—no new notifications. *Who would—?* My heart thudded with a wild mix of dread and hope. I peeped through the hole and found Dom standing there, coat rumpled, eyes dark with something that looked like desperation.

I threw open the door. "Dom?" For a moment, I wanted to tear into him for ghosting me. But the haunted expression on his face doused my anger.

He stepped inside, shutting the door softly behind him. "I'm sorry," he muttered, eyes flicking to the twins. "I tried to keep it together, but I—I need you."

My heart squeezed at the broken note in his voice. I set aside my scolding, nodding stiffly. "Well, I'm here. Tell me what's going on."

He didn't wait for more. His hand cupped my face, and then he kissed me—hard. A needy, desperate kiss that stole my breath. The day's resentment threatened to flare, but it fizzled under the raw intensity of his lips on mine, the way he clung like I was his anchor in a storm. I stumbled back against the wall, letting out a muffled gasp.

"Ella," he whispered, voice cracking on my name. He didn't offer explanations, just pressed his forehead to mine, breathing raggedly. "I can't talk about it tonight. I just..."

He didn't finish, but I knew. The meltdown with Leo, the tension at work, the swirl of guilt about everything. He was drowning, and apparently, he saw me as his lifeline. Part of me wanted to demand he open up, but another part was too relieved he'd come to me at all.

"Come on," I murmured, grabbing his hand and guiding him from the entryway. My living room lamp cast a faint glow on the couch, where I'd been napping. The twins dozed on, oblivious to our late-night reunion. "Are you sure you want this?"

His answer was immediate. He pulled me flush against him, burying his face in my neck. "I need you," he repeated, mouth brushing my skin in a way that turned my knees weak.

Heat flared through me, half from longing, half from unresolved tension. *Damn it, Ella—just let him in.* My hands slid under his coat, pushing it off. The moment his coat hit the floor, he was unbuttoning his shirt, lips slanting over mine with a desperation that bordered on frantic.

We stumbled toward the bedroom, mindful of the sleeping babies. My heart pounded with a wildfire of frustration and desire. I should demand answers, should push him to explain, but every kiss stoked the blaze, overshadowing logic. By the time we reached the foot of the bed, clothes were half-off, breath ragged. The look in his eyes was pure hunger.

"God, I missed you," he mumbled against my collarbone, hands sliding up my shirt to cup my breasts. My head fell back, a soft moan escaping me. Even as doubt gnawed at me, I couldn't resist him.

I tugged off my shirt, right before a bitter thought hit. *He can't just vanish then show up for sex.*

But the ache in his voice, the tension in his body, reminded me he was hurting too. He needed to find comfort in me, and I needed that from him, too.

Moments later, he scooped a hand up my back and guided me onto the bed. The faint city light shone on his handsome face, still lined by something unspoken, but now, too distracted by me to say it. I spread my legs for him as he kneeled there, no more words needed.

He moved over me, his lips, his teeth, his tongue, all of them dancing on my body. It was like he wanted to tour me first. His touch was powerful, possessive. The way he gripped my hip, how his fingers spread me open for him, he owned my body, every last cell, every gasping breath I took. When his mouth met my clit, I bit my fist, trying to keep quiet. Trying and failing.

I dug my other fingers into his scalp, desperate for something to cling to. But then he crawled up me, unable to hold back any longer. He couldn't pick a spot to stay at—his energy too frenetic. He climbed on top of me, and thrust in, fitting tightly. We groaned together—relief? Longing? Both?

It wasn't five strokes before he rolled us over, me on top. He held my hips tightly again, fingertips almost bruising. He needed a roughness to this, so I gave it to him. I bucked on his cock, finding the energy from somewhere deep inside. His eyes rolled back as he thrust up into me, growling, "Yes, baby, that's it. Fuck!"

The more he wanted it, the more I wanted to give it to him. Our limbs tangled, the quiet of the apartment broken by our ragged moans and the rustle of sheets. I felt him tremble, like he was pouring all his turmoil into each thrust, each kiss, needing a physical release from everything unsaid.

I tried not to think about how fleeting this might be— how he might slip away come morning. Instead, I gave in to the torrent of sensation, matching his fervor stroke for stroke. My nails raked his shoulders, the friction of our bodies pushing me into a dizzy spiral of pleasure. When the climax hit, I choked out his name, tears pricking my eyes.

He muffled a groan, clutching at me as he arched his back as he came. A moment later, we collapsed together, breath shuddering in the hush. I turned my face against his chest, inhaling his scent. The coil of unanswered questions tightened again, but at least for now, we were together.

Long minutes passed with no words. I lay there, mind racing even as my body hummed with aftershocks. I wondered about what prompted this visit, half tempted to pry. But the raw look in his eyes when I first opened the door flickered through my memory, so I didn't ask about that.

Eventually, I edged upright, brushing back the sweat-damp hair from his brow. "Dom? Are we...okay?"

"I don't know," he admitted, voice low. "Everything's a mess, but being with you—this helps."

"Then talk to me," I said, letting a slight whine creep in despite my intentions. "I'm not a mind reader."

He squeezed his eyes shut. "I will. Just...not tonight. Let me hold you."

Dammit. Part of me flared with anger, but the bigger part ached at his sincerity. *He's drowning.*

I exhaled, forcing myself to relent. "Okay," I said softly, biting my lip to keep from pushing further. "But soon, Dom. We can't keep...burying everything with sex. No matter how much we both need it."

"Soon," he echoed. The single word lacked conviction, but he pulled me closer, tucking my head under his chin.

I sighed, letting him envelop me. My eyes drifted to the half-open door, where the faint shape of the bassinets reminded me we weren't alone in this. *The twins deserve two parents who don't hide from each other.*

Dom's hand stroked my back methodically, almost like he was lulling himself to sleep with the motion. The tension in his body began to ease, if only slightly, and I felt him settling into the silence. I bit my tongue, swallowing the urge to press for details about Leo or the hospital or his entire life.

Now's not the time, I told myself. *He came to me. I won't drive him away by demanding too much.*

My thoughts didn't settle. Anxiety about tomorrow, about Winner at work, about everything, all jostled for space in my mind. Yet the warmth of his skin, the reassuring weight of his arm around my waist, anchored me enough to keep the fear at bay.

He must've sensed I was still on edge, because he slid his hand lower, fingers kneading gently at my hip, a new spark flaring in his gaze. "C'mere," he whispered, voice husky.

A wave of heat flushed through me. Normally, I might have teased him about not giving me time to recover, but the intensity in his eyes stopped me cold. He needed another escape, or maybe he just wanted to drown himself in sensation. Either way, I found I wanted it, too—anything to feel closer to him, even if it meant ignoring everything else.

I leaned in, kissing him with a slower, deeper urgency this time. We twisted until he licked my neck, claiming me. He groaned my name again, burying his face there, teeth grazing my throat in a way that made me gasp. We moved together in a slow dance, my worries receding under the molten swell of desire.

This time, things were different. Lingering and languorous. He rolled me onto my side, and spooned me, methodically working himself into me from behind, one incredibly slow thrust at a time. His arm belted my waist to keep me close to him, until eventually, his fingers found my clit once again.

The deeper he thrust, the more he played with me there, timing them together. Inches of him stroked me just right on the inside, and those fingertips played me like his favorite instrument. I shuddered against him, unable not to. He growled in my ear, "That's it, baby. You're going to come for me."

I almost gasped that I would, but my breath was stolen by my orgasm as I struggled to breathe. He poured himself into me a moment later as he bit my shoulder.

When it ended, a quieter sort of peace settled around us. He gathered me against his chest, both of us slick with sweat. I inhaled, letting the quiet hum of the city slip back into focus. Outside, traffic rumbled somewhere in the distance, but here, we might as well have been in a cocoon of secret wants and fears.

Dom stroked my hair, breath warm against my ear. He just murmured my name like a prayer, and the slow, steady sound of him drifting toward sleep. The last flicker of frustration in me wanted to shake him, force him to share what was on his mind. But I stayed put, tethered by the solace of his embrace.

Minutes blurred into an hour, or maybe two. I couldn't sleep, mind buzzing with half-formed thoughts of what tomorrow might bring. But as his fingers traced idle patterns on my arm, I felt my resistance crumble under the combined weight of exhaustion and tenderness.

In the end, I let my eyes close, a swirl of emotions locked behind my ribs. *He's complicated. I love him anyway.*

Chapter 32

Dom

You came here to talk.

Instead, the moment I'd seen her—disheveled hair, worry etched on her face—all my plans collapsed under the weight of longing. I'd pounced on her like an animal, desperate to banish my own misery.

She'd let me, too, matching my hunger. I should feel guilty, but the truth is, the guilt had been eating at me for so long, one more piece hardly registered. Besides, I was too busy savoring the feeling of her body pressed against mine, the quiet moans that told me she'd missed me as much as I'd missed her.

God, I'm selfish, I thought, brushing a strand of hair off her cheek. *It's time. I can't leave her in the dark anymore.*

She offered a small, uncertain smile. "You said you couldn't talk before." Her tone was gentle, but I felt the underlying demand. She deserved the truth.

"I was afraid if I opened my mouth, I'd break." My throat felt thick, recalling how I'd stormed into her place, physically starving for contact. "I'm sorry I jumped you like that. I planned on sitting you down, explaining everything about Leonardo..."

She squeezed my hand. "And yet here we are. Naked in my bed." Her attempt at levity didn't hide the concern in her eyes.

I managed a wry smile, pressing a kiss to her knuckles. "I know. I'm an idiot. You deserve better than me mauling you every time I feel cornered."

A gentle laugh escaped her, tension easing a bit. "Dom, I would've kicked you out if I didn't want you. But...I need to know what's going on." With that, she settled against the pillows, gaze fixed on me. *No more stalling*, her face seemed to say.

I raked a hand through my hair, silently cursing the tightness in my chest. "Right. Well, I guess I should start with Jodie, my wife. She died years ago—breast cancer."

Ella's breath caught. "You never told me that part before."

I nodded, jaw tense. "I hate thinking about it. But you deserve to know. She had it, and she hid it from me for a long time. I was so focused on work, surgeries, building my reputation...I barely noticed she was losing weight, or was exhausted all the time. She didn't come to me when she found the lump. She scheduled her own appointments, started chemo without a word."

"But that...how could she hide chemo? She'd need a port for chemo, right?"

I was relieved she knew some things about the process. Explaining things would slow the conversation. "Not everyone tolerates a port. Moreover, I probably wouldn't have seen it." I swallowed hard. "Jodie and I had been sleeping in separate bedrooms for a while, due to my schedule and being on-call. She was a light sleeper, so it made sense for us to have our own bedrooms...which meant our sex life was sporadic, at the best of times. It was winter when she was in treatment, and her long sleeves hid the bruising from the IVs."

"I'm so sorry."

"So am I."

She stroked my arm. "Go on. If you want to."

My hand curled into a fist on the sheet, old rage and guilt rising. "When it finally came out, she said she didn't want to bother me. That my work was obviously more important to me, as I'd been ignoring our family for my work. By the time I realized what was happening, her body was so ravaged by everything that there was nothing my colleagues could do."

Ella's eyes glistened with sympathy. "Dom...that's terrible."

"Leonardo was just a kid. He was old enough to see me as the big-shot doctor who didn't save his mom. And I guess part of him needed someone to blame—cancer doesn't have a face you can yell at. So, he picked my face. He kept saying, 'You're a doctor, how could you not know she was dying?' Honestly...I ask myself that every day."

My voice cracked on the last word, shame flickering through me. Ella sat up, sliding a soothing hand over my arm. I glanced away, focusing on the swirl of the bedsheets. "After that, everything unraveled," I murmured. "Leonardo grew up angry. Gina tried to keep the peace, but he just...he needed an enemy, and I was there."

Ella exhaled, eyes shadowed. "So this is why he hates

you so much. On top of the absentee father thing, he blames you for her, too."

I scoffed, running a hand over my stubbled chin. "Finding out I knocked up his ex-girlfriend didn't help. But that's a separate problem. His resentment runs deep, from way back."

She gave a tiny nod, fingers lacing with mine. "You said you told him about us at brunch. How bad was it?"

My jaw tensed. "He walked out. He's barely responding to Gina, and not at all to me. I've tried every-thing—calls, texts, showing up at his place. He's stonewalling me. Blames me for everything bad in his life, I suppose."

Ella closed her eyes momentarily. "God, I feel like this is my fault for hooking up with him in the first place."

I shook my head vehemently. "No. His meltdown isn't about you. If it wasn't you, he'd find another reason to lash out at me. This is old wounds."

"Still, it can't be helping that I'm, well...me."

A reluctant chuckle rumbled in my chest. "Probably not. But Leonardo has to get past it. I'm not leaving you or our girls just because he's throwing another tantrum."

Ella's expression softened at that, and a faint blush colored her cheeks. She fiddled with a loose thread on the pillow. "You sure? Because he might never accept this."

I grunted, shifting to face her fully. My fingers toyed with a strand of her hair, heart pounding with the gravity of what I was about to say. "I'm sure," I said simply, letting the truth resonate. "Look, I love him—he's my son. But I won't let him dictate my life. I spent too many years chasing after everything—my career, my kids' future—only to realize I had never actually lived."

She studied me, brow furrowed. "What do you mean about their future? How do you chase it? That's kind of their job. It's their lives."

A tight smile pulled at my lips. "I told them both that they had to get medical degrees if they wanted full access to their trust funds. I figured it was a safety net. The idea was, *get the degree, have it as backup, then do what you want.*"

Ella blinked in surprise. "And they didn't do it?"

I shrugged. "They did, actually. But afterward, Leonardo dove into art—and a shit-ton of questionable habits—and Gina took up interior design. Honestly, I supported them, even if it made me roll my eyes at times. The trust funds let them chase their passions, something I wished I'd been able to do when I was their age."

She considered that, biting her lip. "So money isn't an issue for them."

I huffed a silent laugh. "Not at all. Gina's thriving—she's got a big name among Manhattan's elite, magazines want her, TV channels want her. She's living the dream. Leonardo...less so, but still afloat, thanks to the trust. And I find myself wishing I could just set up a trust for you, so you don't have to stress about anything."

Her eyes widened, a spark of indignation flashing. "Dom, don't even think about it. I'm not some...charity case."

I raised both hands in surrender, a wry grin crossing my face. "I know. You're too damn proud. Just telling you where my head's at—sometimes I want to fix everything with money, but I realize I can't."

Ella relaxed, twining her fingers with mine again. "I appreciate the thought, though."

Silence settled, but a gentler one. The gloom in my chest eased, replaced by a quiet warmth that Ella radiated even in her frustrations. I inhaled, letting the faint baby-powder scent from the nursery drift through the door. *This is what I want—peace.*

She angled her head, giving me a searching look. "So... about Seth. Carrie's husband. He knows about you and me now, because Carrie knows."

"I knew it'd come out sooner or later. How did the conversation go?"

A rueful snort escaped her. "She was mad I'd lied to her. But mostly, I'm worried Seth will use your renewed fatherhood as an excuse to block your admin position."

An edge of determination flared in me. "Let him try. I'm not ashamed of having newborns, or of being in love with you. If the board wants to question my dedication, they can watch me outwork every damn candidate."

Ella's lips parted, her eyes widening. "You're in love with me?" she echoed softly, voice a bit wobbly.

My chest tightened, the words hanging in the space between us. *Did I just say it outright?* No going back now. "Yes," I said, forcing myself to meet her eyes. "I am."

For a heartbeat, she stared at me, cheeks flushing. Then she let out a shaky laugh, tears glistening. "Well, I'm in love with you, too, you confusing bastard."

I laughed, unable to hold it back. *She loves me back.* I couldn't stop the grin that spread across my face, or the way my heart drummed with renewed heat. "That's...good to hear."

She smirked, shifting closer, letting her thigh press against mine. "So, Dr. Mortoli," she teased in a low murmur, "you want to show me how much?"

After we made love, I leaned down, kissing Ella's temple, inhaling the faint trace of vanilla in her hair. She snuggled closer, half-drifting. My own pulse slowed, warmth pooling in my chest. *I will do everything in my power to keep this woman and our children safe from the storms.*

Moments later, her breathing evened out, and I felt sleep tugging at me. I let my mind wander to Jodie, to my son, to everything undone. But the heaviness felt more bearable now, cushioned by Ella's breathing's steady rise and fall. *I'm not alone anymore.*

And as I finally drifted off, I realized that, for all my regrets and mistakes, I could still forge a new beginning with Ella, building a family that wouldn't be shattered by silence or secrets. We'd face the ghosts, the resentments, the drama—all of it. Because I had her, and for once, I wouldn't let go.

I should have done this with Jodie. That was my biggest regret regarding my past. If I'd taken the time to truly be with her, to be by her side, she might still be alive. It ate at me every day.

And it should.

I'll never take Ella for granted the way I did Jodie. I've learned that lesson. Sure, I didn't text her more than a few words in the past couple of days, but that was a temporary thing, and not at all how I planned to operate going forward.

With Ella, I will be a real partner to her. A real father to the twins, too. This is my second chance, and I will not screw it up.

Chapter 33

Ella

I 'd once thought telling the truth would be the hardest part—letting people know about Dom and me, about how I used to date his son. In my imagination, the moment we "came out" would be the peak of our anxiety.

But real life had an annoying habit of proving me wrong. Turns out, the telling was easy compared to everyone else's reactions. I felt that weight of disapproval constantly now, as if the whole city had discovered our secret and decided to whisper about it behind our backs.

Even if that wasn't entirely accurate, it was how my nerves interpreted everything. It seemed like every time I glanced around, I caught someone exchanging glances or cutting off a sentence mid-conversation when I walked by. I felt like high school, except now, they had a reason to gossip about me. Maybe I was just paranoid. But I couldn't shake the queasy sense that everything I did was under scrutiny.

At the heart of it, though, my biggest worry was Leo. I had no direct knowledge of how he was handling any of this —Dom refused to spill details about their blowout, but the few things he let slip told me it wasn't good. Leo had stormed out, shut Dom down, and apparently avoided even his sister, Gina.

It was easy to figure out that my involvement made it worse. It'd be one thing if Dom had gone through the steps of accidentally starting a new family with someone else. I was sure that would upset Leo and Gina enough on its own. But adding me into the mix was pouring bleach into the wound. I could almost feel Leo's anger on the horizon, pressing in, even though we hadn't spoken in over a year.

If that wasn't enough to gnaw at my conscience, there was also Gina to consider. I'd never met her—only heard Dom talk about how brilliant she was, how proud he was of her interior design success. Part of me yearned to meet her, to prove I wasn't some manipulative vixen who hopped from son to father.

But another part was terrified she'd despise me on principle. She and Leo were siblings. *Of course, she'd take her brother's side, right?* In her place, I probably would. The thought haunted me, leaving a sour pit in my stomach.

I tried to bury the anxiety by focusing on work at Suivante, but that brought its own brand of misery. Carrie, once my steadfast boss and friend, had become increasingly chummy with Winner, the "temp" who acted more permanent by the day.

I'd look up from my station to see Carrie and Winner laughing over some new labeling system, or reorganizing a shelf side by side, or discussing menu ideas with enthusiastic nods. Meanwhile, I'd stand off to the side, feeling like an outsider in the very kitchen I used to run.

I couldn't shake the sense that Carrie looked at me

differently now—like she was reevaluating my reliability. Sure, she'd forgiven me for lying about Dom at first, but I sensed a hint of reservation in her eyes whenever we talked. Maybe it was my imagination, or maybe it was real. Either way, her newfound closeness with Winner stung.

"Carrie's only worried about Seth stirring up trouble," I told myself, stepping outside for a breather one afternoon. She'd mentioned how Dom's fatherhood might become a weapon in Seth's rivalry. The board might see Dom as too distracted.

At home, things weren't much better. The nanny, Amanda, was an angel with the babies—truly. She had them cooing and giggling like they never did for me. On one hand, I was grateful. On the other hand, it cut me deeply. Whenever I came in from work, she'd have them fed, changed, and happy, and I'd stand there with a forced smile, feeling a hollow pang in my chest.

Aren't I supposed to be the one who soothes them?

But they spent so many hours with her that they'd naturally bonded. It was petty of me to be upset about that. I should have been grateful they were happy and flourishing under her care. But it still hurt.

I'd tried to reassure myself that I was doing the best I could—working to support the twins, and caring for them in the off-hours. But the guilt never left. I'd be at Suivante, mindlessly chopping vegetables, and my mind would drift to the twins.

They must be giggling with Amanda right now. Do they think she's their Mom?

It was a lose-lose scenario. Stay home full-time, and I'd lose my career, not to mention the financial independence I clung to. I saw the parallels to Dom's old struggle, the one that ended with Jodie's illness going unnoticed. Dom had thrown himself into work, and tragedy struck. I didn't want that for our daughters. Yet, ironically, it felt like I was following the same path.

It seemed like all I ever did these days was worry. The good news was I was a hell of a multi-tasker. Stirring a demiglace? I could worry while I stirred. Changing a diaper? Worrying didn't interfere with that, either. Texting Dom? Worrying was a part of every letter, every emoji. As I rocked Marissa in the nursery, my heart aching at how seldom I got to do this, I couldn't shake the question, *am I making Dom's life harder?*

He was up to his neck in hospital drama, adult children issues, a brand-new fatherhood he never expected, and here I was, piling on my insecurities and the weight of my career. Staring at the pastel walls, I murmured to Marissa, "He must be exhausted."

Her cooing response was an agreement. I was sure of that.

Leo's meltdown or not, Dom was dealing with a lot. And I worried that if I wasn't strong enough—if I kept pulling him in different directions—maybe I'd become another Jodie in his eyes. Someone he didn't have time to see crumbling.

That thought cut so deeply I almost dropped Marissa. "Shh," I whispered, pressing a shaky kiss to her soft head. "Mommy's okay." A lie if ever I told one.

Days turned into a blur of half-smiles at work and forced cheer at home. Dom would text me short updates—fewer than before, but occasionally sweet.

Missing you. Everything's chaos. I'll call tonight.

And sometimes he didn't call, leaving me feeling like a rug had been yanked from under my feet. When we did manage a phone conversation, it was quick, overshadowed by beeping hospital machines or me checking on the twins in the background. We rarely addressed the big stuff. There was no time.

One afternoon, Carrie pulled me aside in the kitchen, Winner trailing behind her. "Hey, Ella," she said, trying for a casual tone that didn't fool me. "I understand things are tense for Dom at the hospital."

My stomach sank. "Right," I managed, wiping sweat from my brow with the back of my forearm. "But he's handling it."

Carrie nodded, expression concerned. "He'll try, but you know Seth. He's ruthless."

A flush of anger prickled my skin, but behind it was guilt. "I appreciate the warning. But I'm sure Dom can handle Seth."

Winner, standing a step back, gave me a tight smile. "Things are intense, huh?"

She was the last person on earth I wanted to hear from on the matter. I faked a shrug. "Yeah, well, that's their world, not mine." But the anxiety clung like a burr.

What if Dom is losing ground at the hospital because of me?

After Carrie and Winner moved on, I stood there, an onion half-chopped, tears stinging my eyes not from the onion but from the hopelessness growing in my chest. If Dom's career suffered because we had twins and complicated baggage, that was beyond my control.

Which was not a comforting thought. It was one more thing I couldn't fix.

By the time I got home that night, I felt drained, physically and emotionally. Amanda was singing a lullaby to Summer, who cooed in delight, and I forced a smile. I tried not to begrudge how well the nanny did her job. "Thanks."

"Of course," Amanda said, noticing my strained tone. "You okay?"

"I'm fine," I lied, swallowing the dryness in my throat. "Just a rough day."

When she left, I slumped onto the couch, rubbing my temples. Dom's last text had been two words. *Sleep well.*

How the hell did he expect me to do that?

No mention of visiting, no phone call. The lonely hush of the apartment pressed in. If I left my job, would that solve anything? Then I'd rely on Dom's money—something that made me cringe. If I stayed, the twins grew closer to Amanda by the day. If Dom's job fell apart, that was on me, right?

Every angle of this, I was at fault. And I didn't know how to fix any of it.

Eventually, I padded to the nursery, watching the twins drift in and out of sleep. My heart ached, swirling with guilt and longing. Dom's old struggle, repeated. Leo never forgave him for Jodie's death. Now, *I* was the one with precious little time with my children.

I won't let that happen to us, I thought fiercely, brushing a gentle hand over Marissa's soft hair. *But how do I avoid it, exactly?*

I imagined Dom wrestling himself free from the hospital to rush to my side, only to find me a stressed-out wreck. Or me giving up my career, becoming a resentful shell of myself who might blame him for that choice.

Lose-lose. The realization broke something inside me, tears I'd been holding back all day slipping down my cheeks.

I crouched by the crib, head leaning on the railing, letting quiet sobs rack me. *I'm sorry,* I told them silently. *Mommy doesn't know how to fix this.*

If Dom had soared too high with his ambition, I was being ground between the pillars of motherly duty and my job's demands. Neither path let me breathe.

After a few minutes, I forced myself upright, wiping my face with the edge of my shirt. The twins needed a mom, not a crying mess. "It's okay," I whispered to them, though I didn't believe it. "We'll figure this out."

But as I slipped into bed later, the apartment dark, my phone silent, all I could think was how I might be burdening Dom more than benefitting him. He had enough on his plate. Would he have been better off if I'd never walked into his life?

That thought hurt worse than I expected. *But maybe... I'm making everything worse.*

I stared at the ceiling, listening to the soft breathing of two little lives in the other room on the monitor. I loved them more than I ever thought possible. I loved Dom, too, in a way that scared me with its intensity. But love didn't erase reality—it didn't stop the world from being cruel. My phone stayed dark, the weight in my chest heavier than ever.

So I closed my eyes, tears slipping out anyway, and tried to imagine a future where we all found a balance. Maybe I'll just hang on until Dom finds a solution. Maybe if we hold each other tight enough, the storm will pass.

But storms don't pass just because we want them to. Sometimes, they break us.

For now, I had no plan. No bright fix. Just raw worry that everything was unraveling at once. My job, my babies, Dom's career, and Dom's relationship with his other kids felt precarious. And I was at the center of that storm, tugging him in different directions.

I didn't know if I could keep it up. But I also couldn't bring myself to let go. And I had more questions than answers.

How do I protect the man I love from the chaos I've brought into his life, when I can barely protect myself?

Chapter 34

Dom

I 'd pulled plenty of all-nighters in my career, but today, I was running on less than three hours of decent sleep. A messy combination of newborn duties and an early surgical consult had me chugging coffee just to keep my eyes open.

Typical Monday, I told myself as I headed through the hospital corridors.

At least it was my kind of mess. Better to be exhausted from caring for my daughters and saving lives than...well, any other reason. Still, my shoulders felt stiff from tension. Ella was worried about her job, the girls, and me and Leo. I had my worries, too. Neither of us was good at opening up about what was on our minds. But we'd figure it out.

As I paused near the nurses' station to grab a file, one of the RNs, Marta, hustled over, breathless. "Dr. Mortoli, quick!"

My pulse spiked. "What is it?"

She looked alarmed, gesturing down the hall. "It's Dr.

Boddington. He's hurt—again. He's in the breakroom, bleeding!"

A surge of adrenaline hit me. "Damn it," I muttered, already picturing the old codger. He was on blood thinners for a heart condition, and the last time he'd tried to pop the tab on a soda, he'd sliced his fingers enough to leave half the breakroom spattered red. "I'm coming."

I sprinted behind her, ignoring the way my heart thumped. *Seriously, that man needs a caretaker just to handle soda cans.* It was early—no reason for him to be slicing anything else. Maybe he'd discovered a new method of injuring himself.

The breakroom door loomed, and I shoved it open, calling, "Dr. Boddington, where—"

A roar of voices erupted, nearly stopping me in my tracks. "Surprise!"

Pink confetti rained down, and I almost tripped on the threshold. The entire room was decked in pastel balloons, streamers, and an obnoxious banner that read, "Congratulations on the twins, Dr. Mortoli!"

Seth Bowan stood at the center of it all, beaming like the cat that ate the canary.

I blinked, mind reeling. *What the fuck is this?*

My adrenaline soared in the wrong direction, half from confusion, half from noticing the array of hospital administrators crammed in the corners, sipping punch and smiling politely.

Ah. That's why.

Seth clapped his hands loudly, stepping forward. "Dr. Mortoli! So glad you could join us. Heard about your babies —figured we'd celebrate properly."

My eyes flicked to the cluster of suits near the donut table. They were sipping coffee, observing the goings-on. Noting every glance, every ounce of judgment in their eyes.

My pulse pounded. "Uh," I said, forcing my best professional grin, "this is...wow. Didn't see this coming."

Seth grinned with pure malice in his eyes. "I know."

Dr. Boddington himself wasn't bleeding at all—he stood off to the side, guffawing with a soda in hand. *Great, so they used him as bait.*

Seth clapped a friendly hand on my shoulder, turning me toward the administrators. "We just wanted to show our support, you know? It's not every day a surgeon juggles newborns and work—especially *two* of them."

There is a kind of strain that comes with not sleeping. An all-over muscular tension that leaves you aching by the end of the day. Then there's the kind of strain that your body undergoes when you're doing everything in your power not to punch someone's lights out.

Today, I felt both.

I felt the muscles in my jaw tighten, but I maintained the outward veneer of composure. "Right," I said, scanning the bright pink and blue decor. Some folks had gathered baby gifts, presumably. A stuffed giraffe perched on a far table laden with pastel presents. The thing was massive, and it stared me down as much as Seth did. "Thanks, Dr. Bowan," I managed. "This is thoughtful."

His lips twitched in a smug smile. "Of course. Anything for a colleague. After all, we know you'll be needing extra time off soon, with...special needs, right? Better to celebrate while you still can."

My heartbeat hammered, rage flaring at his insinuation.

"My daughters are perfectly healthy," I said evenly, forcing a small laugh. "No special needs, no complications."

Seth's eyes flicked to the administrators. "Oh? But newborn premature twins require a lot of care. We understand if you're, ah, stepping back from certain responsibilities."

I forced a chuckle that tasted like bile. "Oh, I'm not stepping back at all," I said lightly. "I've got top-notch help at home, and everything's under control."

Roxanne Weiss cleared her throat. "Dom, we're delighted about your new additions, of course. But Seth mentioned you might need extended paternity leave. There's no harm in ensuring you're not overextending yourself."

A bald-faced lie and we all knew it.

I plastered on a polite smile, ignoring the knot of anger in my gut. *Well played, Seth.*

The man was a snake, orchestrating a "baby shower" to publicly corner me. "I appreciate the concern," I said smoothly. "But I assure you, I'm handling everything just fine. The twins have a nanny, and their mother is a fantastic partner. I am just as focused on the hospital as I ever was."

Seth's grip on my shoulder tightened in a show of camaraderie that felt more like a threat. "Yes, well, we all know you have your hands full— *two* premature newborns, a busy schedule...just wanted you to know we respect your decision when you decide it's too much."

Not if I decide it's too much. *When.*

My mind flashed to what Seth would look like with a black eye. Instead, I turned, letting out a measured chuckle for the audience. "And I respect everyone's kindness," I replied, picking up one of the pastel cupcakes from a nearby tray. "This is quite the surprise, and I'm happy to see such support from the hospital administration."

Behind Seth's veneer, I spotted the flicker of frustration. *He wanted me to blow up, or at least confirm I was stepping aside.*

Not happening. I took a deliberate bite of the cupcake, ignoring the swirl of tension in the room, and forced a pleasant hum. "That's delicious," I lied. It tasted like chalky sugar. "Seth, you really went all out."

He gave me a shark-like grin. "Anything for a colleague," he repeated, gazing toward Roxanne and the other suits. "After all, we're a team here, even if some of us have more leadership capacity than others."

You want to play that game? Let's play.

I turned to Roxanne. "Actually, I've found fatherhood has sharpened my focus. My time is precious, so I'm more efficient when I'm here these days. When I was a young father, I had more energy, but less direction. Now, my perspective has shifted. I understand better how to utilize my time here and at home. My increase in patient care is evident in my reports." With a smile, I face off with Seth. "It's a pity you'll never get to experience this kind of clarity, Dr. Bowan. Late-in-life fatherhood is better than Adderall for keeping your head straight."

Because I refused to cave, Seth's smile turned angry, his words clipped. "Well, then. Congratulations."

Roxanne nodded, looking somewhat relieved that I wasn't folding. Another administrator, Dr. Patel, raised a cup of punch. "To Dr. Mortoli, may your daughters thrive, and your career continue to flourish."

The others toasted me, and I forced a grin, lifting my half-eaten cupcake in solidarity. The entire scene felt surreal—a baby shower turned pithy battleground. My mind flitted to Ella, the twins, and how they'd hate being used this way if they saw it.

They deserve better than Seth's petty sabotage.

His expression tightened, but he kept up the charade. "Yes, cheers to Dom. And, of course, if you find the demands of fatherhood too taxing, we'll understand if you bow out gracefully."

A few uncertain laughs. I locked eyes with him, forcing my voice to remain friendly. "Thank you, but I have no intention of bowing out. My family is the reason I work so hard. They're not a hindrance, don't worry."

Roxanne clapped her hands, stepping forward. "Yes, well, we should let Dr. Mortoli get back to his duties," she said, apparently sensing the tension. "This was a lovely gesture, Dr. Bowan, but we can't keep everyone from their rounds."

Seth gave a nod, feigning disappointment. "Of course, we wouldn't want to hinder patient care." His eyes flicked to me, brimming with smug satisfaction. "Dom, truly, congrats on the newborns. We're all behind you."

Of course, he's behind me. Stabbing someone in the back is hard if you're not behind them.

"Thanks, Seth," I said flatly, stepping away from him. My fists clenched behind my back, nails digging into my palms. I scanned the parting crowd, giving quick nods and thanks, ignoring the swirl of whispers I could practically feel behind me.

I had kept my cool, but the damage was done.

As soon as it was polite to do so, I slipped out, heading down the hall at a brisk pace. The breakroom door closed behind me, the clamor of forced celebration fading. I turned a corner, leaning against the cool tile wall to catch my breath. My heart hammered, blood roaring in my ears.

I let out a slow exhale, fighting the urge to punch something. Administrators were a fickle bunch, always reading into every detail. Seeing me blindsided by a baby shower and hearing Seth's insinuations about fatherhood might be enough to plant seeds of doubt.

Exactly what he intended.

A quiet cough from behind startled me. I glanced back to see Roxanne approaching, expression soft. "Dom, I just wanted you to know, we're not idiots. We know what he was doing with the party, and we're not jumping to conclusions about your ability to handle administration."

My spine stiffened, forcing a smile. "I appreciate that."

She hesitated, glancing around. "I know Seth can be intense. He pitched this idea as a morale booster, but I worried it'd devolve into that side show in there." She folded her arms and her face tightened. "I'm not supposed to say anything, but you still have my vote, as things stand currently."

I wasn't sure it was safe to relax yet. "Oh?"

"Even if I didn't prefer you to him before this debacle, I do not want this kind of backbiting, high school bullshit within the administration. We have too much to do for the hospital without someone who plays these sorts of games, and I'm going to say as much as soon as we reconvene."

Relief flickered, though I remained cautious. "Thank

you. I won't let fatherhood compromise my commitment to this hospital."

She offered a small nod, stepping back. "Then show us that. Keep doing your work, keep the department running smoothly. I'm counting on you to be successful, Dom. I do not want that asshole for my colleague."

With that, she left, leaving me with a kernel of hope. *Maybe not all is lost.* But I still felt tainted by Seth's stunt, uneasy at how easy it had been for him to spin my new fatherhood as a liability.

My thoughts darted to Ella, how she'd react if she knew about this fiasco. Probably outraged, maybe guilty, definitely worried. She had enough on her plate—no need to pile more stress. Yet the thought of keeping her in the dark weighed on me. We'd agreed to share our burdens, but I wasn't sure if telling her about Seth's baby shower ambush would just feed her insecurities.

I sighed, pushing off the wall. *Later.* Right now, I had to finish my rounds, then dive into the next meeting. My phone buzzed in my pocket—a text from Gina. *Hey Dad, you busy?*

My heart twisted. Gina reaching out was a small silver lining, but I'd take it. I'd text her back soon, maybe tell her how a breakroom party blindsided her dear father.

At least I'd held my composure. Even if Seth had dealt me a blow, I'd parried. Forced smiles, polite claps, subtle barbs—that was how we survived in this environment. But as I ducked into the next exam room, I couldn't shake the pang of worry that the damage to my admin bid might be deeper than Roxanne let on.

Seth's sly. He didn't go to all this trouble if he didn't expect results.

Frustration flared, but I let it go. I couldn't fix the optics right now. My mind drifted to Ella, longing to hold her again—this time not in a haze of desperation, but with real conversation about everything. We'd left so much unspoken.

She's part of me now, along with the twins. I won't let Seth or anyone twist that into a weakness.

Swallowing my anger, I forced myself to focus on the patient chart in my hand. Saving lives always came first, then I'd worry about saving my promotion. That was the plan, and if Seth wanted to push, I'd push back. Because no fake baby shower or sly insinuations would keep me from climbing to the top. Not when Ella and our daughters were counting on me.

At the end of the day, fatherhood truly wasn't a liability —it was my driving force. And no matter how many balloons and confetti Seth threw at me, I wasn't backing down.

Chapter 35

Ella

It started with a text that made my stomach churn.

Dom: *Hey, I have to tell you about something Seth just pulled. Surprise baby shower at work—basically tried to humiliate me in front of the hospital board. I'm fine, but it was a fiasco.*

Reading those words, a bitter taste filled my mouth. Even without the details, I got the gist. Seth had gone out of his way to sabotage Dom's reputation under the guise of "celebrating" the twins. That absolute asshole.

So, this was to be the new normal. Dom part of hospital politics, Leo despising him, everything falling on him all at once...because of me.

Tension spiked as I typed my reply.

Me: *Are you okay? That's insane.*

Dom: *I'm fine. Just pissed off. We'll talk soon.*

We'll talk soon. The same line I'd heard for weeks. The phone trembled in my hand, my heartbeat pounding a frantic rhythm. I glanced at the twins, both fast asleep in their bassinets.

They're so innocent. They don't know their father's fighting a war at work because of me.

I rose from my couch, setting my phone aside, mind whirling. He wanted that admin position so badly. He wanted it to be able to do more good in the world. And now Seth was using fatherhood to drag him down. Guilt gnawed at my chest.

Is it worth it for him to have me in his life if he's going to lose everything that he cares about?

A cold pit formed in my stomach. By Dom's own admission, his son was shutting him out entirely, furious at the entire situation, me included. The last thing Dom needed was to lose the only sliver of hope he had left with his kids. If I stayed, that's exactly what would happen.

My eyes drifted to the twins again, heartbreak blooming in my chest. I loved them, and I loved Dom. I had to fight for us, didn't I? But I remembered the meltdown Dom described, the pain in his voice when he first mentioned the fallout with Leo. If I truly loved him, wouldn't I free him from the load? Fear wrapped around me like a cold chain, dragging me down beneath the waves of my self-loathing.

If we keep going, and in a year or two when he realizes it's too much, he'll bail.

Then, the twins and I would be devastated, left on our own again. The heartbreak would eat us alive.

Better a clean break now, before we all get further entangled.

Tears pricked at my eyes, but I pushed them back, refusing to drown in self-pity. *I'm a chef, I'm a mother, I can handle this on my own.* My girls won't remember him. They're too young for that. We'd managed before he came along, albeit barely. But I had a better handle on things now. I took a breath, steeling myself, and grabbed my laptop off the side table.

Time to do something irreversible.

I opened my email, checking on my contacts in Chicago. Dom had mentioned his company's headquarters were there, but ironically, he was never around, which meant he'd never find us there, hiding in plain sight. Plus, I had a sister in the suburbs I hadn't spoken to in years, but maybe we could mend things.

I'd already looked for apartments before and saved all the ones I liked. It was a big city but cheaper than Manhattan if you knew where to look.

My fingers hovered over the keyboard, my heart pounding. *Am I really doing this?*

The twins let out a soft coo in their sleep, reminding me I had to keep them safe. I had to do the same for Dom. He was in danger of losing his job, his relationship with Leo was precarious, and I was the catalyst. A fresh wave of determination flared.

Yes, I'm doing this.

I typed a quick message to a couple of restaurants. I described my experience, gave a brief rundown of my culinary style, omitted the personal drama, and hit send, each email feeling like a step toward a cliff's edge.

Just as I started to open a tab to see if any of my preferred apartments were open, an unexpected ping popped into my inbox. One of the places, a mid-range yet highly rated spot called The Steel Kitchen, had replied almost instantly.

The manager wrote: *You've got perfect timing. Our head*

chef just quit on us midweek after a tantrum from a rude customer. If you can start ASAP, we'd love to chat. The sooner the better.

A hollow laugh escaped me. *Who quits over a bratty customer?* Then again, kitchen meltdowns were more common than most folks realized. My heart raced as I typed back, expressing my eagerness to discuss details. *If they're desperate, they'll hire me fast.* That suited my plan. Less time for second-guessing.

I arranged a call, stepping away from the sleeping babies to speak quietly in the kitchen. The manager's voice was frenetic but friendly, telling me all about the fiasco and how they needed someone unafraid of high-pressure nonsense. I half-smiled. "I've worked in Manhattan my whole career. High-pressure nonsense is a daily occurrence."

I can handle anything, as long as I keep Dom from losing everything.

We agreed to terms quickly, almost too easily. The job came with a significant rate increase and a two-bedroom, two-bathroom apartment above the restaurant that cost a dollar per month, something about how city regulations wouldn't allow them to let me live there for free. They cautioned the apartment was small, but it turned out to be five hundred square feet bigger than my current place. They wanted me there in a week, no time wasted. I said yes, ignoring the knots in my stomach.

With a new job and apartment settled, I stared at my phone, heart hammering. That had been almost too easy, and I didn't expect anything else to go as smoothly.

Carrie was my next hurdle. She might be mad or not

care, considering her new favorite chef wasn't leaving, but I still owed her a conversation about my resignation.

That's if she doesn't fire me first.

I sent a quick text requesting a meeting. She immediately replied, telling me to come by at the end of service. Perfect. I glanced at the twins again, tears threatening. I vowed to figure everything out as I stroked their wispy hair.

Work that evening felt surreal, as if I was moving underwater. Each chop of the knife and every swirl of sauce hammered home that this was the last time I'd do this as assistant head chef at Suivante. Winner hovered around, offering suggestions that made me want to fling a spatula at her. I bit my tongue, focusing on the finality of what came next.

The truth was, her sniping would have zero impact on my future now. Once that realization struck, I just smiled and shrugged at her, ignoring her commentary. She tried a little harder to get a rise out of me by "accidentally" swapping grated ginger for grated garlic in my mise, but I caught it in time. "Does your sense of smell work, Winner?"

"Yeah, it was just an accident. Kitchen shit, you know?" She tried to play it off.

"Maybe you should get your eyes checked," I said with as much concern as I could muster. "They're pretty different looking. The fibers in the ginger—"

"I said it was an accident."

"Right, well, I'm telling you how to avoid it in the future. You never know when the next accident could happen to you, if you just keep making them instead of working to avoid them." I smiled as she stared daggers into me. "No sense in letting all my expertise go to waste just to save your ego, you know."

Her eyes lidded into slits, anger pulsing off of her. "I know what grated ginger and garlic look like."

"Which means that accident wasn't an accident. Better luck next time, Loser."

She stomped off for the freezer without another word. Now that I wasn't worried about her bullshit or playing politics, it was easier to handle her. Too bad I hadn't gotten to that point before now.

After service, I knocked on Carrie's office door. She stood behind her desk, flipping through receipts with a frown. "Ella," she said, not looking up. "Come in, shut the door."

I obeyed, heart thudding. For a moment, she kept her eyes on the papers, then set them aside with a sigh, turning to me. "So what's going on? Did Winner do something else to upset you? I keep telling you, she's someone you should mentor, not someone to worry about."

I swallowed, stepping forward. "I'm leaving. I've accepted another position in Chicago."

She blinked, stunned. Then, a harsh laugh escaped her. "You're kidding, right? You've got newborns. You're just settling back in here—"

"Exactly," I cut in, voice tight. "And it's not working. I need a fresh start."

Carrie's gaze sharpened. "Is this because of Dom? Because Seth might make waves? Come on, we can handle it—"

I shook my head firmly. "It's more than that. Look at me, Carrie. I'm juggling too much, and my kids deserve better.

This job is not my safe haven anymore. You and Winner...
you have a good thing going. I'm out."

"I can't believe you're bailing on me. After all the
accommodations, after I covered for you, let you take extra
leave—"

A stab of guilt pierced me, but I swallowed it. "I appreciate everything, truly. You bent over backward for me, and
I'll never forget that. But it's time I move on. It's what I need
to do for my family."

Carrie's eyes narrowed, bitterness lacing her tone. "You
realize you'll be walking into a bigger mess, right? New city,
new environment, no stable connections. And Dom's here—
aren't you two a thing?"

A pang shot through my chest. "That's...complicated," I
managed, looking away. "He'll be fine in Manhattan."

She let out an exasperated huff. "Whatever. Do what
you want. Seth will probably be thrilled to hear you're
breaking up with Dom. One more thing to put him off his
game. Doesn't that bug you?"

I stiffened. "I'm doing it for me and my girls. I can't stay
where everything is...I can't stay." No need to explain
myself to anyone.

"Fine. When do you leave?"

"End of the week," I said, forcing my chin up. "I'd appreciate your keeping it discreet until I finalize everything."

She rolled her eyes. "Sure. Whatever. Good luck in
Chicago, Ella." The sarcasm practically dripped.

My shoulders sagged, but I mustered a polite nod.
"Thanks. I'm sorry, Carrie. Really. I know I'm leaving you
in a tough spot, but Winner can handle it."

"She's good, yeah. But it doesn't mean I trust her fully yet. And you're wrong if you think you'll find some magical fix in Chicago. Problems follow you like chewing gum on your shoe. Running away from home never solved anything."

The remark stung. "I hope you find happiness, Carrie. I truly do."

She looked away, tension in her jaw. "Bye," she muttered, clearly done with this conversation.

My head was a mess when I left her office. *That's that, then.* No going back now. *I severed the last tie.*

Outside, the air hit me with a chill that cut through my jacket. I breathed in, letting the adrenaline drain. A sense of finality loomed.

I'm leaving this place.

My mind flicked to Dom, how he'd react. Probably furious, or maybe sad, or worse...relieved. *He'll hate me short-term, but eventually he'll realize it's best for him.*

I pictured our last conversation, how his eyes lit up when we confessed we loved each other. Tears pricked my eyes again, but I blinked them away. My current emotions didn't matter. If Dom left me and the girls in a year's time, I'd be devastated. The way I felt now was nothing in comparison.

When I got home, the twins were asleep, and Amanda had tidied up their bottles. She deserved a heads-up, in so far as I could manage one. I thanked her in a shaky voice, telling her there might be changes soon. She gave me a curious look but didn't pry.

Once she left, I stood in the quiet living room, phone in

hand, resisting the urge to call Dom. *No. If I hear his voice, I'll lose my resolve.*

So I dropped onto the couch, stared at the faint glimmers of city light through the window, and let tears slide freely. *I can do this.*

I had to. Better a heartbreak now than a total catastrophe later. My daughters deserved a stable mom, not one tugged back and forth by complicated bullshit. Dom deserved a fair shot at his promotion, at repairing things with Leo, without the scandal of fathering twins with his son's ex.

As I finally crawled into bed, I clutched my pillow, feeling the emptiness of the sheets where Dom might have been. With time, he'd understand. *He might even thank me.*

Morning would bring new logistics—packing, final arrangements with the Chicago restaurant, saying goodbye to the city I'd known forever. It felt like too much to handle, but I knew better. People moved all the time, even with kids. This was the right call. I was sure of it. I just had to convince my shattering heart.

Chapter 36

Dom

I'd known something was wrong the moment Ella's texts trailed off into silence. By the time I finished my last surgical consult, I couldn't stand it any longer. I slipped out of the hospital, telling myself I'd surprise her at her apartment, maybe find her on the couch with the twins, too busy or too stressed to reply. A thousand rationalizations.

But as I drove, that hollow ache in my chest only deepened. I climbed the familiar stairwell, each step echoing ominously. At her door, I knocked, heart in my throat.

Silence. No infant cries, no shuffle of footsteps.

A chill ran through me. *Come on, Ella, open the door.* I knocked harder, tried calling her phone—straight to voicemail. Blood pounding in my ears, I debated forcing the lock. That was when I noticed Mrs. Waverly hovering at the end of the hall, grocery bag in hand, concern etched on her features. Hoping for good news, I stepped away from Ella's door.

"Mrs. Waverly," I said, swallowing hard, "have you seen Ella? She hasn't been answering me."

The elderly neighbor offered a sympathetic frown. "I'm sorry, Dr. Mortoli. Ella moved out this morning."

My mind blanked. "What?"

She nodded, eyes full of regret. "Said she was leaving the city altogether."

My pulse thundered. "Did she say why?"

Mrs. Waverly shrugged, face somber. "Only that it was time to move on. Looked like she'd been crying half the night. Poor thing. I'll miss her and the girls."

I managed a stiff nod, mind swirling. "Thank you," I murmured, stepping back.

My gaze flicked to Ella's door one last time—locked tight, no sign of life. *She left me without a word.* My phone buzzed in my pocket, a text that made my heart seize with hope. *Maybe she's telling me to come find her.*

Ella: *I'm sorry, Dom. The girls and I have left NYC. This is what's best for everyone. I'm changing numbers soon, so don't bother texting this one. Please take care of yourself, your work, and your other kids.*

Her final goodbye—no address, no chance to argue. Just a curt apology and a severance of ties. Like I was nothing to her.

I typed a frantic reply anyway, only to receive a "Message not delivered" notice. She must've already shut off her phone. A hollow sensation spread through my chest, each breath a struggle. *She actually left.*

Eventually, I trudged back down the stairs, out into the twilight city. The shock gave way to a swirl of anger at her for bailing, at myself for not seeing it coming, at Seth for piling on the pressure that drove her away, at the hospital for complicating things, at everyone and everything I could think of. By the time I got home, I was numb.

The next few days dragged by in a blur. I went through the motions at the hospital—performing surgeries on autopilot, giving curt nods to staff. Everyone noticed I was off my game, though my hands stayed steady. Years of training kept me from mistakes. When I was not in the OR, I obsessively checked my phone, hoping Ella would reach out again.

She didn't.

The koi pond at the hospital had lost its shine. Everything had. So I took my meals in the breakroom, which left me open to Seth's verbal sparring at random. As I stared at a stale sandwich I couldn't bring myself to eat, he strolled in, smug and smiling.

"Dom," he said, voice dripping with false concern, "I heard your girlfriend took off. Tough break."

My jaw clenched. I forced myself to speak evenly. "This isn't your concern."

He raised his brows in mock innocence. "Just repeating what I heard. Something about her landing a job at a Michelin-starred place—must be quite the career move. Shame she didn't see fit to include you in that plan, huh?"

Ambition? Was that what this was all about? But her text implied she was fleeing for my sake. Could both be true? Was I that naive?

I bit back a retort, shaking my head. "You don't know a damn thing."

Seth shrugged, sipping his coffee. "The admin role demands focus. Hard to keep that when your personal life is a train wreck."

I spun on him, rage flaring. "Stay the hell away from me."

He raised his cup in a mock toast, eyes gleaming with satisfaction.

I'm giving him exactly what he wants. That realization scorched me. *I'm done.*

Storming out, I made it to my office before my knees threatened to buckle. Was he right? Was this some kind of karma for what I'd done with Jodie? I lost one partner because I gave my all to my career, and now I was losing another because she gave her all to her career.

And for what?

Around midday, I just...gave up. After completing a consult, I strode to HR, ignoring the stares of staff who tried to stop me from barging in. Mrs. Fletcher, the HR manager, looked up in alarm as I approached.

"Dr. Mortoli?" She glanced up from her screen. "Is everything—"

"I'm resigning," I said bluntly, my heart hammering. "Effective immediately."

Her eyes widened. "But—your candidacy for admin is still under review—"

I let out a harsh laugh. "I'm done here."

She hesitated, as if searching for the right words. "You're certain? This is...quite sudden."

"Yes, I'm sure. Please email me whatever paperwork you need." My chest felt hollow.

Her expression was heavy with concern. "Sure, but—"

I got up and left, striding out of HR. Staff parted for me in the hallway, eyes flicking with curiosity. *Let them talk. It's not my problem anymore.*

But the freedom felt suspiciously like despair. My mind flitted to the only family I had left here. I got in my car, knuckles white on the steering wheel. My phone pinged once—Gina texting me about brunch next weekend.

I swallowed, thinking how I'd rarely see her if I left. But our brunches had become an excuse for Leo to take his anger out on me and little more than that.

Ella wasn't the only one who needed a fresh start.

I sped all the way there. Once inside the sketchy building, I climbed the rickety stairs, each creak echoing the tension in my nerves. At the door, I pounded with more urgency than usual. After an agonizing minute, it cracked open, revealing Leo's disheveled form.

His eyes flicked over me, annoyance plain. "What do you want now, Dom?" He spat my name like an insult, refusing to call me ad.

I mustered my last few ounces of calm. "I quit the hospital."

He blinked, crossing his arms. "So? Why should I care?"

"Because I might leave the city for good, and you're my son, whether you accept it or not. I need to see if we can bury the hatchet."

Leo's jaw tightened, but he didn't slam the door. "Fine," he muttered, stepping aside. "If you want to talk so bad, make it quick."

Inside, the loft was the same chaotic mess—paint cans all over, reeking of stale smoke. My eyes burned from the acrid smell, but I focused on what I came to say. "Ella left me. Took the twins somewhere. I have no clue where she went."

He raised a brow, expression guarded. "The way you are about your partners, are you really that surprised?"

Pain flared in my chest. "I'm devastated and furious."

Leo shrugged, though something flickered in his gaze. "So you're alone, then. Sucks."

"Listen, I'm not here to guilt you, or talk about Ella. I just...can't leave Manhattan without telling you how sorry I am for everything. I couldn't save your mom, I know you blame me. But I can't rewrite history."

His lips pressed into a thin line, an old bitterness returning. "You should've known she was sick. You're a doctor."

"I know that makes it hard on you—"

He snorted in derision.

"But for once in your life, imagine how that makes me feel."

He blinked up at me. "Not 'imagine how that makes me *look*'?"

I swallowed the guilt of having said that once many years ago. Maybe that was why he hated me. In a rambling grief tirade, I'd said that to him—that her getting ill and my not noticing it meant that other doctors doubted me. Maybe that was why I had so much to prove with the admin promotion.

"I was a shitty man for saying that before, but I was a shitty man who was grieving, and I hope you never know what it's like to say the wrong thing to the wrong person at the wrong time the way I said that to you." I blew out a breath to steady myself. "I would've done anything to save her, Leo. Anything."

He let out a ragged breath, raking his fingers through

unkempt hair. "Even after she was gone, you buried your-self in surgery. Gina and I had no one."

"You had me, and I failed you. You deserved better than that. You both did. I botched everything back then."

"Yeah. You did."

We both exhaled, and our eyes met. "Funny. I think that's the first time we've ever agreed about anything from back then."

He nodded, a ghost of a smile on his face.

"There's more. I'm leaving New York—maybe tomor-row, maybe next week. If you never want to see me again, that's your choice. But I want you in my life, if you want the same thing."

Leo's eyes dropped to the floor, tension radiating from him. "So, is that it? Just 'sorry' and you bail?"

"I'm not bailing on you. After leaving the hospital, I have no reason to stay here—Ella's gone, Gina doesn't need me, and you hate me—"

"You think I hate you?"

"Are you trying to say you don't?"

He swallowed, tears glistening. "I'm...I'm tired of hating you. But I can't just forget everything."

"I'm not asking you to forget. Or even fully forgive. I'll never be able to do that for myself, so how could I ask that of you? But we can move forward."

"Jesus, Dom, you're asking a fucking lot."

Hearing him call me by my name instead of ad was another knife twist, but I bit it back. "I love you and Gina. I just...messed it all up."

He looked ready to argue, but the tension drained from

his shoulders. Slowly, he turned away, dropping onto a paint-stained couch. "What future do we even have?"

I approached, sinking onto the edge of the battered coffee table. "One where we're not strangers. Where I check in on you, and you don't slam the door in my face."

He gave a watery scoff, swiping at his eyes. "That's a low bar."

"We can start low."

For a long moment, we sat in silence, the gritty loft air feeling thick. Then Leo exhaled shakily, glancing at me. "It sucks that you're leaving, but I guess...if that's what you need to do..."

"I can't stay here. Too many memories."

He swallowed, a single tear slipping down his cheek. Then, so quietly I almost missed it, he murmured, "I...I don't hate you, Dad. Not anymore."

The word dad cracked something inside me, tears I'd held back surging. I reached out, and to my shock, he let me hug him. We clung to each other in the musty loft, father and son trying to rebuild a bond shattered by years of grief and anger.

Eventually, we pulled apart, both wiping our eyes. The gloom of the loft seemed less oppressive. I stood, exhaling unsteadily. "I'll let you breathe," I murmured. "But call me anytime, okay? And I'll text you when I figure out where I'm going."

"All right," he said softly, glancing away. "Dom—Dad. Be safe."

A lump rose in my throat. I gave him a final pat on the shoulder, then headed out, leaving behind the echoes of so many regrets. Outside, the city's neon glow felt harsh, but my step was a fraction lighter.

Dad.

At least he and Gina still acknowledged me. Marissa and Summer? Would they ever get the chance?

My chest remained hollow, the sting of Ella's absence gnawing at me. Maybe I'd prove her wrong, track her down eventually. Or maybe, if she truly wanted me out of her life, I'd respect that. The thought crushed me, but I had no fight left in me.

Starting the car, I stared at the flickering city lights, mind swirling with memories of her eyes, her laugh, the twins' soft coos. I resigned from the hospital, made amends with Leo—sort of. That left me...nowhere, standing at the edge of an unknown future.

But for the first time in ages, I felt a strange clarity. I'd learned the hard way that life was too short, that burying guilt in ambition only led to missed chances. If Ella left to spare me from scandal or to chase her own dreams, I couldn't fix it by lingering here.

If fate was kind, maybe it'd lead me back to her someday.

I let the tears slip down my cheeks as I drove into the night, mind on Ella and the twins. My heart ached, but I wasn't broken. Leo had called me Dad. That was worth something.

No. It was worth everything. That little word was a stepping stone on a new path. I had no idea where it would lead me, but it was a first step nonetheless.

Chapter 37

Ella

I'd thought New York was the epitome of chef success, all fast-paced and grueling. But now, I found myself in a brand-new kitchen in Chicago, pausing between flips of an omelet to realize I hadn't even broken a sweat. That used to be unthinkable. Yet the calmer pace didn't feel wrong, just...different.

I wasn't hating my job, which was why it felt strange. But since I wasn't hating it, it also felt really, really good. Maybe not hating my job was an actual success.

"Chef, ticket for table four," called Marcus, my line cook, from across the pass. He was a fantastic line cook, always on time, always ahead of the rest of the kitchen. I would have thought he was handsome if he had another twenty years on him. Dark hair, a day's worth of stubble at all times, nice square shoulders.

But every man under forty looked underbaked these days.

I glanced over, giving him a nod. "On it," I said, plating up eggs benedict with a flourish. As I drizzled spicy hollandaise, my mind briefly wandered to my old life—sliding plated dishes across to Dom when he visited me after hours. I forced the memory aside, focusing on the swirl of sauce.

This is my reality now.

Across from me, Tanya, our pastry chef, approached with a tray of fresh croissants. Her rainbow-colored hair was pinned up in a bandana. She had the personality of a manic pixie dream girl and the body of an anime character. She was short, had big boobs that made it hard for her apron to fit right, and a crooked grin that rarely faded. "Morning rush is wild, but it's less crazy than yesterday."

I gave a half-smile. "I'll take it. Yesterday, I swear we had a dozen orders for those stuffed French toast bombs all at once."

"Hey, that's your fault—advertising them on the specials board, Miss Creative."

I shrugged. "People here love sweet, over-the-top stuff for breakfast."

Jason tapped my shoulder, and I handed him a plate. "Run that out, would you?"

He zipped off, leaving me to reorganize the line. Over the next half-hour, the flow of orders ebbed, and soon the midmorning lull set in.

Almost time to check on the twins.

"Chef, you cool if I prep some fruit compote for tomorrow's brunch?" Tanya asked.

"Go for it," I replied. "I'll be back in a few."

She winked. "Say hi to your babies for me."

I tried not to grin too broadly. "Will do." Then I slipped out of the kitchen, weaving past a few lingering customers to the stairs leading to my apartment. This stairway commute was still surreal, a far cry from the jam-packed sidewalks in Manhattan.

With every step, I thought about my little family. My girls were growing so fast, and I hated that Dom wasn't here to see it. I gulped at the thought, shoved it away. My sister lived in a suburb nearby. I should give her a call. We'd never been close—she was twelve years older than me.

After Katie left home, Mom tried to turn me into a miniature version of herself. I blamed my sister for not being there to protect me from Mom's bullshit, but I knew better now. That wasn't her job. She was just trying to survive.

Maybe I should integrate her into my little family. I didn't even know if she had kids herself. My girls might have cousins.

At my door, I let myself in quietly. Martha, the nanny, glanced up from the floor where she was playing with Marissa and Summer. "Hey there, Chef," she greeted with a warm smile. "Your girls just finished their morning bottle. Perfect timing."

I crouched down, heart softening at Marissa's delighted squeal. "How're my munchkins doing?"

Martha chuckled, pushing a strand of gray hair back. "They're angels. Not a peep of complaint since breakfast." She gestured at the crocheted blanket forming in her lap. "I got half a row done while they rolled around."

I reached out to stroke Summer's cheek, a tiny pang shooting through my chest. *Dom would've loved seeing them so peaceful.* Clearing my throat, I forced a smile.

"Thanks, Martha. I just wanted to pop in and see them. We're in a lull downstairs."

"Take your time," she said softly. "You deserve a little mama moment."

For a minute, I did just that—scooping Summer into my arms, pressing a gentle kiss to her soft hair. Marissa grabbed at my sleeve, babbling. I indulged them with coos and tickles, letting a wave of calm wash over me. Then, too soon, I had to stand up, because the lunch prep beckoned.

"I'll be back up in a couple hours," I told Martha, handing Summer back.

She gave me a knowing nod. "We'll be here."

Back in the kitchen, the lull ended with a flurry of lunch orders—clubs, melts, and the occasional special request for a fancy salad, each with their own spin on the dish. I thrived on that mild chaos, orchestrating the line without feeling crushed by it, which was new. In Manhattan, I'd be gulping coffee, sweating through my chef coat, and praying for a spare minute. Here, I actually had a moment to chat with staff.

"Chef," Marcus called from the stove, "what do you think about adding roasted poblano peppers to the soup tomorrow?"

I checked the simmering pot. "Do it," I said, tasting a spoonful. "We'll call it southwestern tomato bisque. Might spice things up for the dinner crowd."

He gave me a thumbs-up. This dynamic was refreshing —I had the authority to shape the menu and still had the time to collaborate. No Carrie side-eye, no last-minute chaos overshadowing everything.

After the rush calmed, Tanya sidled over, wiping flour

off her hands. "So, chef, you free to grab a coffee after this shift?"

I considered my schedule. "Yeah, I can do that. Martha's got the twins, and I have a couple of hours before dinner."

She grinned. "Awesome. I know a great place around the corner. Cozy vibes, strong coffee."

"Sold. The only coffee I get is quick slugs in the storage room." *At least I'm not inhaling it in sheer panic like I used to.*

Sure enough, after we closed lunch service, I told Marcus to hold the fort, changed into a clean shirt, and followed Tanya out onto the street. The crisp Chicago air felt good against my skin. People passed by with polite nods, a few in business attire, others more casual. The city's vibe was calmer than Manhattan—less tension crackling in the air.

Tanya led me into a small coffee shop with wooden booths and a chalkboard menu. Once we had our drinks, mine a straightforward Americano, hers a caramel latte with extra whipped cream, we grabbed a corner table.

"So," she said, leaning forward, "how are you settling in? Everything going well with the nanny, the apartment, that sort of thing?"

"Surprisingly, yes." I blew on my coffee. "Martha's great. The apartment's bigger than anything I ever had in New York."

She sipped her latte, foam dotting her upper lip. "And emotionally? You know...the breakup."

My chest tightened. The second night at the restaurant, I made the mistake of getting drinks with the staff to get to know everyone and drunkenly confessed what brought me to Chicago after the group had dwindled down to me and Tanya. Thankfully, aside from being a wonderful pastry chef, she worked like our restaurant's HR slash counselor.

"Still sucks," I admitted, tracing the rim of my cup. "Time heals all wounds, right?"

Tanya reached across, patting my forearm. "That's what they say."

A wry laugh escaped me. "Doesn't make the nights any easier, though."

"Give it time. Chicago will grow on you, or maybe the universe has other plans. Could be this heartbreak frees you for something unexpected. You have to stay open to the possibilities of what might come along."

"Yeah," I murmured, forcing a smile. "We'll see." I fought with myself about what to say next. Tanya was always cheery, always positive. I wanted to warn her about living life that way, but I also didn't want to take that away from her. If anyone could get through life happy as a clam, who was I to take that away from them?

We chatted about menu ideas and local festivals—apparently, Chicago had a million street fairs in the summer. Eventually, I headed back, grateful for the new friend I'd made and doing everything I could not to think about Dom.

That evening, I took the elevator up to find Martha humming a lullaby to the twins. She nodded at me, her crochet project still progressing, the twins dozing in a playpen. My heart squeezed. *They look so peaceful.* I saw her off, handing her an envelope with her weekly pay.

After that, I sank onto the sofa, listening to the quiet.

My phone lay on the table, a brand-new Chicago number. No messages from Dom, obviously—he had no way to reach me now.

I forced myself not to think about him, focusing on the twins instead. But as I tucked them into their cribs, the memories rolled in like a tide: the way Dom used to cradle Marissa, how he'd grin whenever Summer grasped his finger. I pressed kisses to their foreheads, stepping back. "Sleep tight, my loves."

In the tiny living room, I flicked on a lamp and picked up a battered notebook of recipes. My new boss was giving me free rein to experiment, so I'd jotted down half a dozen marinade concepts. But the scrawled notes blurred before my eyes, overshadowed by the heartbreak I couldn't quite bury.

A knock on the door startled me. I hurried over, worried the noise might wake the twins. Cracking it open, I found Martha again, sheepish. "Forgot my keys on the counter," she whispered.

I grabbed them from the coffee table, offering an apologetic smile. "No problem."

She lingered, brow furrowing. "You all right, dear? You look...sad."

My heart wobbled. "I'm fine. Just a long day."

She squeezed my hand gently. "Well, if you ever need to talk, I'm next door."

I nodded, unable to speak.

She left, and the apartment felt emptier than before. I gave up on the recipe notebook, deciding a hot bath might clear my head.

In the tub, steam curling around me, Dom's face

invaded my thoughts again. *Was he mad at me or relieved? Did he know I left to protect him?* A tear slipped down my cheek, lost in the bathwater.

The guilt flared the way it did every night. *Maybe he's dealing with Seth alone, maybe he hates me for that. But I had to do it.*

When the water cooled, I trudged to bed, my phone silent on the nightstand. Before turning out the light, I paused to check on the twins. They breathed softly in unison, tiny fists curled. My throat tightened. "It's worth it," I whispered, as if they could understand. "He'll never resent us if we're not there to ruin his life." The words tasted bitter, but I forced them out.

Time went by like that, my days filled with menus, staff camaraderie, short breaks with the twins, and late-night heartbreak. I refined the morning specials, introduced a few dinner items, and started receiving positive reviews from the local neighborhood blogs. "Steel Kitchen was on the rise," the manager said, beaming as he showed me an online write-up praising my "inventive but comforting dishes".

"See?" Tanya teased one afternoon, elbowing me. "The universe is rewarding you for trusting it."

I smiled weakly, stirring a pot of rosemary-infused soup. "Maybe."

That night, before heading home, I ventured out for a quick stroll to the corner store—milk, bread, small essentials. The evening air had that crisp Chicago feel. A few people I passed offered smiles or nods, and I managed to nod back.

On my way back, I paused in front of a window display showcasing baby clothes. A pink onesie with "Chicago's Cutest" scrawled across it caught my eye. Dom would have teased me for buying something so touristy. But I walked in and bought two anyway, telling myself the twins needed new outfits.

Later, in the apartment, I held one of the onesies up to Summer's sleeping form, imagining her wearing it and me texting Dom a photo. Except I couldn't do that to him. No bridging that gap.

My tears splattered on the tiny garment, so I tucked it away. *We'll be okay,* I told myself for the millionth time.

Like Tanya said, the world was full of possibilities and the universe...blah, blah, blah. That girl might have lived a charmed life, and I hoped she was able to continue doing so. But I had kids, so I had to accept the real world.

Crawling into bed, I stared at the ceiling, clutching a pillow. The ache throbbed in my chest, but Chicago had begun to feel like a real home—friendlier staff, a more balanced schedule, a calmer environment for the twins.

All I can do is keep going. I did the right thing. Now, I have to learn to live with it. Sometimes, you have to leave the people you love to save them.

Maybe that was what Katie thought when she left home. If she weren't around, then Mom would stop using her as an accomplice in her scams, so she'd stop scamming. My sister had no reason to think Mom would turn to her youngest child to replace her lost teenager.

We do the best we can with what we've got at the time.

A tear slid down my cheek. I held onto that phrase, letting it lull me into an uneasy sleep. Because if I doubted it for one second, the heartbreak might swallow me whole.

Chapter 38

Dom

I stepped off the elevator into a corridor lined with tinted glass walls and abstract art, feeling oddly weightless. The hush of expensive carpet muffled my footsteps as I approached the sleek reception area, where a practiced smile from the assistant greeted me. She recognized me easily—I was one of the three founders, after all—but there was no trace of warmth in her eyes. This was a world of polite formality, not personal attachment.

"Good morning, Dr. Mortoli," she said, rising from behind her pristine desk. "They're ready for you in the conference room."

"Thank you," I murmured, adjusting my lapel. My stomach churned with a nervous energy that felt misplaced. I had saved countless lives and successfully performed impossible surgeries. There was no reason for a business meeting to shake me this badly. But it did.

She led me down a quiet hallway, each office door etched with the names of people who'd become strangers. I'd once known every face in my company, back when it was a small startup in a cramped suite. Now, in this imposing Chicago high-rise, everything gleamed with corporate polish.

The truth was, this place had stopped feeling like it belonged to me a long time ago.

We arrived at the conference room—one of those glossy glass boxes with a panoramic view of the city skyline. The CFO, the CEO, half a dozen board members, and a handful of lawyers all rose to greet me with polite handshakes. There were murmurs of "Dom, congratulations" or "This is a monumental day."

I forced polite nods, but the hollowness in my gut only grew.

"Come in, have a seat," the CEO said, gesturing to a plush leather chair at the head of the table. That used to be my spot. For the final time, I sat there, hooking my fingertips under the armrests to keep them from trembling.

"We appreciate you coming in person to finalize everything," the CFO began, folding his hands. "Your contributions have been invaluable, and we're honored to take the reins from here."

"Right," I answered, voice low. "I'm...proud of what we accomplished." I'd built this company from scratch, forging prototypes in a small lab, stepping away from my family to push my inventions forward. Now, I was handing it over like a used car, albeit a very profitable one.

Financially speaking. But as much as I loved this company, it took me away from what mattered most.

Though, I suppose that's not the way to look at things. I took me away from them. Not a company, not the hospital. I did that. I let things get out of control.

No more.

The lawyers passed a stack of documents around. "We just need your signature on these forms to formalize the share transfer," one said, pushing a pen toward me. "You'll receive the final deposit by close of business."

I nodded, glancing at the top page. The sum was staggering—enough for multiple lifetimes of comfort for me and every person I knew. I should have been ecstatic. Instead, my chest felt tight. I scribbled my name where indicated and repeated the gesture about half a dozen times until each slip of paper bore my final consent. The CFO's eyes gleamed like he'd just closed the deal of his life. Maybe he had.

"Well," the CEO said, rising with a broad grin. "That's that. A new chapter for the company—and you. We'll uphold your legacy, Dom, I promise."

That was the deal we'd struck, one that guaranteed the company's participation in several charities and university hospitals to bring medical technology to those who might not otherwise have access. It was my only stipulation for the buyout.

Polite claps followed our handshake. The rest of them stood, offering handshakes of their own. There was even a pat on my back. "Retiring so young, huh?" one board member teased lightly. "You'll have to find a new hobby."

"Young?" Hadn't been called that in a while. "I'm almost fifty."

"Retirement is quite an accomplishment at your age."

"Yes," I agreed quietly, returning his handshake. "I suppose so." It didn't feel like one, though. It felt like shedding an old skin. Uncomfortable, but necessary.

"We'll handle press releases in the coming days," the CFO added, guiding me to the door. "If you have any statements, let us know. Otherwise, enjoy your well-deserved rest."

"Thanks," I said, forcing a tight smile. "I'll keep that in mind."

He pressed the elevator button for me, still beaming as if I should be celebrating. The doors opened, and I stepped inside. Before they slid shut, I caught a final glimpse of the CFO and CEO exchanging triumphant grins. *They got what they wanted.* The final chunk of my soul sold off for a fortune I wasn't sure I even wanted.

Outside, I paused on the sidewalk. The Chicago wind nipped at my jacket even as spring was coming to a close. I was done here, but I had nowhere to go. My hotel was a mile away. My flight back to...well, I didn't have one. This was a one-way flight, because I had no plans, no direction.

Once upon a time, I'd have killed for this moment: a huge windfall, no responsibilities. Now, all I felt was an ache for what I'd lost. Ella and the twins.

I'd tried to locate them, once. Hired a private detective to poke around, see if she'd actually gone to a Michelin-starred place, like Seth said. But it felt wrong—like I was invading her privacy. So I called it off before the detective did more than confirm Ella had left Manhattan. That was all I really knew.

I am officially retired. What do I do now?

I'd never realized how disorienting "freedom" could feel until the moment I stepped out of that boardroom. I walked for blocks, hands stuffed in my pockets, head bowed against the breeze. Skyscrapers towered above, the sun reflecting off steel and glass. Part of me admired the city's mix of modern sparkle and old-world grit. Another part just felt numb. Untethered.

At some point, my stomach growled, reminding me I hadn't eaten since a hurried breakfast. I glanced around, spotting a row of shops and cafes. One had a sign boasting *Open Kitchen—Fresh Cuisine.* I cut across the street, letting the idea of a quick lunch distract me from the swirling emptiness in my chest.

Inside, the warmth of the restaurant enveloped me, along with the tang of spices and seared meats. My mouth watered from the scent alone. A hostess greeted me, and I followed her to a small table near the half-circle bar that let diners watch the chefs at work. The chatter of customers blended with the clink of utensils, the occasional hiss of a grill.

"Here you go," she said, handing me a menu. "Your server will be right over."

"Thanks," I mumbled, shrugging off my coat. Scanning the menu, I frowned when a dish named Halekulani Chicken jumped out at me. My pulse gave an uncomfortable flutter at the association. *Halekulani,* that damned tropical drink that had changed my life. Was the universe mocking me? Still, something compelled me to order it, maybe a masochistic attempt to conjure her presence.

Back in Manhattan, I thought I'd seen her twice. Once in a boutique that she'd never have been caught dead in, and once at the bodega near Leonardo's place. The bodega sighting went badly. My private detective had already told me that she'd left Manhattan, yet I couldn't stop following that woman through the shop to make sure it wasn't her.

When she finally turned around, I realized she wasn't Ella just in time for her to mace me right in the face.

I didn't blame her. I was a strange man following her around a bodega. When I explained she looked so similar to the mother of my children and how she'd left me and taken our kids without warning, the woman bought me a black and white cookie to make up for macing me. It was a good cookie, but not that good.

A server slid up with a polite smile, took my order, and then vanished. I leaned back, glancing at the open kitchen. Several line cooks moved in a coordinated dance of plating and garnishing. *Efficient,* I noted absently, but it was a shadow of how mesmerizing it had been watching Ella. My heart twisted again, just as it did every time I thought of her or our girls.

The server brought water. I stared into it, half in a daze. *Retired at fifty, alone, with nowhere to go.* My phone felt heavier by the second, the detective's card inside the case. If I called him now, he'd pick up the search where we left off. But that was the opposite of giving Ella space. And if she discovered I'd hired someone to track her? She'd never forgive me.

When the server returned with the Halekulani chicken, the sweet citrus aroma strangled me with nostalgia. I forced a bite, waiting for anger or sadness to subside. Instead, numbness blanketed me. At least I was feeding my body, even if my soul felt starved.

Then, about halfway through the meal, I saw movement at the edge of the open kitchen. A figure slid into view from behind a stack of boxes, briefly hidden by a large rack of pastries. My pulse spiked.

The posture...something about the tilt of her head, the way she studied a sauce pot. The resemblance clawed at me.

But the memory of being maced came back in full force. The last time I *just had to see*, I ended up not being able to see much for about twenty minutes. It was a full hour before my eyes stopped tearing down my cheeks.

There was no reason to think Ella was in Chicago, much less in this restaurant. This place did not have a Michelin star. It wasn't as high-end as her last job. She wouldn't move here to step down a notch in her career.

But even as every reasonable voice in my head demanded I stay put, my heart was loud and clear.

I couldn't help it. I set my fork down, heart thumping. The woman moved to a station, rummaging for utensils. Her hair was pinned back in a low bun—dark, thick, with stray curls at the nape. *It's just another cook.* My mind insisted, but my body disobeyed, standing abruptly. A few customers glanced up at me, confusion on their faces.

What am I doing?

Feet propelled me forward, weaving around tables. The server blinked at me, alarmed. "Sir? Is something wrong with your—"

"I'm fine," I muttered, my gaze glued to that silhouette in the kitchen. I pushed open the half door that read "Staff Only", ignoring a startled busboy. Inside, the heat of stoves and the clang of metal pans rushed me, line cooks throwing me confused looks. One started to protest, telling me to leave. I didn't hear them.

All I saw was her.

She was leaning over a simmering pot, writing notes in a

small spiral notebook. As she turned slightly, I caught sight of her profile. *That jawline, those lashes...oh God.* My heart thundered, knees threatening to buckle.

Ella.

A line cook shouted, "Hey, you can't be in here!" But I was already stepping closer, breath locked in my lungs. The closer I became, the slower my steps, as though some primal fear said this had to be an illusion.

But it wasn't.

Finally noticing the commotion, she snapped upright, frustration in her tone. "What's going on? We can't just have—" She turned, eyes landing on me.

In an instant, all the noise vanished into a muted roar. Our eyes locked, and my entire universe stopped.

Ella.

Her hazel green eyes widened in disbelief, the spoon in her hand trembling until it clattered onto the metal counter. My chest felt like it would explode.

She's here...she's really here.

What the fuck do I do now?

Chapter 39

Ella

He's here.

The entire kitchen felt like it was spinning. My brain hollowed out with one thought rattling around in it. *The universe has a sense of humor.*

Marcus took a step toward me. "Chef, need me to get him out of here?" A cleaver gleamed in his hand.

Still staring at Dom, I whispered, "No."

He glanced between the both of us, seeming to understand. "Go on break. We've got this. Take the rest of the day off if—"

I barely heard him. My lungs burned as if I'd forgotten to breathe, locked in a stare with the man I'd torn myself away from. Dom's hair was a bit longer, with a few more strands of gray at the temples. His jacket hung open, revealing a rumpled shirt beneath. He looked as disoriented as I felt, his eyes flicking from me to the door as if he couldn't decide whether to bolt or close the distance between us.

"Marcus, take over the line. Tony, watch the pass." My

heart hammered, and I felt sure they could see it pounding beneath my chef's coat.

Dom took a half-step closer, swallowing hard. "Ella—"

Without a word, I grabbed his sleeve, leading him away from prying eyes. The only place that made sense was the side door leading to the stairwell. He followed silently, tension radiating off him in waves.

He found me. I didn't know what it meant, and I didn't want to speculate. I had to know why.

We emerged into the stairwell, the metal door cutting off the kitchen's noise. The hush blanketed my ears as I stared at him, adrenaline coursing. "I live upstairs," I blurted, breathless. "We can't talk here..."

"Lead the way," he said, voice rough, as if talking cost him great effort.

I started up the stairs, my chef's clogs echoing on the concrete steps, Dom just behind me. It felt surreal. My heart pounded, each step an effort not to glance over my shoulder at his face, because if I did, I might cry.

At my door, I fumbled with the keys, my fingers shaking. The lock gave, and I pushed the door open to reveal my modest, yet larger-than-Manhattan apartment. Shutting it behind us, I realized how quiet it was—no nanny, no babies. *They must be at Martha's place next door. Small favors.*

He stood in the entryway, coat still in hand, scanning the living room. "It's...nice."

"Rent is included in the job," I said automatically, crossing my arms to still the trembling in my hands. "The nanny is watching the girls right now...they're next door."

His gaze snapped to me at the mention of the twins. For an agonizing moment, we just stared. I wanted to explain everything, or maybe I wanted to scream at him for appearing unannounced or just collapse in his arms. My thoughts whirled so wildly I couldn't pin down a single one.

He opened his mouth, but no words came out. Something raw flickered in his eyes, mirrored in my own. Words seemed too complicated, too messy. And apparently, Dom felt the same.

"I don't..."

"I'm not..."

Silence fell again. He wasn't screaming at me, angry for taking his daughters away. He wasn't being snide or saying something bitter about me leaving him. He stood before me, sadness and longing on his face. A man steeped in the same pain as me.

One minute, we were two people in a silent apartment. The next, we were colliding—lips on lips, arms around each other as though we'd spent months swimming in an endless ocean and finally reached shore. I gasped into the kiss, tears stinging my eyes, because it was Dom, *my* Dom, here, and I'd missed him with an ache that never dulled.

He clutched my waist, pulling me close, and I gripped the front of his shirt like a lifeline. My mind screamed that this was a bad idea—we needed to talk first. But the heat of his mouth on mine obliterated logic.

I whimpered, pressing up against him, letting the raw need overshadow everything else. We stumbled backward, crashing into the couch. I barely remembered letting go of his jacket before we were tugging at each other's clothes, breath ragged.

I tugged off my chef's coat, feeling his hands slip under my shirt, palms exploring my skin like a man starved. A moan tore from my throat, and I could feel him trembling, too. Longing ignited into a frantic hunger. Words weren't enough. This was primal, unstoppable. He tried to speak, maybe say my name, but I cut him off with another desperate kiss, pouring all the sorrow and guilt into it.

Buttons popped. I half-laughed, half-cried as I realized we were tearing at each other's clothes like teenagers in a rush. His stubble grazed my chest, and I breathed in the faint smell of the aftershave I remembered so well, feeling tears burn behind my eyelids.

Somehow we found our way onto the rug in front of the couch. I had no sense of direction, only the press of Dom's skin against mine, his breath hitching as we finished stripping each other bare. There were no words. There was no time for them. He didn't ask the question or wait for an answer.

Neither did I. The moment he was in position, I wrapped my legs around him and pulled him close, aiming myself at him as he thrust into me. I dragged my nails down his back as I arched mine. This. I had missed this so damn much.

We made love like drowning people gasping for air—fast, raw, a tangle of limbs and sweat. The world faded to the sound of our heartbeats thudding, my moans muffled by his shoulder, his harsh groans in my ear. Tears slipped from my eyes at the sheer intensity of it all, but I didn't hold back. Neither did he.

Back and forth, on top, behind, on the couch, on the floor again. Neither of us could get enough. When I was on top of him the second time, we were on the floor. He turned me around until his mouth was on my pussy, and I swallowed him down. His arms banded around me, holding me to his mouth as if I moved away, he might die.

His tongue met my clit every chance he had, and when I came on his face, he lost control down my throat. It didn't stop us, though. Mere foreplay.

Eventually, we landed with him on top once more, and there, I saw it on his face. The heartbreak of what I'd done to him. I knew that expression because I saw it in the mirror every morning.

I took his face in my hands, kissing him long and deep while he slowed his strokes, languid and bittersweet. Then I tasted salt. Not my tears this time. His.

I wrapped him up in me, arms and legs like a vise to keep him close. I didn't know what this meant for us. All I knew was that I needed him this way. I needed him to be mine, even if only for this moment and maybe the next one.

When the next climax hit, it felt like the first real breath I'd taken since leaving Manhattan. My entire body shuddered with release, a thousand unspoken emotions surging as we both came. He crushed me to him, trembling, his breath ragged on my neck. Then we collapsed, chest to chest, hearts still pounding as if they couldn't believe we'd finally closed the distance.

Minutes passed in a haze of gasps and tangled legs. Eventually, I found the strength to shift onto my side. The late afternoon light filtered through the curtains. Dom's eyes locked onto mine, brimming with tears, and my own did the same. We didn't speak, just stared for a while.

Finally, he broke the silence, voice hoarse. "Ella..."

The guilt slammed me. "What...what are you doing here?"

He exhaled shakily, still half-lying across my thigh. "I was in Chicago to finalize the sale of my company shares. And to figure out my future. I ended up at the restaurant by pure chance." A weak laugh escaped him, overshadowed by sorrow. "I think the universe is laughing at me."

I clenched my jaw, curling my fingers against the rug. *He sold his shares?* That was always part of his plan, once the hospital promotion was locked in. My plan worked. He got what he always wanted. I swallowed. "I guess congratulations are in order. You must be thrilled about the promotion—"

He shook his head. "I quit, actually. No admin position. Nothing."

My stomach lurched. Panic churned. "Because of me?"

He pushed himself upright slightly, cradling my cheek. "Yes and no. Because losing you made me realize what I was doing—sacrificing everything for ambition. I'd done it once before, with my wife, and I lost her without noticing how sick she was, thanks to working all the time. Then I lost you and the twins because there were too many conflicts between us and the hospital...it all clicked."

I stared, tears threatening again. "Dom, I...that was exactly what I wanted to prevent. I didn't want to ruin your career or your family life—"

He gave a shaky laugh, leaning in to rest his forehead against mine. "Ella, you didn't ruin anything. You saved me from repeating the same damn mistakes. I lost Jodie in part because I was too blind, too wrapped up in my ambition to see her illness. And I lost you because of it, too. But it took losing you to see the pattern."

I felt sick. "But you loved it there."

"The hospital was a job. The company was a business. Loving something that can't love you back leaves you lonely. So I left....the hospital, the device company."

Warmth and guilt warred in my chest. I'd told myself I was doing the right thing by leaving. But now, I wasn't sure. "I feel like I painted you into a corner, and I never meant to do that."

"I needed that wake-up call. History repeats itself because we do the same stupid shit over and over, and that's what I was doing. You forced me to see what truly matters— family. Now, I have the resources to live without working another day if that's what I choose." He swallowed hard. "If that's what my *family* chooses."

That word clung to me. I let out a ragged sob, tears spilling again. "Dom...I left so you wouldn't resent me, so you could fix things with Leo, keep your career track. I never imagined you'd quit everything. I never wanted you to do that for me—"

"Not for you," he interjected, a fierce gentleness in his tone. "For *us*. For me. For all the times I put work before the people who mattered." He stroked my hair, kissing away the tears on my cheek. "Leo and I...we're on better terms now. I apologized for what I'd done, for our past, for all of it. We're trying to move forward. Gina's good, like always. She's happy I'm making these changes. She thinks they're a long time coming. They want me to be happy. And...I'm only happy with you."

His arms enveloped me as I trembled, face buried against his chest. I wanted him again so badly, but we had to talk this out. Didn't we? At first, I let him hold me. Talking be damned.

Eventually, though, the words came. "I never wanted you to lose your dream. But if...if that wasn't your dream after all—"

He pressed a gentle kiss to my forehead. "My dream was to do good, to save lives, to feel purpose. I've done that, and I can still do that, maybe in volunteer work or philanthropic efforts. But the admin role, the corporate battles... that part of my life is over, and I'm glad for it. Now, I can spend time with the people who matter most."

I gulped and met his eyes with a teasing smirk. "Gina and Leo?"

He met my smirk with his own. "And you. And our girls. If you'll have me."

My heart fluttered, tears still leaking. "I...love you. I never stopped. But I thought staying would cost you everything you care about."

"You didn't cost me a thing," he insisted. "You made me see what was important. I want to know my daughters. I want us to be a family, in whatever shape we can manage."

"I want that, too." Fresh tears blurred my vision. After a moment, I pulled back slightly, a watery laugh escaping my lips. "You realize we're naked on my living room floor, right?"

His gaze flicked downward, realization dawning with a faint smile. "That would explain the rubber duckie under my ass. We might want to move. Or get dressed."

Once I slipped on some clothes—an old T-shirt and comfy pants—I turned to find him seated on the edge of my bed in his trousers, buttoning his shirt. I came up behind him, pressed a soft kiss to his shoulder. "So," I whispered, settling beside him. "What now?"

"You tell me. I'd love to see the twins as soon as possible. Then...maybe we figure out if we can relocate, or if we stay in Chicago, or whatever."

I blinked tears away, nodding slowly. "They're next door with Martha, my nanny." My chest squeezed with simultaneous fear and excitement. Then I remembered the restaurant. "But first, I should probably tell the kitchen I'm not returning today."

"Marcus, right? My competition with a cleaver."

I swatted his arm lightly. "He's staff, not your competition."

"You sure you won't trade me in for a younger model?"

I laughed. "Nope. Same question."

He snorted. "Never."

"Then, we're good." It shorted out my brain that he was in my apartment. "Dom...I can't believe you're here."

He cupped my cheek, brushing away a stray tear. "I can't believe I found you. Or that fate brought us back together again." He paused, swallowing. "It keeps doing that."

"Yeah. It seems to." The knot of guilt slowly eased, replaced by a cautious euphoria. *Maybe this really is meant to be.*

We sat there a long time, just breathing in each other's presence. Eventually, I rose, grabbed my phone to shoot Marcus a quick text to say I wasn't coming back today. "Should we...go see the twins?"

"Please."

Just before stepping out, he reached over my shoulder and closed the door. I turned. "What is it?"

"One more thing. I'm sorry I lied to you."

"What?"

He blew out a breath. "I told you in the hospital the day the girls were born that I'd never let you out of my sight. But that wasn't true." He paused, thinking, searching. "I did. I thought everything was good between us, so I took you for granted—"

"Dom, it wasn't like that—"

"I did, Ella. I won't make that mistake again." He pressed his forehead to mine, breath unsteady. "I love you. And I won't let you out of my sight. In a healthy, respectful way."

A shaky laugh escaped me. With that, I opened the door, my heart pounding with anticipation. We stepped into the hallway, ready to introduce Dom to the life he never got to share, but hopefully would from this moment on. Because sometimes, second chances do exist, and maybe we'd just found ours.

Epilogue

Ella

I'd never planned to come back to New York, certainly not like this. Yet here I was, stepping onto a sprawling lawn, holding one of my twins while the other wriggled in Dom's arms.

My heart hammered in my chest at the sheer vastness of his family home. Oaks and maples dotted the property, and the wraparound porch framed an enormous house with more windows than I'd be bothered to count. It felt like stepping into a pastoral painting.

"Are you nervous?" Dom asked gently, shifting Marissa higher on his hip. He must've seen my knuckles go white around Summer's little jacket.

"Yeah," I admitted, blowing out a shaky breath. "I've never...had a big family get-together like this. And we're about to meet your kids—all at once. Well, your older kids."

"You've already met one," Dom said with a small smile. "Just not under the best circumstances."

"You can say that again. Leo..." My stomach flipped remembering the last time I'd seen him—angry, bitter.

Dom reached over, touched my shoulder. "He's changed. Rehab helped. He told me he's ready to be a brother to Marissa and Summer. He's even looking forward to meeting you sober."

"*Sober*," I echoed in a murmur, glancing down at Summer. Her big eyes peered back at me, as if telling me not to worry. Maybe she was right.

Martha trotted over, craning her neck at the house's third story. "So this is the upstate mansion, huh? My word. You told me it was big, but this is something else."

"Welcome, Martha," Dom said warmly. "Plenty of space for you, too. I've got your room all set upstairs."

She brushed a strand of gray hair from her face and grinned. "I've never been upstate. As soon as the babies are settled, I might wander around, see if it's as pretty as I've heard."

"Go for it," I said, adjusting Summer. "We'll handle the introductions to Dom's kids."

"I'll leave the complicated stuff to you two." She winked, heading inside ahead of us, presumably to find her quarters.

As Dom guided me through the front doors, I couldn't help letting out a soft gasp at the wide foyer with polished wooden floors. Family photos lined the entry with Mortolis throughout the years. The house exuded history, warmth, and a touch of sorrow.

I pressed my lips together, passing the pictures. "I never realized you had such a big place."

Dom nodded, glancing at one photo of Gina as a teenager, her arms folded in teenage rebellion. "I like a lot of space."

He paused at the mantle, where a more recent photo of Gina—her on the cover of a design magazine. Next to it, a frame with a picture of me holding Marissa and Summer, taken in Chicago during the Friday Fried-Dough Festival.

My chest constricted. I had no idea Dom had put that up. Gently, I brushed a finger over the photo's edge. *We're part of this home now.*

Summer squirmed in my arms, letting out a small whine. "Ready for the big meet-and-greet, baby girl?" I murmured, bouncing her lightly. She responded by drooling on my shoulder.

Just then, the doorbell chimed—a clear, old-fashioned ring echoing through the halls. My heart jumped. Dom smiled. "Let's do this."

He led the way back to the foyer, and I trailed him, trying to quell the flutter in my stomach. Gina's familiar voice drifted through the door as Dom swung it open.

"Dad, hello!" Her sing-song greeting carried into the house before she stepped in, rolling a pair of suitcases behind her. In person, Gina was tall, with stylish boots and a sleek bob. She took one look at me holding Summer and practically squealed. "Oh my God, they're so cute in real life!"

I managed a smile, letting her swoop in for a hug. Her enthusiasm was like a warm hug. She patted Summer's back, cooing softly. "Hi, sweet baby. Your big sister has a whole bag of goodies for you!" Then she looked at me, eyes bright. "Ella, finally! It's so great to meet you face-to-face."

"You too," I said, my tension easing at her genuine excitement. "Thanks for, uh, not being weird about all this."

Gina tossed her hair with a laugh. "Please. I can't wait to get to know you and the girls." Then she beckoned Dom closer, hooking an arm around him in a quick side hug. "Hey, old man," she teased, "glad to see you not scowling for once."

Dom rolled his eyes affectionately. "I'm not that old. Where's the rest of your stuff?"

"In the trunk, but I can get it later," Gina said, waving a dismissive hand. She turned back to me, rummaging through one of her suitcases. "I brought these for the babies." She pulled out a pair of tiny designer dresses, the labels making my eyes widen. "Some more for them to grow into as well, but I couldn't resist, they were on sale."

"Wow," I breathed, gingerly touching the soft fabric. "These are...fancy."

She laughed. "I know, right? But they'll look adorable." Turning to Summer, she brandished one of the dresses like a toy. The baby reached out, squealing. Gina's face lit up. "See, she likes it already."

I huffed a small laugh, a knot loosening in my chest. "Thank you, Gina. This is really kind of you."

"No biggie," she chirped. Then her gaze flitted around. "Is Martha here? I want to meet the legendary nanny who keeps these two angels in line."

Dom smirked. "She's probably upstairs settling in. You'll run into her soon enough."

Gina nodded, then noticed a slight tension in my posture. "It's Leo who's the big question, right?"

I swallowed hard, grateful she'd spoken about the elephant in the room. "Yeah, I guess so. I mean...we didn't end on great terms when we dated. And now—"

"Now you're with Dad, which is...complicated," Gina finished, not unkindly. "But he's in a much better place these days."

I mustered a shaky nod. "Dom told me about rehab and everything. Still, I'm bracing myself."

"I completely understand."

Dom cleared his throat, adjusting Marissa in his arms. "Gina, want to hold your sister?"

Her eyes lit up. "Absolutely!" She accepted Marissa gingerly, cooing as our baby stared at her with wide eyes. "Hello, sweetheart. I'm your sister, can you believe that?"

Marissa stuck out her tongue in response, eliciting giggles all around.

For a moment, warmth filled the room as Gina introduced herself to the twins, half-babbling nonsense words and making faces that had Summer cackling in my arms. My pulse settled. Maybe this would all be fine. Then the doorbell chimed again.

"That's Leo," Dom said softly, sharing a quick, meaningful glance with me. The flutter in my stomach returned full force.

He opened the door, revealing Leo stepping in hesitantly. I was shocked. He looked...good. Healthy, in fact. His hair was pulled back, and he wore casual clothes—none of the damaged designer swagger from before. He clutched a paper bag, glancing around awkwardly.

"Hey, Dad," he said, hugging Dom lightly. Then his eyes flicked to me, where I stood holding Summer. I swallowed, waiting for the tension to explode.

Instead, Leo offered a small smile. "Hey, Mariella. Good to see you."

I blinked. "Uh, yeah. You too." Not the greeting I expected from my ex—no hostility, no sarcasm.

He waved the paper bag. "I, uh, brought some baby toys. Thought...maybe they'd like them. I'm not exactly a baby expert, but the lady at the store said they're good for their age."

I stepped forward, adjusting Summer so I had a free hand. "That's very thoughtful. Thank you."

Leo swallowed, eyes darting between Dom, Gina, and the twins. "So...guess we're all one big family, huh?" His tone held uncertainty, but I noticed sincerity in his expression.

Dom nodded, placing a hand on Leo's shoulder. "We are. And it's about time you met your little sisters properly."

Leo exhaled, then crouched down beside Gina, who still sat on the floor with Marissa. He placed the paper bag in front of them, pulling out a set of rattles, plush animals, and teething rings. Marissa's eyes lit up, and Gina laughed, guiding Marissa's hand to a soft plush lamb. Summer babbled in my arms, so I lowered her as well, letting her crawl a bit.

"Whoa," Leo said softly, eyes shining as Summer tried to clamber over his foot. "They're so tiny."

"That's usually how they come out," Gina teased.

He smirked and rolled his eyes, before standing to face me, guilt in his eyes. "About before...I'm sorry for how I treated you back when we dated. I was angry at Dad, angry at everything. I took it out on you, said things that...didn't even make any sense."

I blinked rapidly, surprise rocking me. "Leo, it's okay. We both—"

He shook his head. "No, let me say this. I spent ninety days in rehab, had a lot of therapy. Realized I scapegoated Dad for Mom's death, and blamed you for stuff that was my own doing. It was messed up, and when I said that thing about...about your body, about settling...God, I was an asshole to you."

"You could have been nicer," I said with a shrug, trying to let him off the hook.

But he leveled a look at me that reminded me of Dom. "Don't brush this under the rug. I was an asshole. If you want to yell at me, or—"

I laughed. "No. That was ages ago, and I'm pretty sure we're different people now. Water under the bridge."

He let it rest there and looked at Dom, swallowing. "I'm glad you two found each other, weird as it might've been initially."

A strange laugh escaped my throat, tears threatening. "Weird, yeah," I agreed softly, "but apparently what the universe had in mind."

Leo grinned, picking up Summer carefully. She grabbed his nose, giggling. "The universe has weird aim, huh?"

Dom let out a relieved chuckle, stepping closer to rest a hand on my back. "It got us here, so I think it's okay." He nodded at me, and I swallowed my fear down as I pulled the engagement ring out of my pocket, sliding it on. "Leonardo, we're—"

"You're engaged?"

"What?" Gina squealed.

Nervously, I nodded, and before I could finish, Leo hauled me to him for a hug. "That's amazing!"

"Really?"

He held me at arm's length. "Dad's getting old. He'll need someone to take care of him, and I didn't want to do it."

I laughed, and Dom slugged him in the shoulder. "Hey!"

Leo grinned, and then Gina swooped in for her hugs and congratulations.

I didn't realize my whole body had been tense this entire time until then. But the tension melted away as they went back to playing with the babies. Leo made silly faces at Summer, who squealed in delight. Gina bounced Marissa on her knee, and the two older siblings launched into a playful argument about who got to hold which twin. Dom and I locked eyes, tears in both our gazes. I'd never expected this to be so...natural.

Soon, we moved into the dining room, where a brunch spread was laid out: fresh pastries, fruit, scrambled eggs, and coffee. Martha reappeared, exclaiming over the grandness of the table setup. Gina teased her father about going over-board, and he shot back that Gina could pay for the next feast with her design money. Leo chimed in with a joke about how he'd sponsor dessert if it meant sugary chaos. The twins gurgled happily, as though used to all the banter.

I sat there, heart so full I thought it might burst. Was this what a family was supposed to be? I'd always wanted one, but had never really known what I was asking for.

When the meal wound down, Dom glanced around, clearing his throat. "We should show Ella the orchard, right?" he suggested, eyes lingering on me. "It's sort of a tradition."

Gina snorted. "Dad and his orchard. Just watch out for the donkey."

"The donkey?"

Leo raised an eyebrow, finishing the last sip of his coffee. "Still no official donkey sighting, though. It's basically cryptid territory."

I blinked, confused. "There's a donkey cryptid?"

Dom chuckled. "Apparently, two donkey farms used to be around here somewhere, and now, people say there are donkeys that got loose and roam around. We'll figure that out eventually."

The goodbyes were surprisingly emotional, with Gina hugging me and the babies, and Leo making me promise we'd FaceTime so he could read the girls some bedtime stories in his silly voices. My chest ached with gratitude as I watched them drive off. The quiet that followed felt warm, not empty.

Dom and I carried Marissa and Summer outside, into the golden afternoon light. The orchard sprawled behind the south end of the mansion, scatterings of apple trees in all directions. Martha excused herself to unpack more, so it was just the four of us again.

I inhaled the crisp air, glancing sidelong at Dom, who balanced Marissa in his arms while I toted Summer. "You sure about all this?" I asked softly, though my tone was playful. "Rural living? Orchard donkey hunts?"

He grinned, brushing his shoulder against mine. "Positive. As long as you and the girls are here."

Summer let out a squeal at a flutter of leaves overhead. Dom paused beneath a tree, shifting Marissa so he could tuck me under his arm. The babies watched each other, babbling. I looked up at Dom's face, finding the gentle warmth I'd come to rely on.

"Thank you," I whispered, tears pricking my eyes. "For letting me stay in Chicago until I was ready, for giving Leo time to come around, for making today possible."

He kissed my forehead. "Thank you for being here with me. And for promising to never, ever do what you think is best for us without talking to me first."

"Funny—I don't remember promising that."

He arched a brow and waited. Marissa squeaked, flailing a tiny fist. Summer promptly tried to grab it, and both babies ended up giggling in incoherent baby chatter. Dom and I laughed, pressing our foreheads together. I gave in. "Okay. I promise."

We resumed walking among the trees, letting the girls absorb the rustling leaves and dappled sunlight. My fear of Leo's reaction, my guilt over leaving Dom, all of it dissipated into the sweet orchard air. I finally had the big, loving family I'd longed for my entire life, odd as it might be.

Dom's gaze caught mine. "Happy?"

"More than I ever thought possible."

"Me too."

After a little while, the babies got fussy. We headed back, turning toward the house. Dom stepped close, his free hand curling around my waist. "Let's go inside," he murmured. "We can lay them down for a nap, then maybe we can have a little time to ourselves."

"I'd like that."

His grin was soft as he leaned in, pressing a kiss to my lips—a quiet promise of this life we were building.

I'd traded a life of clattering pans and scorching burners for one full of orchard donkey rumors, a couple of complicated adults, a man I loved so much it was hard to breathe around him, and two precious babies who united us all.

It wasn't the life path I'd planned, but it was the best possible one I could imagine.

THE END

Read more SILVER FOXES from the Accidentally Yours bestselling series, exclusive on Amazon:

Accidental Vegas Vows: A Silver Fox Boss Romance
(Damien and Olivia)

Accidental Twins: A Silver Fox Dad's Best Friend
Romance
(Adrian and Ava)

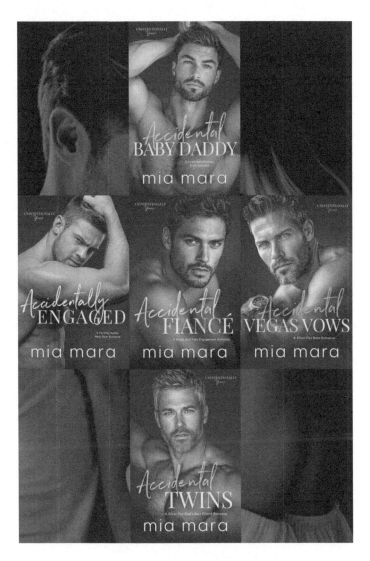

Unintentionally Yours Series

Get ready to fire up your kindle with these cinnamon-roll billionaires! When spicy, sugarcoated accidental engagements, marriages, and babies bring opposites together.

Each book follows the story of their own couple and are standalones with a very satisfying HEA.

Read the Unintentionally Yours series on Amazon:

Unintentionally Yours series page

Accidentally Engaged: A Fertility Doctor Next Door Romance
(Hudson and Sophie)

Accidental Vegas Vows: A Silver Fox Boss Romance
(Damien and Olivia)

Accidental Twins: A Silver Fox Dad's Best Friend Romance
(Adrian and Ava)

Accidental Baby Daddy: A Single Dad Runaway Bride Romance
(Oliver and Lexie)

Accidental Fiancé: A Single Dad Fake Engagement Romance
(Julian and Maggie)

Happy reading!

xx

Mia

Made in the USA
Columbia, SC
05 December 2025